# Passionate Determination

Alan Hewison

First published in Great Britain as a softback original in 2020



All characters and events in this publication, other than those clearly in the public domain, are fictitious and any resemblance to real persons, living or dead, is purely coincidental.



Typeset in Palatino

Editing, design, typesetting and publishing by UK Book Publishing

www.ukbookpublishing.com

ISBN: 978-1-913179-65-6

*I would like to give very grateful thanks to Gerry Knox.*

*All the lovely clever members in the Attleborough Writers Group.*

*And especially to My Beautiful Wife, Linda.*

# Passionate Determination

# Chapter one

Summer had breezed into autumn, autumn had blown itself into winter and winter had crawled into spring. The hot, beautiful months were now ahead of us.

The millennium had just changed hands and a new era was gallantly bracing itself in front of us. My wife Daphne and I were presently snuggled up warm and cosy under our massive duvet. Unfortunately, the light from the bottom of the shuttered window bounced itself across my face, and caused one of my eyes to open. The eye wasn't very keen on this bright intrusion and closed tighter, which didn't help very much because now the brain had awoken. This was most disappointing, because sleep was enjoyable, especially when the opportunity arose to continue.

A blurred peep at the clock registered minutes before eight. Daphers stirred beside me, wriggled and shuffled her shoulders and half sat up. I followed her and we kissed, which was always a good start to a day.

She was the first to speak.

"Nice to see the sunshine so early, I'll go and make the tea." She put on her dressing gown and elegantly walked through to the kitchen.

I sat and made a pyramid out of my fingers and pondered on how our lives had been shaped over the past years and came to the conclusion 'it's not possible to dictate to life, it is only possible to manipulate it'. This thought remained with me for some time until my arrival back at the present.

Today was the thirteenth anniversary of our retirement and the move here to the Loire in the west of France. After having lived all our working lives in the East of England, we had retired in our mid-fifties and opted for the easy life and the warmer climes. Many years ago during our married life, we suffered a deplorably distressing, tragic loss, something so cruel and devastating, it had taken a long, long time for Daphne and myself to find a way to carry on living. We first absorbed ourselves in our work. Family and friends gave us great support and helped with the overwhelming sadness, but it lingered and always remained. On retiring, we again tried to continue to come to terms with what had happened, but we found it difficult. After much thought, we came to the conclusion it might be a good idea to start a new life in different surroundings, maybe in a different country, so at the end of a very cold winter in England, we sold our house and bought an old farmhouse in France, and moved over, lock, stock, and barrel. By doing this Daphers and I drew closer together, and gained in strength from each other.

My meditation on the subject was disturbed by my wife entering the bedroom carrying two mugs of tea and the phrase:

"I haven't put any more logs on the fire, because it's warm and I've switched the immersion heater on for the hot water."

Daphers in my eyes were beautiful, and like me was fit for her age. She plonked herself next to me on the bed and looked expectant of conversation. I obliged by saying,

"It seems the sun is going to shine all day, let's set lunch for everybody outside on the veranda. Will it make any difference to the meal you are preparing if we do that?"

"No, I'll do all the cooking, you do all the drinks, including the coffee at the end."

"It's a deal; right, I'll cut the grass first, then I'll bottle some cider."

I'd showered the previous evening, so only a quick visit to the bathroom was necessary. Working clothes with long trousers were the order for this morning, not quite warm enough for shorts.

I passed through the lounge, opened the French doors, walked across the veranda and stood hands in pockets looking out onto the garden. The air was fresh without wind and the sun was rising, beaming its rays on the orchard in front of me. The apple-trees were doing a good job producing leaf, and the plum trees had achieved blossom. It was obvious they were looking forward to improving their display, and it was stunningly beautiful.

With great reluctance, I withdrew my hands from my pockets, took a deep breath and briskly walked round to the rear garden. In the far left corner after more trees was an old brick built barn, which housed the grass-cutting tractor. I swung myself on to the seat, turned the key and drove around the side of the house, set the cutters in mid-position and started to cut the grass.

It wasn't my intention to cut the whole of the orchard, but I got carried away, and stopped by Daphers waving a surrendering white towel, indicating it was time for me to prepare the drinks.

Time seems to pass so quickly.

After carefully parking the tractor in the barn, I walked over to the far corner where a large barrel, measuring about two feet in diameter and about three feet long stood on a wooden frame. This was full of fermenting cider, really good scrumpy. At the end of last autumn, we collected all the apples from the trees and the ground and called the cider-lorry man. He came and set his pipe from the bottom of his tank into the hole in our empty barrel. Then Daphers, myself and our neighbours filled buckets with apples and passed the buckets from hand to hand up to the top of the lorry and tipped them into the chute on the top of the tank. The machine, after chewing all the apples, squeezed them and pumped the juice through the pipe into our barrel, where for the last six months, every three or four days, I have taken the bung out of the top, and on instruction from all the locals, bashed the top of the barrel with a rubber mallet to remove the air then topped it up with water.

In the previous years, the postman and his family had arrived at the appropriate time and taken all the apples away in his lorry. In the New Year, we always received bottles of cider as recompense and a bottle of 'Eau de Vie', 'water of life', which varied from forty-five to fifty-five percent proof in alcoholic content. His illegal still was in a back room of his garage, away from the prying eyes of the police. We only whispered about 'Eau de Vie' through tight lips and flashing eyes. This was the first year I had taken the responsibility of making the cider myself.

A tap poked its nose out at the bottom of the barrel, and on occasions, I sampled the contents, and on each occasion, it tasted good; as a matter of fact, it was steadily improving. All the cider received over the years had been successfully dealt with through various parties, and the empty bottles were kept, washed and stored in the barn in wooden boxes.

After carrying out another, unnecessary taste, I filtered the liquid and poured it into twelve bottles and placed them into a wooden crate, then tugged it into the house, placing four bottles in the fridge.

The table was set on the veranda for six, with the starter already in place. It was very impressive how Daphers made such a difficult task look so easy, I never tired of telling her.

She was delicious.

The first guests to arrive, Marc and Marie, brought wine and flowers, as did Andre and Fanny. Both couples were typically French, the men short in stature, the ladies slim and well-dressed. They greeted us in the usual French manner.

Having lunch in France was a glorious, elaborate affair, which usually went on well into the evening. Today was going to be no exception. It was normal to have an aperitif first, usually whisky or Ricard, but on this occasion it was to be the genuine home-made cider, agreed by all to be a pleasant change. Daphers and I spoke French very well and understood most of what went on, although some of the jokes involving cucumbers and bananas told by the lady guests, very nearly passed me by.

After the main course, we all had a stroll around the planted wooded area behind the house, returning to the table for dessert. The whole thing culminated in the game of 'boule', which was often played in France after lunches.

I remember on one occasion we went to a nearby hamlet and assisted Johno and his friends and family to pick the grapes from his vines. The task took all morning, and on returning to the house, we were rewarded for our labours with lunch outside on a long table, and the duty of finishing the remains of last year's wine. Rather groggily, after the meal, all the men decided to play 'boule', and two teams were selected. The game is similar to bowls, only the 'boules' are steel and sometimes thrown from a great height, the 'Cochon' or 'piggy' is the target, and this was bombarded rather rashly, especially after everyone had quaffed further glasses of last year's grapes.

The nearest 'boule' to the Cochon gains more points. Unfortunately, a fracas developed between the two nominated captains over the measurements to determine the winner. This was followed by a lot of pushing and shoving and finally ended with both players brawling on the gravel. This was great entertainment for the rest of us; pleasingly, in the end, nobody was hurt. Afterwards, hugs and handshakes were even more elaborate than usual, and it was all typically French.

The gentle game outside our veranda was between the ladies and the gentlemen and was full of high fives and silliness. In the end, nobody knew who won and nobody cared.

The cider received a bit of a bashing, the men attended to the drinks, while the ladies swiftly returned the table to its normal appearance.

The afternoon curved its way sweetly into the evening, and we all sat inside the veranda on the cushion-laden wicker-chairs, drinking coffee with maybe a touch of 'Eau de Vie'.

Fanny was the first to feel the chill of the hour and rose. A small discussion took place as to whether Marc would make the walk home or whether he would maybe require help. A wheelbarrow was always on hand for those unsteady on their feet, and with the addition of a cushion was the perfect shape for the recipient to be trundled home. In the end determination and pride took over, and he joined the others in the walk down the drive. We stood on the veranda and watched the chattering group descend along the path. The closing of the gate signified frantic waves all around.

What little was left of the evening was spent by Daphers and I mulling over the various humorous happenings of the afternoon, talking about whether they had enjoyed it, and of course tidying up. I quickly set and lit the log-burner and while doing this my mind wandered back to that horrible dreadful time in England, questioning if we would ever be able to get over it.

# Chapter Two

The following morning we overslept and rushed around doing ablutions and things, with no time for the log-burner. I was in the bedroom changing into my going-out clothes when Daphers poked her head around the door.

"What are you wearing?"

"A shirt with a white collar, dark blue trousers, and a jacket." I was always bewildered as to why she wanted to know.

We had been invited to attend a lunch today, at the house of Tom and Yvonne who are English and friends of a friend. We had both forgotten the reason for the party, possibly Yvonne's birthday. Because of this, our strategy is to take a really good bottle of wine and the best flowers we can find and bluff them into thinking we know why we have been invited, and possibly avoid appearing rude.

Things were put in the car, and we drove for about an hour. French houses are notoriously difficult to find, and this one was no exception. It was up a lane, down a dirt track, and finally culminated in the courtyard of a very nice stone-built property of indiscernible age.

Pleasingly we were not the first to arrive. Our male host Tom greeted us at the door, and we gave him the wine; luckily for us he said:

"The birthday girl is through there in the lounge." We went where he pointed and gave the present to Yvonne, plus kisses galore.

The lounge was full of people, some we knew but most we didn't know, which made me slightly unsure why we had been invited to this little clique of English people living in France; it was unusual. I was given champagne, Daphers had sparkling water, indicating it was her turn to drive home. We joined the party and were catching up on the news and gossip when we were requested to go into the dining room, which was set for twelve.

The lunch and wine were extremely agreeable, and as the coffee was served, a lady introduced by our host, began giving a talk on her holiday in an out-of-way place in Africa. God, it was boring, and I was just about to feign illness when she finally finished. Afterwards, we broke away into small groups and chatted with various people.

I found myself talking to a couple we had met around a year earlier, who lived in South-East England and were friends of the hosts. Through the haze of general chit-chat, they began to talk about the growing crime in England, and a particular crime committed not far from where they lived. I listened intently, as they told me what had occurred. It involved two men, who stopped a girl and her old grandfather in a car near a wood on the outskirts of a town late at night. One of the men dragged the girl out of the car, the other man attacked the grandfather. Both the grandfather and the girl managed to put up such a fight, the men eventually backed off enough to allow the old man, who kept the car-engine running, to drive forward in an attempt to run one of the attackers down. He was partially successful, and in the end, the two men gave up and disappeared into the darkness. The girl was left bruised and shaken, with her clothes ripped. The local paper printed the story, but the description of the men was vague, and they were never found. Extensive searches and inquiries were carried out, but no arrests were ever made.

At this point, we were joined by Gary, a friend of the hosts. He was a tall, slightly red-faced, balding man about forty-odd, who introduced himself, and we shook hands.

"I overheard what you were talking about," he said. "I know someone who lives close to the villages and rumour has it, all the problem stems from one family, who were forced to move there a few years ago."

Suddenly, from inside, I experienced a stab of frightening recollection, a past memory. Something crawled up from the base of my spine, along my back to the nape of my neck, and at that moment enormous amounts of adrenalin flowed. Was this too much of a coincidence? My curiosity was forcibly aroused.

Compelling myself not to appear too interested, but staying ever so slightly enthusiastic, I calmly and casually asked:

"It must be awful to live near people like that. Is the family at loggerheads with everyone in the village, or are they only at loggerheads with one another?"

Gary looked at me and replied, "From what I have heard, they are apparently at loggerheads with everyone. They are in it together, two brothers, nasty pieces of work. I suppose you could say they are as thick as thieves together, although from all accounts a lot worse than that."

This conversation now had my full attention and was getting fearsomely engrossing. I needed desperately to calm down, but also to glean additional information from Gary, but it had to be done gently and without him knowing exactly why. This wasn't my field at all, so I feebly ventured:

"Mind you, it is a beautiful part of England that South-East corner, not an area Daphers and I have ventured into much. We have passed through it many times, but never stayed."

This comment was not very good, but it did provoke a response, possibly influenced by the amount of champagne and wine Gary had consumed.

"Are you the fellow who was a Captain in the Merchant Navy?"

"Yes," I said.

"I bet you have been around the world a few times."

"Yes, a few times."

"Yet you have never stayed down in Kent."

I had listened to and had these sort of conversations before, especially from somebody who had enjoyed the internal contents of a bottle, so I very gently produced:

"Well, we have passed through, to catch the ferry at Dover."

"You have never stayed around Canterbury then?"

Before I could speak he turned his head and looked around the room. My eyes followed his, he waved to someone and called out:

"Doris."

A smart attractive woman slightly older than he acknowledged the wave, politely excused herself from the company and came over.

"Doris, I want you to meet Matthew. He's been around the world and visited all sorts of places, but never visited Canterbury or Kent. He has passed through to catch the ferry, but never stayed."

This was a 'too much to drink' conversation and was going nowhere. Fortunately, Tom arrived and filled our empty glasses with wine. Doris took a sip from her glass, then ventured:

"Next time you come over to England on the ferry, pop in and see us."

Her husband interjected. "Why don't you come over for the wedding? Our daughter is getting married in a few weeks," then as an after-thought said, "Tom and Yvonne are coming, it would be nice if you came too."

Doris added: "We can recommend some wonderful hotels in Canterbury."

For my part, the conversation had suddenly taken a turn for the better. It did sound like a chance to find out more about this irritatingly gruesome family that somehow seemed familiar, also to have a look at the Kent countryside, maybe even get to see some cricket.

"I shall have a word with my wife Daphne, and scan the diary; it does sound a rather splendid idea to me. Can I have your email address?"

Gary handed me a printed card with all his details, and I popped it into my top pocket. "I'll go and see if I can find my wife," I said and wandered off, vaguely searching different rooms.

After a while I found her talking to Yvonne, sidling over allowed the chat to tail off. When it did, I asked Daphers the question:

"Gary and Doris have invited us to the wedding of their daughter, in a few weeks in Kent – what do you think?"

She looked at me in a puzzled manner and I could see from the expression on her face she had too many questions and not enough answers. Also, she was surprised to see I was keen to go to this wedding knowing weddings were not my favourite type of entertainment.

Returning to her usual calmness, she smiled and commented: "Let's go and see Gary and Doris."

We three returned to the other room where Gary was pouring himself another glass of wine. Doris looked up and saw us approaching, an introduction was made and female-type conversation immediately followed.

It was a time for me to take a back seat and contemplate the situation. An awful lot had happened in the last half-hour. I was feeling excitement, anger and curiosity all at the same time and it was a devil of a job trying to keep them under control. To help I side-stepped my way into a deserted part of the garden and followed the path around the lawn. It was time for some serious thinking.

Apart from the Kent area and the wedding being rather pleasant I suppose, it might produce some subjective transient information. However, there was a big question to contend with. If all this information about these brothers was relevant, what was I going to do with it? I was feeling a bit uncomfortable with this perturbing snippet of knowledge.

My rambling around the garden finally returned me back to the house. Daphers approached me, softly gripped my left elbow and whispered in my ear.

"I'm sure we are free on the day of the wedding. We could go the day before and leave the day after, and have a relaxing tour around Canterbury – what do you think?"

All for it, but not wanting Daphers to suspect my ulterior motive, and also trying to curb my enthusiasm, I replied:

"I think that's a fine idea. We can contact everyone by email when we get home."

The wine had finally registered fully with Gary and was now delivering the full alcohol content to his upper region, and with a slight list to one side, he mumbled:

"I'll give your husband a card."

He handed me another card and I placed it in my top pocket with its companion and pretended not to have received the first. This incident indicated to me it was time to go; fortunately, other guests were showing similar signs by heading for the front door, all getting ready for the usual elaborate farewell exit.

We thanked Tom and Yvonne and as we slid into the car to a multitude of waves, somebody shouted.

"Don't forget to come to the wedding." It may have been Gary.

On the way home, we had the customary discussion on the preceding events. I decided against mentioning the story of the awful incident in the wood. It wasn't the right time.

# Chapter Three

The following day after checking the diary, we contacted Gary, informing him we would be free for the wedding, and arranged a hotel to stay for a few days. It wasn't until some time afterward, that a communication arrived, telling us they were pleased we could make the wedding and looked forward to seeing us. About an hour later, more information arrived telling us they had a problem, and went into an elaborate explanation of why the church organist for the wedding had called off; also how they were unable to get a replacement in time. They were aware Daphne played the piano and organ and hoped it wasn't cheeky, but was it possible she could play the organ at the wedding?

We were having coffee on the veranda when I read the message out. My wife wrinkled her brow. She was a totally independent soul and had played music professionally all her working life. However, she did sometimes take offence at people assuming she would play any time in any place. Fortunately also one of her virtues was tolerance, so I wasn't surprised to hear her say:

"Write back and tell them I would be delighted."

Later she asked me to add: "Can you please ask them to arrange for me to meet with the vicar, late afternoon the day before the wedding, to show me the organ and also the music for the ceremony?"

"That sounds very official to me."

Her reply was rather stern: "If I don't arrange it, they tend to dilly dally and end up doing nothing, then when it all goes wrong on the day, they blame the organist. It is very important to get things right at a wedding."

Then, more softly she added: "This is an attempt to avoid embarrassment all round. I have learned these things from past experience."

Sitting for a moment and sipping coffee, I wrote another email to her instructions, and thought, 'blimey when they receive this message, there will be no messing about'.

Arranging trips to England were usually left to me. My customary preference was the ferry, but on this occasion, we needed a quick crossing, so we gave the train a go and used our French car.

It was always a pleasure to be in England, although as we entered the first road, my heart fell for a moment. Changing over to driving on the left-hand side of the road with a left-hand drive car takes discipline, especially at the first roundabout. It is a must to remember to turn left rather than right. Once this has been achieved driving becomes easier.

Before going to the hotel, we went to the house of Gary and Doris so Daphers could visit the church and verify musical arrangements with the vicar. Luckily these arrangements excluded Gary and myself, and as we were at a loose end, I turned to Gary and quietly ventured:

"How about we drive to a village pub and have a pint? I've not had a pint in an English pub for ages."

This was a well-thought-out ploy on my part and a great opportunity to try and produce more information about this violent attack on the girl and her grandfather nearby, so I probed for a bit more:

"Do you remember when you were at the house of Tom and Yvonne in France, and you talked about those horrible brothers? Can we go and have a look, just for curiosity and see what sort of squalor they live in?"

Gary took the bait very easily. I wasn't sure whether he was interested in it for himself, or simply wanted to get away from the talk of weddings for a while.

"I'll ring Dave, he's a good friend, he'll show us."

He disappeared out of the room, returning within a few minutes with the news that we were to meet Dave in the Dog and Duck in Brogdon, a little village close to Epscomont, the village of this family of the two brothers.

We sidled up to the two ladies and Gary explained he didn't want to go to the church again and preferred to meet up with Dave in the local pub.

I approached Daphers. "We won't be any use wandering around the church when you are practising the organ."

Both ladies looked at us with trepidation. They could see the logic in the separation. Neither were surprised at our suggestion and could see we would only be a nuisance to them by hanging about in the church.

Doris looked directly at Gary.

"It might be wise not to have too many pints." She stopped and started again. "Oh and don't be too long, Matthew and Daphne have to check into their hotel this afternoon."

"We'll go in my car," piped up Gary, as we went through the front door.

I enjoyed seeing the beautiful English countryside on the way to the Dog and Duck, which turned out to be a typical English pub with low beams, old comfortable furniture, and a good atmosphere.

Dave, seeing us enter, put his pint down, stepped forward, greeted Gary, then shook hands vigorously with me. He was around the same age as Gary, only broader in the shoulders with a lot more hair and wearing a rather snazzy jumper. He was full of questions.

"What are you going to have, Matthew? I'll get you the usual, Gary. How is the wedding going?"

We remained standing at the bar. The two pals chatted about the present happenings in their lives; I listened politely, nodding when appropriate. It was a pleasure to see good friends enjoying each other's company. When the chat subsided Dave turned his attention to me.

"I hear you want to have a look and see where these bloody awful blokes live."

Reluctant and not to draw too much attention to those bloody awful blokes, I apologetically mumbled:

"Yes, just to see how different they are, and how they live. Also, it might be nice to see more of the English countryside, you fellows see every day. How about a short guided tour around a few villages, to the next pub."

My inquiry and requests were lame ones, but they did the trick, and we downed our pints and walked out into the sunlit courtyard.

Before getting into the car, Gary thoughtfully asked:

"Are you and Daphne thinking of leaving France and moving back here to the old country? If you are, there isn't a better place to live than here."

What an idea, I thought, at our age anything is possible. Stumped for a reply, I plumped for a bit of flattery.

"You never know, Gary, from what I have seen so far, this area is so lovely, probably the best part of England."

People always enjoy hearing the area where they live to be picturesque, so I considered it not a bad reply.

Sitting in the back of the car and watching the fields, hedges and woods go by in this lovely county of Kent was enthralling. My thoughts were interrupted by Dave whispering:

"We are not far away from the place where these blokes live."

I wrinkled my brow – why was he whispering? Surely nobody could hear us from inside the car. Gary slowed to a crawl and drove close to the kerb, then continued even slower around a bend, not quite daring to enter the road properly. From the right-hand back-seat side window, I could see the road edging its way down into a cul-de-sac. As we crept along, a shiny silver Mercedes overtook us at speed as it rounded the bend, then cut straight in front of us, and Gary braked heavily. Although we weren't going very fast, we all strained into the seat belts and watched worryingly engrossed in the action of the speeding Mercedes.

Dave recovered first. "What was that? What a bloody idiot!"

I said: "Watch where he goes; there you see, into the drive of the semi-detached house, next to the one that looks empty."

At that, Dave stared down at the steering wheel. "Jesus I'm glad I didn't hit him."

I responded. "It wasn't your fault."

"Maybe not, but I'm sure that's the house where one of the blokes live. I suspect if we had hit him, we would have had a load of road rage – anyone connected to these people are to be avoided at all costs."

Breathing out heavily, he went on: "What the hell are we doing here anyway?"

Dave and Gary in the front were both shaken.

I felt embarrassed because it was I who had directed them here. My lack of knowledge of these people did me a favour. "Wait," I said, "someone's coming out."

A thin youth with close-cropped hair, and wearing trainers, ran out of the drive, then headed away from us down the road, crossing over as he did so.

This time I saw Dave breathe a sigh of relief, probably very pleased he wasn't coming our way.

I put my hand on his shoulder. "Just wait for another minute, let's see where he goes."

We all watched, as he ran to the very end of the cul-de-sac close to the edge of the wood, and disappeared into the far house on the left.

Dave put the car into gear. "I've had enough," he said, then made a 'U' turn and drove off as quietly as he could.

I leaned forward between the front seats.

"You fellows are genuinely frightened, aren't you? What on earth is going on here?"

Neither of the men in the front chose to say anything. Dave continued to drive, now rather more quickly than before. After a while, Gary spoke up.

"I reckon on top of what's just happened and the rumours we hear, the place is justified in giving me the jitters. I vote we have another pint in a pub a little closer to home."

This was unanimously agreed upon.

The Bell was busy at the bar, so we took our drinks and sat by the window, and soon the conversation returned to humorous normality. We didn't say anything more about the silver Mercedes incident; I found this a little strange, although understandable for the people living in that cul-de-sac were a long way from the world of Gary and Dave. To them, these people were only a rumour, and they much preferred to leave it that way and dismiss them from their minds.

I was unable to dismiss it from mine.

After our beers, Gary and I returned to Daphers and Doris. Both ladies greeted us, and told us, all had gone well at the church. Nothing whatever was asked about our outing, and we chose not to venture any information.

The following day the wedding ceremony went without a hitch, and Daphers received compliments about her organ-playing. The reception in the village hall was full of drink, food, and good wishes, and we saw the newly-married couple leave on honeymoon. The following day we said our thanks and goodbyes to Gary and Doris.

# Chapter Four

Maximum concentration on directions for the beginning of the journey was necessary; it wasn't until we entered the motorway that Daphers gathered herself together:

"Something has happened, hasn't it?"

I wasn't keen at this stage to let my assumptions free, wanting to keep them to myself until knowing a little more – well, a lot more really. Bringing up the past at this point would be bad timing, so in a rather vague and silly voice, I enquired:

"How do you mean?"

"Matthew, I have known you long enough now, to know when there is something going on in your mind, and this is such an occasion. I don't think anyone else detected it, because they had other things to think about, but they don't know you as well as I, and from time to time your mind was occupied elsewhere, and moreover, it still is."

She stopped speaking for a moment, so I butted in.

"Look, love, you're right. Something has happened." I glanced over to her and thought it might be a good idea to add a little more.

"I want to have a really good think about things, before saying anything further, if that's alright with you?"

"You are agonisingly secretive sometimes, Matthew, but of course it is. Oh, we turn right here and follow the signs until we come to the barrier."

The train was quick and boring and the journey passed reading a newspaper. We discharged ourselves at the other end of the tunnel and sped home down the French motorways.

As we approached the entrance to our house, we both spotted a little furry creature, sitting in front of the gate. I stopped the car, and Daphers got out. We could see it was a cat, not the prettiest thing I had ever seen, as it had multi-coloured fur and a face like a bulldog.

The animal was unmoved. Daphers opened the gate, then focused her attention on the cat, steadily inching towards it.

She turned to me. "I don't think it's very well."

Squeezing the car through the gap between the cat and the gatepost, I drove down the drive and parked by the side of the house.

Daphers eventually followed down the drive on foot.

"I'm going to take it some milk first and see what happens."

The cat was still sitting by the gate; it seemed a sorrowful sad little figure, but strangely content. Daphers arrived with the milk and placed it in front of the cat; there was only a moment's hesitation before lapping action commenced.

On returning to the house she looked at me and contemplated the situation out loud.

"I think it's just hungry, I'm going to see if I can find something for it to eat," and she disappeared into the kitchen.

Within a moment she was back. "I've found a tin of chicken." She opened it, spooned it into a small dish and placed it at the front of the veranda.

Popping inside the house, I made a couple of gin and tonics and returned outside. We both sat watching and waiting with expectation. It wasn't long before the smell of the chicken reached the nostrils of our new friend. With increasing speed it moved down the drive; the food must have been alright because it was fully consumed within a very short space of time.

The look on my wife's face was worth a fortune. "I'm going to put this cushion on the floor by the front door, maybe it will sleep on it."

We went back inside the house, reluctantly closing the door. More gin and tonics and occasional inspection of the cushion kept us busy until we went to bed. After all that had happened over the last few days, we slept very well on our own mattress.

The following morning Daphers was up first and I could hear her in the kitchen, then walking on the veranda.

The door to the bedroom opened. "Matthew, I thought he'd gone, but I put the rest of the chicken out, and he's now eating it."

I smiled: "He's a he, is he? What are you going to call him?"

"I've no idea, you are usually good with names, what do you think?"

"Well, I think we should call him Rainbow or Bulldog."

She stood with the door ajar. "Ah, if we choose either of those names he might not stay."

The normal day carried on, Daphers mostly fussing after the cat. It was fairly obvious they were both getting on rather well.

I busied myself in the garden, as well as thinking about the strange happenings in England which were enough to more than raise strong, fiery feelings inside me. All my reflections were irritably sensitive and had grown stronger over the past few days instead of fading, possibly because of what had happened a long time ago. Now I'm older, these feelings have become more dominant and the beginning of anger has raised its ugly head. Maybe it was time to do something more serious in life, rather than just go to lunches and listen to holiday talks. This business in England needed looking into further, my mind told me things needed to be done. If we were going to do anything it would mean getting away and leaving these very comfortable surroundings.

During a glass of wine on the veranda with Daphers in the evening, I voiced my thoughts.

"This is a strange thing to say, but there is no other way of putting it. What do you think about selling the house and moving?"

She didn't look as shocked as I thought she would and replied: "I knew there was something on your mind – why do you want to move?"

It was necessary to tell a bit of a fib. "It might be nice to move further south for the warmth and it also might be a good idea to bank the money and rent a house. It would create a lovely sense of freedom for us, just to do what we want to do."

She looked at me, picked up her glass of wine, took a sip, then with a hint of a smile replied: "Maybe that's not such a bad idea. I like the idea of freedom, and money in the bank, yes, it would allow us to do anything we wanted."

The conversation continued wandering around the nooks and crannies of both our brains. In the end, we decided it was a good idea to move.

Before we went to bed, we talked about a name for our newly-found friend, who had by now moved in. Because of his facial features, it was decided his name would be 'Bulldog'.

The following morning arrangements were made for an estate agent to attend the house. He eventually came and priced the house including the usual eleven percent agency fee.

Before the 'For Sale' sign went up, we asked all our neighbours to come for an evening aperitif. When they arrived and were all gathered together, we thought a speech from me was necessary so I stood and informed them we were going to move. Immediately after I said it, a surprising silence of dismay descended amongst all assembled. Then someone asked the question in a disgruntled manner:

"Where are you going, back to England?"

This was rather unexpected, so I quickly added:

"No, we are going to seek warmer weather down in the south of France."

This changed the mood completely, and all became amicable again. The distance between the French and English will never diminish.

In the early summer evening, the drinks flowed and we all sat and enjoyed the occasion. I do believe two wheelbarrows were necessary.

Selling a house in France is not an easy process, and we were a little surprised when the agent called to say there was an interested party. We scampered around the house, trying to make everything as inviting and ship-shape as possible. When they arrived the agent shook our hand, but introductions to the viewers never came. At first Daphers and I sat on the veranda watching and listening to this little trio, with a certain amount of curiosity. The viewers consisted of an oldish woman and a man in his thirties. The most noticeable thing about the man was that he was wearing a flowered shirt, buttoned on the girl's side and he wandered around away from the other two. We occasionally heard his mother shouting to him in a high pitch voice.

"Lulu, come here Lulu," in French, of course. Each time she did this, it brought a broad grin to us both, also an inclination to take more notice of the proceedings which caused us to peer around corners of the house to see what they were doing. I felt like a naughty schoolboy. There was a distinct lack of interest paid to the important issues like the condition of the house – they seemed to dwell on the style of the house inside, and the flowers in the garden.

After they left, we were suspicious of the motive of these two people to come and view. One of our inquisitive neighbours waved to us and indicated for us to go for an aperitif. Scurrying over, we told them of the strange disinterest shown in the house by the mother and son. Both our neighbours were aware of this ploy, and additional light was shed on the issue. They explained the viewers were either people who the agents used to view any house on a regular basis, to show they were doing their job properly, or it was the mother and son who were nosy and wanted to see how English people furnished the inside of our house. We couldn't understand why; however, after elongated explanations from our neighbours, we arrived at the conclusion, it was purely and simply because we were English. They wanted to see how we lived before we departed. Similar I suppose to peasants around the guillotine during the reign of terror, it was an opportunity for them to see how we lived, they wanted to see us before we went. The agent had brought a pair of gloaters.

Fortunately, within a matter of months, friends of a friend telephoned and asked if they could come and view the house. They turned out to be Jean-Jacques and Madeleine; he a Major in the French army and his partner a fitness trainer, both delightful people.

After showing them around, we negotiated a total price for the house, with one or two unmanageable heavy pieces of French furniture thrown in as a bonus, most of which were far too heavy and expensive to move anyway.

The estate agent was duly informed, and the complicated French process of buying and selling a house was left to the agent and the Notaire to finalise.

# Chapter Five

Over the years we had, like everyone else, inadvertently collected an abundant amount of essential and non-essential items, some personal, some useful and some just stuff. The most treasured possessions, which did not amount to a great deal, we kept, the rest we gathered together in the garage and decided to try our hand at 'car-booting'. On the evening of announcing to our neighbours our intention of moving, we also informed them of the idea of getting rid of all unwanted items, by getting a pitch at a car boot sale. Something in our translation must have failed, for the whole of the hamlet suddenly involved itself in this escapade, and commenced bringing to us the items they wanted to sell.

I am certain many wars between the French and the English most probably started through the misinterpretation of the languages, plus of course an inordinate amount of greed.

Our car was evicted from the garage and replaced with what could only be described as a great pile of junk. When standing in front of it, at an ungodly hour on the morning of the sale, wondering if we would ever get it all in the back of our pick-up truck, my thoughts were interrupted by a van coming down the drive. Albert lived in a village close by attached to ours by a short road and he had obviously been seconded by the hamlet as their organizer and go-between. He was a very jovial man, well-liked, stockily built, not very tall, born and bred in the village, and certainly an asset.

As he got out of his rather old vehicle, I noticed he was wearing shorts. This was a little surprising to me because he had an aluminium leg, a well-worn aluminium leg. Occasionally, when assisting me in the past, he had always worn trousers, today I tried very hard not to look at his false leg, but was unable to stop myself, and he noticed. We embroiled ourselves in the usual French greetings and pleasantries, lingering on the handshake a second longer than normal, and eventually, he pointed to his leg.

"I've brought my safe with me today, to put the big banknotes in."

At that, he lifted the leg of his shorts higher, then to my amazement opened a little trap-door in the top of his aluminium leg.

"Keeps the important coloured paper money out of harm's way," he said.

He then shut the trap-door, smiled a broad smile and went on further to explain all the details of the plan for the morning. Arrangements had been made for us to have two pitches on a site in a town not too far away, and Marc and Marie would be here in a minute to help load all the stuff into the pick-up and the van.

It wasn't long before the two neighbours arrived with more bags, this time mainly full of things to eat and drink. With renewed enthusiasm and everyone pulling together, the van and the truck were soon full. Last to go on top of everything were the trestles and boards for quick assembly of the stall tables on arrival.

Before getting into the pick-up, I found myself standing by the side of it, staring cross-eyed at nothing, focusing on nothing, slightly panicking, wondering whether this massive change in our lives was the right thing to do, questioning if all this was eventually going to be for a just cause. Something secretly within myself was driving me forward; the worst thing of all was knowing I needed to pursue this thing right to the end, there was no going back!

My attention was brought to the present by a female voice from inside the cab saying:

"Are you going to get in and drive, love?"

We set off in convoy, Albert who was familiar with the route, leading the way, then Daphers me and our neighbours in the pick-up behind. Soon we were heading through the entrance of a very large field designated for the sale, then on to our two allotted positions. We parked behind the markers and wasted no time in erecting our counters.

Daphers and I had experienced car-boot sales before in England and were sure they would be the same here. We were right, the rummagers were the first people to arrive; they are like moles only with eyes, groping inside the back of the pick-up, never giving anyone time to get things arranged on display. To combat this, I had placed an old sheepskin coat destined for the bin on top of the boxes of small items, to try and hide their contents in an effort to side-stepping these infernal searchers, but it was to no avail, they were there, and very active.

Out of the corner of my eye, I noticed one particular competitor with a short Van-Dyck beard, taking more than a passing interest in the aforementioned sheepskin coat. My initial reaction was to advise him, if he would like it for nothing, he could have it. I was about to say this to him, when suddenly with one deft movement of his arms, he swished the coat around his shoulders like a cavalier, and strutted backward and forwards a few paces trying to seek a mirror and admire himself. At this point, I decided it was time for me to play the game and pretend not to be interested in his capers. I busied myself with other things, whilst secretly thinking maybe, 'the horseshoe of good fortune' was cantering towards us'. The more our rummager strutted about the place, the more the price went up. The coat was now off the shoulders and was being worn properly; I must say it did fit him rather well.

Unfortunately, the time arrived where we needed all the items from the back of the truck, so it was necessary for me to approach the catwalk area. He tried to curb his enthusiasm, but it was no good, I had seen it, and he knew.

"How much?" he said gruffly in French.

I was now so embroiled in this fiasco, I cheekily said: "Forty euros." He turned, admired himself in the mirror once more, dipped his hand into his pocket, withdrew two twenty-euro notes, delivered them into my hand and walked off.

'The horseshoe of good fortune' had satisfactorily deposited a little bonus into my wallet.

We did very brisk trade right up to lunch when of course everything stopped – or rather, slowed down. Our little group consumed plenty of wine and food, which resulted in some over-exuberant selling in the afternoon.

The door in Albert's leg opened and closed on many occasions.

Towards the end of the day, on hearing raised female voices from the other table, I twisted around and saw a middle-aged woman running past me with a frying-pan clutched in her right hand. This startled me because it was not a sight I had come across often. The woman was closely followed by Marie shouting, "Arret, arret, stop stop." Some of the other language she shouted escaped my hearing, but I don't think it was, 'could you please stop, you have pinched our frying pan'.

Due to the weight of the fairly sizeable item, Marie soon caught up with the woman, and a fierce argument between them ensued. Feeling somewhat responsible for the situation because the frying pan belonged to us, I dispatched myself towards this fracas, thinking this could easily turn into a very awkward incident, and tried my best to step in between the two women. As I did this a man approached from out of the crowd. He appeared to be of a similar background to the woman, and I adjudged him to be a possible relation. Luckily for us, the woman, on seeing the man, for some reason changed her mind about the frying pan and threw it to the ground. This extremely heavy iron object didn't manage to hit the ground, only the foot of the newly arrived relative, and resulted in him jumping up and down, holding his foot and shouting a lot of words in French and other languages not in the dictionary. He also commenced wagging his finger at her in a forcefully aggressive fashion, which was not really necessary. In the increased general mayhem, she saw her chance, and shot off away from the group at a far greater speed than before, possibly because she was now not impeded by the heavy weight of the frying pan.

The man, for some unknown reason, now blamed his sore foot on me, and gesticulated wildly, speaking in French quickly, and with an accent, and staring at me very close face to face. It was patently obvious he suffered very badly from halitosis, which was extremely unpleasant. Not knowing what to say, I just stood my ground and endured more bad breath. The tension was suddenly broken when he whirled around and painfully limped away following the path of the woman. Why on earth she had plunged the frying pan onto his foot was beyond me. Looking at the back of him hobbling off, I thought, I'm sure walking in the other direction would be a better idea.

Marie recovered the frying pan and put it back on the stall. She spoke heatedly in French to her husband Marc, who had not moved from his position but had watched the entertainment placidly from afar.

When everything had calmed down, Daphers winched herself over to me.

"You could have ended up in a lot of trouble there, trying to part two excitable women and a very excitable man."

"I felt responsible, the frying pan is ours, and Marie is only little."

"From what I have just seen, I am sure she can take care of herself."

It was a strange incident. Why should the woman steal a frying pan? Was there more to it? Had I saved the man from being beaten to death with the frying pan in the middle of the night? The woman had deliberately dropped the pan on the man's foot and it looked very painful. Also, where had my sudden act of bravery come from? I hadn't been able to stop myself, it had just seemed the right thing to do.

A combination of cheap selling and giving items away for free, left only the trestle tables, boards and empty bags remaining in the back of the pick-up truck.

When we arrived home, it was pleasing to see Albert's van looking fuller and plumper as it chugged down our drive and parked up; I think he might have been a bit of a hoarder. We all sat around the veranda in comfy chairs, drinking beer and chilled wine. The door in Albert's aluminium leg produced a surprising amount of folded money. Amicable divisions were given to everyone of the days' takings. The illustrious farewells were a great reflection on the outcome of the day.

# Chapter Six

One morning sometime during the following months, our French friend Jean-Claude telephoned. He and his wife Genevieve lived in a house very close to the city of Toulouse in the south of France. After the usual niceties at the beginning of the call, he came to the point, saying we had not been to see them for a while, and it was time for us to visit. I filled in a few details and told him of our intention to sell our house here in the Loire. This provoked an onslaught of comment, one of which was a definite insistence to go and see them.

"Matthew," he said, "Genevieve and my mother are visiting my mother's sister, and they are going to stay with her for a couple of days, so my mother's house is empty. Why don't you both come and join me, in her house in the little village of Eeee."

Both Jean-Claude and Genevieve were a delightful adventurous couple, both retired, slightly younger than us. They had visited and stayed with us on many occasions, and we had reciprocated by holidaying with them in their house in Toulouse. The village of Eeee was situated in and around the borders of the Pyrenees and they had talked about it in the past and portrayed it with enthusiasm. Our conversation continued on the phone until I finished by saying, "I will ring you back after talking with Daphers." He thought this was a good idea and said, "Don't leave it too long."

During lunch, Daphers and I chatted about the invitation from Jean-Claude. She indicated a preference to stay at home and monitor the progress of the agent and solicitors in selling the house. I also secretly believed there were two more reasons: firstly she wanted to leave the boys together, and secondly, she wanted to remain and look after and be with 'Bulldog', who had grown into a most honourable cat, and on reflection, deserved to be called another name. Nevertheless, he did respond to Bulldog when called, be it in his own time. He was unable to change his facial features, however – everybody who visited admired him, asked his name and when told, smiled a smile of acknowledgment, although many edges of the smiles had a tinge of pity. He had surprisingly quickly become one of the family.

I didn't leave the return call to our friend too long and was slightly unsure of his reaction to my coming alone. His tone told me he didn't seem to mind at all and gave me the impression something was afoot; maybe Daphers was right, all boys together might be good. This was clarified by his remark:

"Bring some really strong boots and don't bring anything smart."

It was agreed I should take the car to travel to Toulouse and leave the pick-up-truck for Daphers. She was never keen on touring around in the pick-up-truck with its right-hand drive and cumbersome oversize cargo space at the back, although whenever she drove it, she always returned with a smile on her face. I think it was something to do with the reaction of the French men, who found it marginally irritating to see a woman in command of such a large vehicle.

Unsure of what Jean-Claude had in mind and using my knowledge of previous experiences with him, I filled my holdall with everything I thought best and placed additional strong boots in the car along with a case of my favourite Bordeaux wine.

Daphers waved me off from the veranda with 'Bulldog' sitting by her side, like one of those adored porcelain cat figures, tail tucked in, aware that things were afoot but impervious as to why.

I disappeared down the drive, through the gates, and along the lane, waving frantically. My intention was to join the autoroute as soon as possible – it was expensive but a darn sight quicker than the ordinary roads and perfect for people like me, who found driving a bit of a chore.

I was very pleased to arrive at the townhouse of Jean-Claude and Genevieve, without the mandatory slow crawl. The gates to the drive were open for me, and the house was bathed in glorious sunshine. While I was stretching my legs and stamping my feet, Jean-Claude came out through the French doors, and an eruption of greeting commenced; a delight I never tired of.

He was younger and shorter than I, slightly built but strong-looking, with a full head of hair, and a good stride. Both his dogs followed him and jumped up and greeted me, then lost interest and wandered off, sniffing at various unknown doggy things in the garden.

He started speaking to me in English, reeling off a practised little speech, having put some thought into our initial meeting but soon lapsed back into French as the conversation became more involved. After all the pleasantries about families and an account of my journey, he proclaimed, "I have made some soup for us, before we go to Eeee, OK?"

I gestured an agreement as we went through into the kitchen. During our meal, he asked why Daphers and I were moving. I fibbed a bit and told him we wanted warmer weather, and maybe a move further south was on the cards. He rather liked this, and with arms raised, suggested there was no better place than the area around Toulouse; my smiling and nodding brought a huge grin to his face. He also enthused about the forest, the mountains and cottage in the stillness of the Pyrenees and further chatted about his family home and explained how he had enjoyed his childhood, then left in his teens to go to university. Later he married, bought a house and only went back to his tiny house in Eeee from time to time, saying there wasn't enough space in the tiny house for him and his family to stay and sleep.

We were both keen to start our journey down to Eeee, and decided it a good idea for me to follow him down in my car. The dogs were used to his car and had their special blanket over the back seat.

Reflecting on the history of his life and wondering what the house would be like, certainly enabled me to pass the time and it was approaching nightfall when we arrived.

# Chapter Seven

We entered the village of Eeee on what looked like the main road, and slowed down to a crawl, turned right into a gate-less pebbled grassy sort of drive, and parked my car away from the house close to a very old outbuilding that seemed to be barely clinging to life.

As we opened the car doors, the dogs were out and about. Jean-Claude and I slipped around the side and entered the house from the rear. The cottage was on one level, not very big; basically, four rooms, consisting of two bedrooms a toilet and bathroom, a main room which was quite large acting as a sort of lounge and kitchen combined.

Dumping the gear in the bedrooms, we placed all the wine on the table and the food Jean-Claude had brought in the kitchen area. The house itself, had a cosiness about it, with an open fire, which gave the room a snugness and warm feeling of old-world charm.

Steak, salad and a bottle of wine appeared and we ate, drank and talked. At a break in the conversation, Jean-Claude looked at me quizzically, paused for an immeasurably long time.

"Matthew, for many years I have been coming here to my family home, and nearly every time I'm here I search the mountains for a special Cepes, and have never been able to find them. You are aware these are the best mushrooms in France and are highly prized by everyone. The ones my father found and collected are a very special variety, having the most exquisite flavour."

I didn't know a great deal about this particular fungus, always regarding mushrooms as a dangerous species of vegetable. I mentioned this to him and he drew a small book from a shelf and thumbed through it. First, he showed me the edible Cepes mushroom, then he moved on to others which grew in the forest not far from where we were. He turned to the page showing a photograph of the deadliest mushroom of all in France, which had the scary name 'le chalice de la mort' or in English 'the chalice of death'. It didn't look particularly gruesome but when I asked if we could collect some, Jean-Claude looked directly at me and raised an eyebrow.

"Why do you want some 'chalice de la mort', Matthew?" He maintained his eyebrow in the raised position, slowly adding a faint quizzical smile.

The real reason I wanted a sample of these deadly mushrooms was because they were able to kill people, quietly and silently, without anyone visibly noticing. It was an idea that could possibly come in handy in the not too distant future, but I couldn't under any circumstances tell Jean-Claude, so I quickly and calmly said:

"Just to keep them in a box and show our neighbours."

It was a pathetic response to try and move the conversation along, so I quickly asked the question, "Where are all these mushrooms?"

To my surprise, he hesitated and winced just a little.

"I can find the 'Chalice de mort', but only have a reasonable idea where the best Cepes mushrooms are. Tomorrow I would like us both to start early, and go and try to find the special places where this rare variety is hidden away."

He then went quiet and very serious.

"Look, the forest can be very dangerous. Every time I venture deep inside, it seems to change, especially if we go off the beaten track. Sometimes it can be full of unpleasant surprises, and unforeseen dangers and many wild beasts prowling about."

He stopped for a moment, poured more wine into his glass, took a good gulp, then continued.

"It is always better for two people to go together, it is why I'm asking you to go with me tomorrow, it is always better to have two. If one gets into difficulty, the other can go for help. It is easy to fall down the slopes. The problem is, once you fall and start rolling, it is sometimes extremely difficult to stop unless you slam into a tree to break your fall. Unfortunately, that usually breaks something and it's never the tree."

It suddenly dawned on me, this was why he had called. I was somewhat taken aback by his seriousness and paid a lot more attention than usual. I was aware his father had died rather young but was unaware of the circumstances. There were questions on my mind, but I chose not to ask and sat very still in silence.

His face showed sadness, and he began to speak again.

"My father was a carpenter and had a workshop in the village, he worked very hard for the family and managed to send me to university."

Jean-Claude took more than a sip from his wine glass, then still staring at the table, elaborated on his history:

"I loved him and was grateful to him, he gave me the best start in life. The question which is always lingering in my mind; was I grateful enough? The house here is very, very small, and so visiting and staying was difficult, there was never enough room for myself and the children. Should I have visited more often? There always seemed to be other things to do with my own family."

He stopped speaking and tried to control himself, but was unable to, and a tear appeared in both his eyes; he cleared his throat. "One day he went deep into the forest by himself and by nightfall he hadn't returned."

Now tears began running freely down his cheeks; he didn't try to suppress them, but let them flow as if he wanted to do that. He silently took his wine glass in both hands and held it up in front of himself, as if he was studying its contents but he wasn't. The flow of tears relented, and he looked straight at me.

"My mother rang me, I came straight away. One of the search party found him; the village was full of speculation as to why and how he died."

Again another silence. "I should have visited more often."

There are occasions when men need to cry. I don't think it was planned, it just happened.

Eventually, he left the table and went into the bathroom.

He was in the bathroom for a long time. I took this time out to contemplate what to say to him on his return. When he came out, he went to his bag, took out a bottle of whisky, two glasses from the cupboard and sat once more at the table, poured two generous glasses of whisky and handed one of the tumblers to me.

"Thanks for listening," he said.

We downed our whisky in one go. "Another?" he said.

"Yes," I replied, "slightly less generous."

This brought a smile to his face, which caused me to smile. We shook hands with upright arms close to the chest; it sort of sealed our friendship.

The nights were sharp, and because the house was without adequate insulation, a heavy duvet and a large blanket were an essential covering on the bed. While thinking about what had happened in the evening, and what was going to happen the following day, my thoughts were interrupted by sleep, thankfully.

# Chapter Eight

I slept extremely well; it could have had something to do with the long drive, or more likely the wine and the whisky. Poking my nose out of the duvet and looking around the bedroom in the morning, revealed a small room by modern standards with an old-fashioned wardrobe sitting in the corner, which reduced the amount of floor space considerably, also a chair at one side which did the same. I abandoned the morning shower and stepped straight into the clothes from my bag, putting on two pairs of socks before my heavy boots, the temperature inside indicating it would likely be even more chilly outside.

On wandering into the main room of the house, I found the smell of toast and coffee in abundance. Jean-Claude greeted me with a firm, genuine shake of his hand, my sincere reciprocal response gave me a satisfactory glow; what a lovely start to the day! The breakfast was as scrumptious as the smell it produced. When it was finished, I made a short telephone call to Daphers. She indicated everything was alright with the house sale, and Bulldog was behaving himself, so all was well.

After the breakfast things were cleared away, Jean-Claude moved about checking cupboards and the attic for useful equipment to enable us to go on our adventurous voyage into the forest. His main aim amongst other things being the old family rucksacks. He eventually found what he was seeking, and set them on the kitchen table. He then filled them with food for the day for us and the dogs, and other essential items. We donned jumpers and hats to ward off the chill of the early morning in the Pyrenees and ambled to the door with shoulders loaded up. The eagerness of the dogs to go outside was excitingly apparent.

On opening the door we were greeted by a misty early morning freshness, and a sensation in the air warranting a moment's hesitation. It was worth delaying to enjoy a concentrated awareness of an unidentifiable chorus of sounds far away. It was the first time I had heard such harmony and found it extremely difficult to describe, sounding like a conglomeration of cries, whistles, rustles, and other indecipherable noises. Probably common in many forests of the world, but present here, high in the mountains of the Pyrenees.

I stood still for a moment, and a tingling sensation ran through the whole of my body. Jean-Claude immediately sensed the same air of anticipation; he turned towards me and gripped my shoulder.

"Matthew, the forest is alive."

We lingered longer and stood subdued, listening intently. I suspected he could hear things distinctly familiar above the noisy stillness, far beyond the realms of my hearing. The dogs were already waiting at the garden gate; I opened it and let them bound enthusiastically along the track to freedom, but a call from their master soon brought them back to heel.

We made steady progress into the forest, mainly climbing along past huge bushes and tall trees so thick with leaf, they blocked out any light. My friend in front suddenly changed direction and traversed sideways along a not so well used route, then continued down a steep slope. I could see how easy it would be to get lost in this dense forest – for me it would need a great deal of time, a compass and a set of very good navigation charts to find my way back to the house.

We had been walking for quite a long time, when a movement beyond the bushes way off, startled us to attention. We both stopped frozen stiff; Jean-Claude and I looked at each other in surprise, apprehension and excitement. He put a hand out for the dogs to stay; they stayed.

"Maybe a sanglier," he said gleefully.

Daphers and I had encountered sanglier or wild boar before briefly when we had been cutting timber for the fire in a wood near where we lived. Wild boar were not the most friendly of creatures, especially if they had young with them. It had happened when we were driving home in the pick-up truck down a remote path. A very large male had defiantly decided we were a threat to him and had resolved to make his presence felt by bulldozing into us as we slowly nudged our way in between the trees. Although our pick-up truck was large, this brute of a beast desperately wanted us to move away and commenced barging and buffeting Daphne's side door. Darkness had been approaching which made the situation even more difficult and the whole thing became very, very frightening. The noise of him hitting into the truck continued until he left us alone when we were clear of the trees. It hadn't been one of our most pleasant experiences. These creatures were not afraid of anything, or anybody, if annoyed.

Jean-Claude held my arm; the dogs didn't move. It was a tense moment and my eyes squinted, trying to discover any image at a distance in the bushes. A large male wild boar would possibly stand his ground, even with two dogs present. It was a curious and scary moment for me, as these surroundings were unfamiliar, a tiny bead of sweat ran its way down from the nape of my neck the small of my back. A bit of tension now and again was alright, but this was lasting a lot longer than necessary and was beginning to get uncomfortable. Surely if it was a wild boar, the dogs would be out of control and running frantically towards the rustling noise, but they stayed as commanded, looking in the direction of the movement.

Gradually into view above the bushes from the left, appeared what looked like a pink baseball cap travelling along the top of the hedge line. It was rather a strange sight, like a puppet bobbing up and down. It continued to the right, then came closer and closer; by now Jean-Claude was laughing.

A man carrying a gun came into view, I joined Jean-Claude in laughter, but my laughter was not as bold as my friend's, it was kind of unsure and half-hearted, because the man was unknown to me and had a gun in his hand. He was a big strapping fellow, over six foot tall with a well turned out moustache, bushy eyebrows, a crooked nose and wearing a pink baseball cap. In any team competition, he was the type of chap you wanted on your side. He also looked very much at ease carrying a gun, and my previous unsure fears quickly disappeared.

Jean-Claude shook him by the hand and embraced him, and treated him like a long lost brother. When the two finally separated, he introduced me to his friend. His name was Christian; the rustling of the trees obliterated his surname, hopefully, it wasn't important. His handshake was less vigorous for a chap his size, also his straining eyes and wrinkled brow told me he didn't care much for the English. How he knew I was English was a mystery, maybe it was the startlingly fast messages sent up the grapevine in the village. It was obvious the two pals hadn't seen each other for a considerable time and they chatted excitedly about everything.

Eventually, Christian brought up the subject of why we were carrying rucksacks and wearing walking gear. Jean-Claude explained to him by saying:

"I am determined to find the really pungent mushrooms my father discovered all those years ago, so we are going to look deeper in the forest."

"Ah," he remarked with a smile. "You've been trying to find them for years."

It was said in a kind of sarcastic way, I took this to be a little bit of French banter. Jean-Claude took it in good part, then gently probed Christian:

"Any sign of wild boar on your travels?"

Christian's moustache twitched. "I've seen movements, nothing positive, although I am sure they are about."

He then spoke very quickly, using a strong French accent, probably trying to hide the conversation from me. Familiar with this type of thing, especially from strangers, I hung on in there and found he was giving further gentle banter to my friend, insinuating he would never find these rare mushrooms and added:

"Maybe it's a good idea to take an Englishman with you, to find them for you."

This brought more laughter from the pair. I smiled and wagged my finger from side to side, indicating acknowledgment of understanding the language, this brought even further laughter. The laughter from the lips of Jean-Claude was kind of forced.

Christian, still musing over what he had said, took our hands and shook them, and asked if we were both going to the bar tonight for the England-France Six Nations rugby match. We both said we wouldn't miss it.

"See you there then, don't be late!" he said, and started to walk away, then suddenly remembered something, turned and raised his eyebrows.

"Maybe I can win my money back after the Wales versus France game."

He then chuckled and disappeared along the path. I couldn't help wondering which of these two men had bet on Wales.

Jean-Claude by now had recovered from his teasing and stared ahead into the distance. Then lifting his arm and pointing, he indicated the direction in which we should go.

"Let's go along that way, through those trees on the right."

We began walking up an incline but didn't travel very far before he stopped, hesitated, looked roundabout then back at me. His demeanour told me he was unsure where to go next. It was evidently necessary for us to search for new places; we were not going to find these mushrooms in all the old places he had previously searched.

After walking for a considerable distance, we crossed a gulley, slowed down and stopped. He stood motionless with an inquisitive expression on his face. The closeness of trees and bushes in the forest made it very difficult to distinguish between one area and another – paths or any form of track had now disappeared altogether.

He looked at me. "We are looking for a very old gnarled oak tree, I have a reasonable idea where it is, but have never been able to find it. The mushrooms are not directly underneath, they are near-by; the old tree is only a guide. We'll try this way, shout if you want a rest."

We plunged further into the forest and the dogs took the opportunity to scurry off into the undergrowth out of sight, then return back in line, passing frequently in between us. As we moved along, shafts of light from the sun penetrated through the gaps in the trees, and the leaves swivelled on the branches, the display the forest produced was spectacular.

We eventually found a gathering of tree stumps and stopped to have lunch. It was a pleasant relief to offload our backpacks containing the ham and cheese baguettes as well as the bottles of Bordeaux wine.

The dogs were not forgotten and gulped down all they were given.

With rucksacks back in place, we continued, veering away from the track, striding further and further through the trees. Before long a mist appeared, and the forest felt quite ghostly. Jean-Claude forged ahead, I followed closely in his wake like a tug boat assisting in berthing a big ship, but also trying to take in the beauty of the forest at the same time. As we climbed a knoll, a shaft of light caught a black shape to my left; I immediately thought it was a large statue. Eventually, the penny dropped and I realised it must be the gnarled oak, so I shouted to Jean-Claude to wait.

He stopped, and I pointed in the direction of the black shape. He looked across, but from where he was standing, it may not have been possible for him to see it because of the intrusion of a couple of large bushes.

The oak tree itself had died many years ago, but the bulk of it remained and was now a gigantic structure trying to retain its dignity. It was situated off the beaten track, and difficult to see. Luck had played a part in my discovery, for it was easier following behind and scanning the forest, than concentrating and deciding where to go.

Jean-Claude walked back and stood beside me, staring where I was pointing. At first, he was cautious, then suddenly he broke forth into life, glaring with sheer joy at the object and clasping me around the shoulders. Before I could move, he was off scrambling between the bushes and trees towards the large blackened shape, and I followed him, stumbling over dead branches and old trees and suddenly there was sky in front of us.

The death of the great oak had allowed sunlight to shine through, and rain to fall freely on the ground around the base of the trunk. My French friend could not contain himself; his eyes were like organ stops searching the ground. Luckily, Jean-Claude was the first to go and explore behind the massive trunk – it would have been dreadful if I had found the mushrooms first. It was imperative that he be the one to successfully find the treasure. I heard him yell: "Matthew, Matthew here, here."

I went to the other side of the trunk and gazed at the light-brown solid-looking mushrooms, and was amazed at their enormous size.

We placed our rucksacks on the ground nearby and removed the special containers Jean-Claude had confidently packed. He showed me the way to pluck the mushrooms from the soil, by picking them firmly from the base, and putting them into the containers, top to toe, every one a prize in itself.

They had a pungent scent and a relatively leathery texture on the outer skin. I was fully aware these delicate fungi were going to be eaten by me later in the day. I secretly hoped they were going to be as good as he said.

We secured the containers in the rucksacks and strapped them on our backs. Before we started our return journey back to the delightful cottage, I asked in a soft voice whether we could search for the 'chalice de la mort' mushrooms.

He shook his head from side to side ever so slightly. I could see his eyes had an enquiring look in them, but he smiled and said:

"Yes, I know where they are, we need to go this way."

We traversed a slope and walked along a line of trees. He suddenly turned behind one of them and pointed to the ground. "There," he said.

The mushrooms he pointed at were white with a bit of orange on the top and didn't look in any way dangerous or lethal.

"They look like normal mushrooms to me."

"Yes, that's why they are so deadly. Do you still want some?"

"Yes," I said not even thinking about it. I just said it with a new kind of determination in my voice, which I was surprisingly pleased about.

I took a container from my rucksack, placed in it several 'Chalice of death' and sealed the lid.

Once we hit the main track, the dogs took over the lead and hurried and harried us on our way back to the cottage, trying to encourage additional speed with the possibility of more food. The path rambled and zigzagged continuously all the way. Why weren't the footpaths ever straight? Maybe the first men who made them drank excessively.

# Chapter Nine

On the journey along the winding track back to the cottage, my brain ambled into pondering and thinking on things and lingered on my action of selling the house. Was it the very first step on a very long ladder? I knew it would inevitably lead to the possibility of difficult, demanding and fearsome alterations in our lives. I felt under the circumstances it was a move we absolutely had to take, words buzzed around in my mind, one of which was selfishness; it rolled around for a while. Although Daphers had agreed to all I suggested, love and the utmost care with her must be given in large doses in all things from now on. We were both of an age where fitness was going to be a companion for only so long. If we were going to do some really serious things, I felt now was the time to do it – doing nothing was not going to achieve anything, something definitely had to be done. As I walked it occupied a corner of my mind and wouldn't go away. I wanted and required a very important second step, which was not in view yet. Patience was annoyingly needed; it was a waiting game. I told myself to just carry on and be patient, hopefully, able to recognise the second step when it arrived.

My brain returned to negotiating the ground ahead, and we made steady progress down the track, eventually arriving at Jean-Claude's lovely family home. The dogs ran excitedly to the gate and flew through when it was opened; I guessed it was the expectation of food. The ultimate rattle of tin plates indicated I was right.

We unpacked our precious cargo from the rucksacks onto the kitchen work-surface, and I occupied myself by making the fire. On beginning to lay the table for a very late lunch, a tablecloth was handed to me; crikey, I thought, this is a special occasion.

Jean-Claude did magic things by introducing eggs and the precious mushrooms into a large frying pan. We sat at the table, ate and talked about our little adventure, opened a second bottle of Bordeaux wine, savoured it, talked about its colour, smoothness and lingering flavour, then eventually drank it. The mushrooms were delicious thankfully, and compliments were given to a very fine chef.

Through the whole of the morning and the meal, our conversation never mentioned nor queried what had happened in the outside world on that day, it didn't seem to matter somehow, and made everything idyllic and satisfying.

"Shall we have another bottle of wine?" he enquired.

A cork was extracted from another bottle, and the contents were dispatched with ease. I looked at Jean-Claude.

"I think it is time to bank the fire up, select one of your comfy chairs by the fireplace, and make a lengthy inspection of the ceiling."

The phrase didn't flow very well in French, being rather difficult for me to translate, and he wrinkled his brow, indicating he didn't understand, so I put my hands together at my cheek and simplified the phrase. After this, he agreed wholeheartedly and thought it a good idea. We both settled down in the chairs, the fire glowed and just made things much more cosy causing instant slumber.

The dogs woke me on their entrance back into the house, with their snuffling, and wandering around checking things. Although it wasn't cold outside, they enjoyed the warmth inside and flopped down by the fireplace. Jean-Claude had woken earlier and let them in, and they loved it.

The special occasion was evidently going to continue, for the table cloth remained in place. I changed my clothes and put on shoes and a warm jacket, my friend did a similar thing. The dogs were instructed to go to their kennels, and we commenced walking down the road to the bar.

The village itself was a close-knit affair, the houses although individual and apart, formed a continuous road with other single junctions streaming off. The surrounding forest snuggled it together. The further we walked, the larger the village became – it seemed to grow in size as we went along.

I asked. "Will there be many in the bar tonight?"

"It will be full and very lively, especially when there's a rugby match on. There is a big television in the corner of the main bar, and as you know tonight England play France, for me it couldn't be better." And he rubbed his hands together and grinned. "I think you might get a bit of a ribbing; we will probably have the odd friendly bet as well if you are you up for it?" And he increased his grin to a broad smile of expectation.

"Yes, I'm up for it, a bit of banter won't go astray either."

I smiled back at him. After that, we walked more briskly, and it did not take long before we arrived.

From the outside, the bar looked typically French, and as we pushed the doors open the light from inside cascaded out, giving a welcome invitation. I could already hear the lively atmosphere inside, and the promise of a very entertaining evening ahead enticed me to go in.

Upon our entrance, the place erupted into a great deal of shouting and waving of arms. Jean-Claude waved back, then automatically went to a table surrounded by six empty chairs, which were obviously reserved for us. The jubilant atmosphere present in the room gave me a glorious tingling feeling.

We took our places facing the television, and were about to sit down, when the outside door opened and in strode Christian. After waving to everyone else in the bar, he immediately joined us, greeted us and parked himself next to me. He seemed bigger than when I had first met him in the forest and stockier. Disappointedly he wasn't wearing his pink cap.

Drinks were bought and placed on the table, then with shouts of Santé and the elaborate clinking of glasses, we finally sat down.

The rugby wasn't due to start for a while, so I took the opportunity to ask Christian a question.

"When you go shooting, do you always wear a pink cap? I've only seen yellow ones in the Loire."

He raised his head for the explanation. "The cap is very important, all the shooting groups wear them. Everyone in the 'chasse' who carries a gun must wear one, it shows a kind of responsibility, and displays to everyone around we are serious at what we are doing, and obey the rules."

He stopped for a second, thought about it, then went on: "Here, in the Pyrenees, we have a pink cap, some of the other groups wear different colours."

Ever since seeing the pink cap bobbing up and down along the top of the hedge, my thought had been, it might be nice to own one, so I asked:

"Is there any chance at all, there might be one for me?"

He looked at me quizzically straight in the eyes and enquired directly with a sort of judgment, "Did you and Jean-Claude find any Cepes mushrooms today."

"Yes we did," was my reply.

"Who was it who actually found them? Was it you or Jean-Claude?"

Not completely understanding what the pink cap and the Cepes had to do with each other, and thinking it was far too complicated to ask any further questions, I simply replied:

"It was Jean-Claude."

He again looked at me quizzically. "Therefore I will do my best to get you a cap for tomorrow."

I beamed. "That would be absolutely marvellous, thanks very much." On saying this, an uncertainty arose in my mind: 'would I be brave enough to wear it anywhere other than here?' It also struck me, 'what are we doing tomorrow?'

But before I could ask, he said, "What kind of gun do you like?"

The question was a bit sudden, causing me to stammer and hesitate before replying.

"I have fired a shotgun, also a Browning sub-machine gun, and a 'three-0-three rifle'," failing to tell him it was many years ago on my Marine training.

He enquired further: "What kind of gun do you prefer?"

He looked at me and must have seen the stunned look on my face, for he voluntarily continued: "I have many guns. My favourite is a two-two rifle which has a smaller bullet size than the 'three-0-three' and would do fatal damage at five hundred metres. I also have a shotgun; maybe that is the one for you tomorrow." And he turned away to talk to Jean-Claude, which allowed my thoughts to wander.

'Wow.' Considering the distance of the two-two rifle, over a quarter of a mile for the bullet to fly, it was a long way and very accurate. It got me wondering 'would the passage of the bullet be affected by the wind, and could I possibly smuggle the rifle in and out of England without anybody noticing?' It would be a very handy weapon, something worth bearing in mind. These very serious thoughts kept entering my head; fortunately, my mind flashed back again to the moment. What on earth was I thinking about? All I wanted was a pink baseball cap, and this two-two rifle had lodged itself in my brain. Along with deadly mushrooms, there was more to my thoughts than meets the eye, I knew these thoughts were going somewhere but not sure where.

We were interrupted by the bar doors bursting open, and in through them, with an air of confidence and a jovial look on his face, came a thickset muscular, shortish, obvious Frenchman. He would have been perfect if he had had a beret on and a sliver of a moustache on his upper lip. Glancing around, he saw Jean-Claude and Christian, and with a radiant look on his face, threw his arms in the air and came towards us.

There were hugs for all his friends, and a firm shake of the hand for me, with a shout of, "C'est moi, Auguste."

"Matthew," I said using the French pronunciation.

One of his pals asked him a question, and he became embroiled in chatter.

While the three friends parleyed together excitedly about this evening's rugby match, I sneaked off to the bar, bought another round of drinks and four glasses of Ricard, a favourite French aniseed drink. On returning to the throng, water was added to the Ricard, and we all stood together with glasses raised and 'good health' was loudly and boldly proclaimed.

# Chapter Ten

Christian and Auguste commenced telling Jean-Claude about the happenings in the village during his absence. The spoken conversation between them was far too quick for me to follow without intense concentration, and this wasn't the time for intense concentration. The French have a habit of speaking all at the same time. I, in turn, had developed an on-off switch, which consisted of not listening, but maintaining an interesting facial expression.

The gist of the conversation was about things and people I did not know. After a while, it eventually meandered round to the rugby match this evening, as it inevitably would.

Christian, Jean-Claude, and Auguste together all said, "Our money is on France."

"Right," I said, "I'll have England," then added, " you all seem to be more knowledgeable on this subject than I; what chance have England got?"

"No chance," came a chorus of replies.

Auguste had a sheepish look on his face, it slowly brightened to a smile and he said: "I've changed my mind, I shall have England. What do you think, Matthew?"

"Good idea," I said, "welcome aboard." I could see he liked the phrase, for he beamed and shook my hand.

We all began to settle down waiting for the game to begin. It was an opportunity for me to glance around and survey the rest of the people in the bar. I assessed I must have been the only Englishman there. My musing took me to the two empty chairs and who were going to occupy them. Maybe other members of the 'chasse,' probably the same enthusiastic, likeable village men.

At that instant, the bar doors opened and in walked two village people. These two were not what I had imagined at all; they eyed us and sort of flounced towards us, slowly, developing a smile as they approached. He was quite small and rotund, with not a lot of hair and rather large ears for a man of his size. His shirt was buttoned at the top, close to his uniquely smooth neck. He wore a tie, and probably to keep the chill away, he wore a grey V-necked jumper, which, incidentally, matched his well-creased grey trousers. In my opinion, he was very well turned out indeed. The other noticeable feature about this man as he walked in, was his very well polished shoes which reflected in what light there was in the room.

Beside him, was what I presumed to be his wife, who was ever so slightly smaller than he. The most prominent feature about her was her chest, which was contained in a very tight sweater and stuck out substantially with pointed ends which made her look as if she was going to a 'rock and roll' dance. She was obviously very proud of this feature, for there was more than a small percentage of this part of her anatomy squeezed together and sticking out over the top of her 'v' neck sweater. It was also rather strange, because the left part of the chest was sticking straight out, and oddly the right part was angled away from the centre a little, which was surprising really, as a lot of attention had been placed around this area. She had dangling earrings, a lot of make-up, dyed hair and beads around her neck; her skirt was in the fashion of the fifties billowing out at the bottom. She also possessed a huge smile.

The couple, I estimated, were in their mid-sixties and looked very jolly together. The man turned out to be Louis, who shook hands with everyone else, then finally with me. It is sometimes possible to tell a lot from a handshake, and his was a generous one.

His wife was called Nicole. She kissed Jean-Claude, Christian, Auguste and ultimately me. I got a bit of a hug as well.

A visit to the bar brought another round of drinks, this time including a bottle of red wine and two extra glasses for the jolly couple.

Louis thanked me for the wine and asked, "How long are you staying in Eeee?" He appeared to know a little about me; the village telegraph had again been efficient.

"Three or four days, until Jean-Claude's mother comes back; actually as long as I can, it is a beautiful place."

"Yes," he said.

"Where in the village do you live?" I asked.

"Not far from where you're staying, we live a little nearer on the other side of the road. You must come and see us before you go." An invitation I was surprised to hear because we had only just met, but it brought a smile of delight to my face.

At that moment the noise level in the room increased as the match kicked off: We watched it on the television and all joined in the general revelry. The side-bets laid on the result were only small amounts, but played a major part in the proceedings.

We drank more Ricard, then a little more wine.

Tucked away about his person Auguste had a glass bottle similar to the size of a hip flask, which he produced from time to time, and handed round for us to enjoy the luxury of its contents. He told us it was his own home-made 'eau de vie,' 'water of life,' from plums. I estimated the alcohol level of this delicious liquid to be about forty percent, which was a lot more than the average bottle of wine. I had my share and thought it very nice indeed. It was noticeable how generous he was with the bottle's contents.

The married couple were good company, and like most French people, were very knowledgeable about rugby, and stood and cheered with everybody else, thoroughly enjoying the company and camaraderie. They also enjoyed drinking, and during the evening drank a considerable amount of wine, Ricard and 'water of life'; whilst engrossed in all the excitement, their glasses were emptied and filled again and again.

The match was eventually won by England and there was the usual post-mortem at our table on how the French full-back could have played better, and the hooker could have fed the ball in a more inventive way.

Christian was the only one to create a fuss, and loudly shouted: "France was easily the better side, the English team was very lucky to win, we have the better players."

He stood up, looked directly at me, then with some disdain placed all the winnings of the bet onto the table in front of me. The others went suddenly very quiet and for a moment I was taken aback. Under normal circumstances, I would have merely smiled, but having quaffed my fair share of fruit and grape, I rose to my full height and stood facing him in my most defiant manner; it was surprising what drink could do. Now Christian was a big man, but not as tall as myself, and my height was definitely an advantage. No words were spoken for some time, eventually both our heads moved ever so slightly backward, and our facial features moderated. I picked up the money from the table and said:

"There might be some truth in what you say, Christian. Let's put these winnings in the charity box on the bar. Would you like to do it?"

I gave him the money. It made him stand back and consider what I had said. He waited then walked to the bar and slotted the whole lot into the box. On his return to the table, he stretched out his hand for me to shake. I took it and breathed a gentle unnoticeable sigh of relief. I turned to Auguste to try and receive some acknowledgement, hoping he would agree with what we had done.

He nodded in agreement.

During this little episode, we had incurred a second or two of awkward silence. This was broken thankfully by Nicole and Louis, who, with some effort, attempted to stand up. They were successful to a point, and just about maintained their dignity, but were unable to gain absolute full stability. The pair were not as steady on their feet as when they first arrived; nevertheless, the huge grin on their faces showed they were capable of getting themselves home.

The gesture on their part of rising from the table gave an indication to our party that the evening's entertainment was drawing to a close.

We shook hands. Nicole embraced me and whispered very close in my ear, "Well done, Matthew, England were the better team," and gave me an extra kiss.

Many of the other revellers, as they passed, were gracious in defeat, some even gave my hand a healthy shake. I was quite taken by this genial attitude, and felt rather humbled, well by some of the French anyway.

Walking to the door, Nicole and Louis tottered and swayed like a couple of ballroom dancers; surely help would be needed to get them home. They were not falling about, but their cup undoubtedly was running over, as a matter of fact, I think most of it had been spilled.

When I mentioned this to Jean-Claude, he remarked:

"They have a cottage just down the road, we passed it on the way here; they will be alright, their 2 CV motor car knows its way home." I looked at Jean-Claude, and we exchanged stares.

As I watched Nicole and Louis totter to the door and stumble out, my mouth curled up and I shook my head from side to side, and thought, let's hope Jean-Claude is right.

We sat down again and Christian started to fidget, glancing around the room. Eventually, he rose from his chair, quickly shook hands with everyone, said his goodbyes and disappeared. I looked quizzically at Jean-Claude, and he answered my query by saying:

"I do believe the landlady of the bar is the attraction!"

"Aha," I said.

Jean-Claude, Auguste and myself were the last to leave, and as we did so, we heard the bolt on the inside of the door behind us slide into place; mmm, I thought, the landlady was keen as well.

The night air had a slight misty chill about it, and the moon shone its glow with reluctance.

We conversed our way down the road, the stocky Auguste walking on ahead, Jean-Claude and I strolling peacefully behind.

# Chapter Eleven

As we approached the bend, Auguste suddenly blurted out, "Mon Dieu!" and pointed furiously over to the left-hand side of the road. In the faint moonlight just before two large brick-built gate posts, I could see a 2 CV motor car, buried in the ditch front first. Possibly, because of the night air, wine and 'eau de vie', the car of Louis and Nicole had been unable to find its own way home.

It took me a few seconds to figure out what had happened. The car had missed the way into their drive and now was encamped in the ditch before the drive's first entrance post. The back wheels of the car were dangling in the air, the lights were on and the engine was stopped.

We three immediately surrounded the car and decided a rescue mission was necessary, hoping things weren't as bad as they looked.

Jean-Claude and I with some considerable effort scrambled down the ditch to the driver's side and Auguste did the same to the passenger side. Opening the car doors at the same time we found our evening companions in the car looking nonplussed, but otherwise surprisingly calm.

"Are you all right?" Jean-Claude asked them both.

"Yes," came the slurred reply from Louis, "but we can't get out."

Our two gallant, inebriated friends were both slumped forward, one flopping over the steering wheel and the other over the dashboard, like a couple of Marionette puppets. In the fading moonlight, it was difficult to see what sort of condition they were in, but they both appeared to be uninjured.

Louis turned his head towards Jean-Claude and I, and helplessly again repeated: "We are alright, but we can't get out."

I glanced over to the passenger seat, Nicole nodded her head, and appeared also to be uninjured, but seemingly unable to move.

Jean-Claude edged me out of the way and took over.

"I'll grip him around the shoulders and pull him towards us. When I get him to the door, can you get hold of his right arm? I'll take his left arm and we can gently lift him out of the car. Is that OK?"

"That's fine with me," I replied.

He leaned into the car and did as he had said. With me assisting as requested and with a bit of huffing and puffing, Louis gradually popped out. We held him under his arms, standing him upright like a typical marionette waiting to perform.

"Can you put me into bed please?" he said; then added: "Can you put us both into bed please?"

Jean-Claude turned to me. I nodded. "Yes, we will," he said.

I heard Auguste rather enthusiastically say from the other side:

"Of course we can, it will be no problem at all."

He was glancing about, trying to figure out how to extract Nicole, so I tapped on the roof of the car to draw his attention.

"Can you go back onto the road and help us pull Louis out of the ditch first? We will push his arms upward, then if we hand him up to you, can you support him for us, until we get out of the ditch?"

"I'll give it a try," he said and scrambled on all fours back up the bank to the roadside, where he stood at the top of the ditch on the grass verge legs apart, like a goalkeeper waiting for a penalty to be taken.

"Right!" he announced.

Jean-Claude and I placed one hand under each armpit of Louis to maintain him upright, the other hand we placed on his forearm aiming his hands in the direction of Auguste. We heaved him up towards the roadside, where Auguste, in position, immediately grasped Louis by both hands and pulled hard. He pulled a bit too much at first, for this caused Jean-Claude and I to let go, and in turn made Auguste fall backwards. Fortunately, he managed to hold on to the hands of Louis, who then slithered up the bank to the grass verge. The good thing about this action was, it plummeted Louis nearly out of the ditch, a push on his feet by us improved his position even more, and Auguste hauled him out completely. Jean-Claude and I then climbed out of the ditch and pulled the two men back into the upright position.

Having had too much to drink was affecting us all by now, and everything seemed to take a lot longer than usual. Jean-Claude, a little unsteady on his feet, murmured:

"I've got him and I'll keep him upright."

We now had the problem of Nicole, who was still slumped inside the car. After a short pondering, I thoughtfully turned to all and declared:

"Why don't Auguste and I do the same thing with Nicole as we did with Louis?"

Auguste put his hands up in the air and grinned.

"No, no, I'll go down into the ditch, I think I'll be able to lift her out by myself, she is a lot lighter than Louis, even with that chest. You stay up top here and get ready to grab her and haul her up on to the road."

The smile on his face turned slowly into a gleeful grin. I thought it a brilliant idea and gave him the thumbs up.

He made his way down to the bottom of the ditch on the passenger side of the car, leaned inside and after a moment's fumbling, positioned her in a sort of fireman's lift, and withdrew her gently out of the car. As he did so she bumped her head on the door frame, squealed a bit and looked up at me. This was encouraging and reassuring because it meant she was still alive and conscious. I watched and readied myself for the hauling, copying the goalkeeper's stance.

When coming fully out of the car, she automatically put her arms out; seeing this, I leaned over to try and grab them. Unfortunately, l leaned a little too far, and just for a split second had the horrible heady panicking sensation of falling into the ditch myself. This would have been impossible to cope with, as I would have fallen right on top of the pair already down there. It would have been a disaster of ridiculous proportions, but luckily I gained my balance in time and steadied myself; this enabled me to get hold of the hands of Nicole and pull her up the bank. Her front made contact with the side of the ditch, and on standing her up, I could see in the moonlight that all her clothes were a little soiled.

Auguste scampered up after her. "I'll take Nicole," he said. "You help Jean-Claude with Louis."

He then gently placed her left arm over his shoulder and took her weight by putting his right arm around her waist, gently holding onto her. As he did so he smiled, a smile of mischievous satisfaction, I secretly hoped he wasn't going to be a naughty boy.

Jean-Claude and I arranged our arms round Louis, and we began moving forward. As we walked towards the driveway entrance we stopped and looked back at the stricken vehicle. He glanced at me.

"Let's leave the car where it is until the morning, best we get them inside the house first."

The car looked even stranger than before because now both doors were open giving the impression of a head with two enormous ears.

We stumbled along the drive, Jean-Claude, me and Louis in front and the other two bringing up the rear, a certain amount of staggering and wobbling was involved in this procession, but finally, we all arrived at the front door.

The porch was lit by a dull orange light. Jean-Claude stepped forward.

"Have you got hold of him?"

I nodded and he tried the door.

"It's locked, are the keys in his pocket?"

I rummaged through both pockets. "No, they must be still in the car."

Jean-Claude issued a cry of irritation.

"Looks like I'm in the ditch again," he said and set off down the drive, wobbling slowly from side to side, with a slight list to starboard.

Auguste turned to me with an expression on his face somewhere between enjoyment and wonderment. I was slightly unsure as to why this was. We both stood in the porch not speaking, looking from one to the other, holding up a couple of live dummies for what seemed an age.

# Chapter twelve

At long last, we heard the arrival of Jean-Claude as he stumbled towards us.

"I fell down into the ditch, and was only saved at the bottom by the car door, hope I haven't damaged it, I've got the keys, they were in the ignition."

He stepped up onto the porch and turned the retrieved key in the lock. Fortuitously it worked and he opened the door and walked inside, then stood and held the door open for the rest of us to pass through. After myself and Louis, the twosome of Auguste and Nicole made their way inside. I naturally assumed Jean-Claude had been in this house before, which was confirmed when he found the light switch and illuminated the hall.

It was then we all realized, what a messy motley crew we were, everyone was now wearing grubby dirtied clothing. Nicole was undoubtedly the worst because when she had fallen forward, her chest had got in the way and was covered in mud – it did look peculiar, but it couldn't be helped.

Jean-Claude whispered to Auguste:

"We ought to get them up to the bedroom, it will be far better than leaving them down here." And he glanced about checking for the way up. "You see the stairs over there, we'll take them up there, the bedroom I think is on the right."

Auguste obeyed and took a firmer hold of his feminine cargo, and gently manoeuvred her towards the stairs. I watched as they slowly advanced, and was pleased to notice a movement of her legs, which meant she was not totally unconscious but also not totally conscious. Perhaps the alcohol, the night air and the exploration in the ditch had taken its toll. She looked as though she was not far away from a deep sleep.

Jean-Claude and I took another grip of Louis under his armpits and gently hauled him after the other two up the stairs. I was certain he was getting heavier – either that or my strength was weakening. It was all becoming a bit of a struggle, and by the time we arrived on the landing, we were both puffed. The evening had elongated because of the missed gate, and we could see our ditch victims were definitely ready for sleep.

Eventually, we all entered the bedroom; again Jean-Claude took the initiative and marched or rather wandered, still with a slight list to starboard, over to the other side of the room and switched on the light. The lampshade spread a glow with an immediately strong influence of pink, giving the room a very French boudoir effect.

"There you go, I thought so," reflected Auguste responding to the pink light.

I didn't quite understand what he meant by that.

"Let's lay them on the bed," he said, then placing one arm around the waist of Nicole, and the other arm under her knees, he lifted her as gently as possible onto the bed. Her head instantly took enormous pleasure in resting on the pillow, and she closed her eyes immediately. He tucked her legs in and put her feet together, then stood back for a second, to see what to do next. Her 'sixties fashionable ballooning skirt' rose slightly in the air, then settled itself down again. He watched this with considerable interest. Then Auguste deliberately bent forward and took her shoes off.

When he finished, he came round and joined us on our side of the bed. Jean Claude and I laid Louis on the bed in the same way and removed his shoes. His eyes had been shut when he was standing, so he instantly fell asleep as soon as his head touched the pillow.

"We will have to take his trousers off, they are covered in mud."

Auguste spoke these words while smiling and eyeing Jean-Claude.

From these glances and the glint in their eyes, it was impossible for me not to see there was something in the past, of which I was not aware – the words were said with far too much chicanery, guile, and enthusiasm. I was intrigued by this and was of the impression there was definitely mischief afoot. Auguste then unbuckled the belt holding up the trousers of Louis and drew them down to his knees. As he did this, there appeared an expression on Auguste's face, first of shock, then of delight, and finally finished in a huge grin and a broad smile.

"I knew it," he said quietly, "I knew it!"

The glow of the lamp allowed us all to see, firmly fitted on the hips of Louis, were a pair of floral, frilly, pink knickers.

Auguste again repeated the phrase, "I knew it! I knew it!" His face emanated a huge grin.

Thank goodness Louis was out for the count, not unconscious, only fast asleep. If he had woken, the embarrassment for us all would have been hard to bear.

Auguste lowered the trousers of Louis even further and finally took them off completely. He then with some exaggeration lifted the legs of Louis and placed them more neatly on the bed. At this point, I was hopeful Auguste had finished his inspection; but no, he delicately and with the precision of a dentist, inserted his fingers in the elasticated top of Louis's floral, frilly, pink knickers.

He then keenly, although gingerly, looked up at me and with great care eased the panties down to a position where he had a full view of the contents. A beaming smile appeared on his face and he whispered:

"He's definitely a bloke all right, it's like an elephant's trunk in there, not Jewish either."

With even greater care, so as not to wake him, he returned the elasticated top of the knickers back to their rightful position, then stood up, turned to us and in a whispered voice said:

"Well, that's half the rumour sorted, let's see if we can find out about the other half!"

I was already feeling apprehensive about the situation, possibly leaning heavily towards the side of embarrassment. Questions sprang into my mind. Did I want to be part of what was happening? How far was this going to go? Could I interrupt as a stranger into this close-knit friendship, and stop the proceedings.? On the other hand, intrigue and drink had taken over, and my interest had strayed to what the other half could possibly involve. My attempt to say something failed, and it ended with me stepping backwards, as curiosity activated itself.

Auguste walked round to the other side of the bed, leaned over and gingerly took hold of the hem of Nicole's billowing skirt and slowly raised it at a slight angle, so the light shone on the area of his interest, again repeating the same phrase.

"I knew it! I knew it!" Not so quietly this time.

Jean Claude put his finger to his lips. I couldn't resist looking under the skirt of Nicole. There in the glow of the lamp, and in full view, were a pair of men's blue and white striped underpants.

He whispered, "We were right! He wore hers and she wore his!"

In our inebriated state, we all tried to quell our laughter; it resulted in us bursting forth with a squeaky type of smiling utterance, and we all put our hands over our mouths in an attempt to muffle the sound. This turned into one of those stifled silence efforts, everyone trying very hard not to laugh aloud. We were like three naughty little schoolboys.

When we regained control of ourselves, Auguste began talking fairly normally again by saying:

"Now we are this far, let's find out if the rest is true."

My eyes passed from the underpants to the eyes of Auguste.

His face was a mask of rascality and devilment coupled with determination, his mouth was fashioned horizontally with a hint of a smile, his teeth hidden from me, but I would have put money on them being clenched, and the whites of his eyes flashed in the dim light.

He lifted the skirt of Nicole up, so it nearly covered her chest and face.

I thought, surely not; this is a bridge too far. If we are found out doing what we are doing and end up in court, we will be branded, 'the trio of perverts'.

But there was no stopping him now. I know I should have tried to intervene, it was one of those situations when you know you should, but you can't, also what was not right; in my drunken condition, I watched.

With even more delicacy then before, he lowered his hands and inserted a finger of each hand into the elastic top of the blue and white striped underpants, then with surprising dexterity he slowly lifted the elastic up, then pulled it daintily down towards her knees.

It was one of those times when looking should have been forbidden; however, no matter how I tried, I couldn't stop myself. Again the limp excuse of having far too much to drink flashed through my brain. It was definitely bordering on being one of the most ashamed moments in my life.

Auguste deftly pulled the underpants down past her hips and even further until the tiny gap between the legs arrived. We all could see the smooth grey hair, quite a lot for a woman of her age.

Auguste turned to us both and said: "Look, she's a woman!"

There was a note of despair in his voice, the distinct indications were, he really would have liked and preferred a different result. His comment completely mystified me; maybe later it might even be possible to discover the reason for this extraordinary affair, in this little village of Eeee, in the Pyrenees? Cupping my hand to my chin and shaking my head from side to side, I slowly contemplated the situation, and a huge smile of bewilderment appeared on my face.

Auguste, with the same daintiness as before, returned the blue and white underpants to their original position and pulled the skirt down. All was returned to normal, well, as normal as it could be for us.

As we were about to leave, I said, "Just a moment," and leaned over the bed, unable to resist checking and making absolutely certain they were both breathing, delaying our exit until I was perfectly sure they were both alive. We pulled the blanket over the pair to cover them; it was agreed between us to leave the light on.

It suited the delightful French pair in a way, together in bed in a pink boudoir.

At the door, we all stopped and peered back at the same time. For me, it was to make sure neither of them had woken; fortunately, we found both were sound asleep. As I closed the bedroom door, a thought struck me – 'was it possible one of them had been awake and aware of all that went on, and only chose to appear to be asleep? Or even worse, both had been awake all the time and only pretended to be asleep and even now as the door was closed, were looking at each other and winking, with a delicious broad grin on their faces?'

The three of us made our way down the stairs to the hall, then out through the front door and into the night. Taking a deep breath was really a bad idea, for dizziness entered my head and wandered around; it was necessary for me to hold on to the others. We all stood there facing each other with double-glazed eyes and muffled gleeful laughter.

Jean Claude produced the set of keys from his pocket and locked the door behind us, then pondered.

"I'm sure they have a spare front-door key, and another set for the car."

The air outside ultimately freshened us, and our little trio without any conversation or comment hurried along down the path and onto the road. We halted at the gate and gazed at the car in the ditch – it really did look a sorry sight.

Auguste spoke first: "We must come in the morning and pull it out."

Jean-Claude nodded in agreement. "Yes, it's the right thing to do."

I wasn't absolutely sure what he meant by that but didn't make any remark, only agreed it would be a good thing to pull it out in the morning, and began walking home with the other two.

Not far along the road Auguste said goodnight and vanished by turning to the right and disappearing around the corner.

Before I knew it, I was tucked up in bed and fast asleep in the lovely cottage of Jean-Claude's mum.

# Chapter Thirteen

I was woken by the noise of scuffling paws on concrete, and feet tramping about outside. The inside of my head had a kind of numbing buzz, which I hoped would diminish as time passed. To say I was feeling a little worse for wear was a dreadful, dreadful understatement!

All this rather forced me to lie back and gently place my head on the pillow for a minute and reflect on what had happened the night before. It had turned out to be an evening of revealing and interesting events, all totally unexpected. It was no good wondering if in the bedroom of Louis and Nicole, in the shade of the pink lamp, we had overstepped the mark. If we had, it was too late now to do anything about it, and an apology to them would be completely absurd. What we had done, we had done. I was nearly sure in the bedroom they had both been out for the count and known nothing. It had been one of those occasions when it is most advisable for all concerned to remain silent and keep what we had seen to ourselves. But oh dear, on the other hand, I had this slightly nervous feeling lurking within me, that both Louis and Nicole were not quite as naive as they made out. This thought persisted and for the moment would not disappear from my head.

Eventually, I dismissed all these thoughts and sat on the edge of the bed with my head in my hands. It wasn't very warm in the bedroom, so I put my clothes on as quickly as possible, and ventured through the lounge part into the kitchen, where the smell of coffee and toast gave me a warm glow. As always, Jean-Claude shook hands with me, and we asked each other how we were. After various affable comments, it was established we were at least ready for the day. The buzz in my head was slowly waning to an acceptable level thankfully, and we sank into the coffee, toast, jam, and white, soft, sliced cake.

The conversation sauntered round to the journey home last night and the pantomime in the bedroom. It soon turned into laughter, with the antics of Auguste featuring heavily. He had intrigued me, and I was keen to find out more about him; it seemed an appropriate time for me to enquire from Jean-Claude about his background.

He was pleased to explain and told me a lot about Auguste, how he had spent most of his life as a farm labourer in a village not far from Toulouse and in time had acquired the little plot of land around the corner where he grew vegetables and kept a variety of animals and fowl. He made the old barn into a garage and has taken on repairing of the village houses and most of the transport. If you want your car maintaining or your plumbing fixing, he is the man to go to. Jean-Claude was sure he was happy and content with himself and his business, then he finished by saying:

"I have known him ever since he came here, we have always been good friends."

"What about before he came here?" I asked.

This brought forth a further deluge of information and he continued. "He was born and lived a distance away from here as I said, he played some sort of role with the Resistance in the Second World War, and learned all about hiding and about waiting to strike at the right time. He was very young then. What happened in those dark days he never talks about in any detail."

This was interesting, and so I gently pressed him for more.

"I think he also played a part in the Algerian-French War and parachuted into various parts, fought and witnessed dreadful atrocities on both sides."

It is always surprising when you hear something like this, and I was slightly taken aback, but as I listened further Jean-Claude generalized Auguste to be astonishingly stable, despite all he had done and seen. Thinking back to the previous evening, I had an idea of how he had achieved that stability, as he obviously enjoyed doing things other people shied away from. He also was not afraid to see things through to the finish and he certainly wasn't bashful. For the short time of knowing him and learning about his exploits, I was beginning to quite like this stocky little farm labourer-cum-garage owner, and wondered, since he had agreed to bet on England at the rugby match with me, if the feeling was possibly mutual.

Whenever England came into my thoughts those two horrible men in the village across the water, always sprang into my mind. Were they the two men who had been responsible for our terrible tragedy? I had endured these thoughts for such a long time and my heart was getting heavier and heavier. These thoughts were now accompanied by a wave of anger and a determination to do something about it, but I knew patience was needed and also possibly some help. I had never been a violent man – on the contrary when faced with confrontation I always preferred to use words. In this case, my peaceful passive attitude was slowly disappearing.

Jean-Claude left the table, and my previous thoughts were invaded by other things to do, one of which was to ring Daphers. She answered the phone immediately, and told me she had cut the front lawn the day before, and all was under control concerning the house sale. I suspected she was enjoying some peace and quiet. Our little pussy-cat was fine and had learned a new trick, which was not possible to explain over the phone. Thinking it prudent not to mention the goings-on last night, I merely gave an account of the pub and the rugby match. After all the changes in her life recently, it was nice to know everything was fine with my wife. There was a strong possibility a lot more changes were going to happen in the future, and I sincerely, and desperately, hoped she would be able to cope with them.

# Chapter Fourteen

Returning to the table and sitting down, I continued to enjoy the calmness of the morning. Then suddenly Jean-Claude spoke up.

"I'll telephone Auguste and arrange to help him pull the car out of the ditch."

He said it in such a matter of fact manner as if it happened every day.

I heard one end of the telephone discussion and understood we were to meet in an hour, and Jean-Claude was to take his heavy car. I mused over why a vehicle from Auguste was not to be used? Having a garage, surely he would have had the perfect motor, but I let it pass and didn't pursue it.

We both decided to wear our soiled clothes and big boots to carry out the recovery and drove to where the 2CV was entrenched in the ditch.

Auguste had already attached a rope around a substantial rear part of the stricken French motor, and waved for Jean-Claude to drive forward between the gateposts of the drive, then indicated he should reverse back along the road towards the rear end of the motionless car. We each stepped out of the car and greeted Auguste; little was said, only handshakes and huge smiles from all three. After last night's activities, comments were apparently not necessary.

Auguste turned to Jean-Claude. "Tie the end of this rope around the towing knob on the rear of your car–" and he elaborately pointed to it.

It seemed he had taken over the situation for he pointed again, this time at the stricken car in the ditch and spoke to Jean-Claude.

"I think the front bumper is trapped under the bank on the other side of the ditch, I'm going to jump up and down on the back bumper to try and free it while you drive forward and steadily pull it out."

He turned to me.

"Matthew."

"Yes," I said.

"Get the keys from Jean-Claude."

"I've got them."

"Right, can you sit in the car and try and steer it out of the ditch when we get it moving."

We all took our places, I clambered down into the ditch and squeezed myself into the cramped space behind the steering wheel of the 2CV and gripped it tightly. When I was comfortable, I turned and looked behind to see if Auguste was in position standing on the back bumper. On doing this I noticed two badminton rackets lying on the back seat and thought to myself, this couple were an active pair, badminton is an energetic sport.

When the car started to rock back and forth, I braced myself and heard the revving of the heavy car and an indication of movement astern, more revs, more bobbing up and down by Auguste and suddenly a violent shift backward and skyward. As we hit the top of the ditch it caused me to turn the steering wheel the right way and we luckily bounced onto the road. Instinct made me put my foot on the foot-brake and pull on the hand-brake. I did this just in time to avoid a collision with the rear of Jean-Claude's car. Fortunately, he had sussed the situation and maintained forward momentum, thus narrowly avoiding a back-to-back bump. There erupted a deafening cheer from all concerned as we came to a halt, which terminated in Auguste joyfully leaping down from the back bumper and waving his arms about in triumph. He certainly was a man who could be very, very useful in any situation.

After opening the 2CV car door and stepping out of the driver's seat, I became aware of a loud buzzing noise; it was more than that, it was an extremely loud buzzing noise. A sizeable hornet made its presence felt by carrying out a couple of fly-pasts on either side of my head.

Having never been overly keen on these creatures, and as the 2CV car door was still partially open, I reached in and grabbed one of the rackets from the back seat. Then, taking a firm stance on the road and eyeing up my opponent, I swung the racket with almighty force and gave the hornet a hefty whack. My aim was true, and it whistled through the air, hit the side window of Jean-Claude's car and slowly dropped down onto the tarmac road.

At that moment both Frenchmen excitedly and aghast shouted: "No, no," but it was too late, I'd done it.

As I swung around Auguste raced towards me, grabbed me by the elbow, opened the rear door of Jean-Claude's car, pushed me inside then tumbled in after me, shutting the car door behind us as he did so.

We three sat inside the car in complete silence, Jean-Claude and Auguste put a finger to their lips, I obeyed the command and stayed very quiet and still.

The silence continued until my enquiring eyebrows and eyes provoked an answer.

There was a lot of pointing from the front seats, as a small identified flying object hit the side window next to me with a smack.

Jean-Claude, now in the comfort of the car, whispered.

"That hitting the window is the hornet you thought you had killed, it has come back to life. You know, the one you smashed with the racket." He winced. "We call them 'Pit-bulls' and they, unfortunately, don't die very easily."

I had the definite feeling a minor bollocking had been bestowed upon me.

Unable to believe my perfectly executed forearm smash had not taken out my gallant opponent, I found it necessary to strain my neck and peer on the ground where it should have been. There was no sign of it, so I surveyed the one buzzing at the window; it had hostility in its little eyes and looked very familiar. The creature I recently smacked with the racket was a size bigger than the ones up in the Loire; these creatures down here in the South were like little aliens.

It suddenly became worse because the first 'pit-bull' was joined by a few friends, who seemed to be larger, and more determined than the original invader. The situation became serious and more frightening, as the buzzing grew stronger and the fly-pasts more frequent. It was like standing in the middle of Heathrow airport on a bad day. Here we were, three grown men sitting in a car, not saying a word to each other, cringing and breathing quietly.

Suddenly, and with aforethought, Jean-Claude reached over and pressed the switch to lock all the car doors. Now it might have been very wrong of me, but I could not possibly see how an insect would be able to open a car door and fly in. The action of him doing this created a huge smile on my face and a titter in the back of my throat. I tried like the devil to prevent it from blossoming and coming out, but failed, and it slowly and finally arrived out through my mouth in a burst of uncontrollable laughter.

The other two looked at me in astonishment. I pointed to the door-switch and imitated him pressing the button for locking the doors; fortunately, they saw the funny side of it and both burst forth in laughter. The noise lasted for some time, as three old fellows rolled about in exuberance, laughing and patting each other on the back.

The rowdiness must have caused the 'pit bulls' to fly off to bother someone else, for they disappeared. We scanned the outside of the car to make sure our foes had completely flown away and were not hiding somewhere in wait.

Jean-Claude whispered, "I think they've gone."

Auguste added: "Thank goodness for that, they have a very nasty and sometimes fatal sting, not nice at all."

I saw now why they had both shouted, 'No' after I whacked it.

We all carefully, with watchful eyes, crept out of the car and gingerly surveyed the scene around us. Yes, thankfully, the hornets had gone.

Auguste organised us again. "If we push the Citroen into the drive, I'll see if I can fix it later this afternoon. Can you get in the driver's seat and steer it, Matthew, please?"

I climbed back behind the wheel of the 2CV again, and with them pushing, we managed to park it in a convenient place on the drive.

As I stepped out of the car, the three of us were gathered together in a little group, and in a moment of synchronisation, each stood with a face of mischievous apprehension looking back in the direction of the house, seeking any movement. There didn't seem to be any. Jean-Claude winced again, Auguste wiped his forehead, and we all quietly sauntered back up the drive and out through the gates.

As Auguste walked off in the direction of his garage, he shouted:

"Don't forget we are going into the forest tomorrow, get everything ready."

Jean-Claude acknowledged this by waving his hand and we jumped into his car and headed for the village store. It was an opportunity for me to return some of Jean-Claude's gracious hospitality, and as it was a special occasion, we chose the best of everything. After a great deal of objection on his part, he finally agreed to allow me to pay, and I jabbed my pin number into the machine.

# Chapter Fifteen

Returning to the house, we tucked into an excellent late lunch and a bottle of wine.

Right in the middle of my afternoon nap, a knock on the front door woke me and as Jean-Claude was not about, it was up to me to go and open the door. There is something not quite right about opening someone else's front door, but on this occasion, there was no alternative, so with great reluctance, I ventured forth and opened it. Auguste was standing there.

"We've been summoned," he said. "An aperitif tonight at 6 o'clock!"

"Where?" I said.

"At Louis and Nicole's house."

"Do you know why?" I enquired, looking slightly concerned and a bit guilty. "Is it about what happened in the bedroom last night?"

"I don't know," he said, squinting his face into a funny shape. Then a quick. "See you later," and he was off.

There were times when Auguste was a man of too few words.

I closed the door and sat back down in the chair, 'well, well'.

Jean-Claude appeared and saw me sitting with a preoccupied, troubled expression on my face and enquired:

"Was that Auguste I heard?"

"Yes, we've been invited to Louis and Nicole's at 6 o'clock tonight."

The same concerned look materialised on the face of Jean-Claude accompanied by an impish smile. "Oh shit, what do you think; is it about what happened last night?"

"I asked that, he doesn't know, I'm afraid we will have to all go and face the music."

He glanced at his watch. "Let's start getting ready now because we will need a couple of glasses of Dutch courage before we set off."

We busied ourselves, and left the house ten minutes before six, and met up with Auguste at the gates of Louis and Nicole's, where we all nervously shook hands. Auguste scratched his head in the usual way.

"I really, really hope it isn't what we think it is."

We all nodded in agreement and made our way towards the front door.

I could sense the tension between us, hoping what we were about to face wasn't going to be as unpleasant as we imagined. To increase our anguish; as we arrived in the porch, the front door of the house started to open without us knocking and the trim neat couple appeared. They had been waiting.

Oh dear, this was getting worse; our nervousness increased.

When the door was fully open, we could see to our amazement and utter surprise, Louis and Nicole standing there with smiles on their faces and welcome greetings. Handshakes and kisses were followed by an invitation for us to go inside. Following the pair through the hall, we couldn't help throwing sideways glances at each other, all of them with wrinkled brows.

As we entered the lounge, champagne was handed round and Louis raised his glass and prepared himself for a speech.

"Madam et Messieurs, this champagne is to thank all three of you, for what you did for us last night."

It took a massive concentrated effort on my part not to burst out laughing because I was unable to quite believe he was thanking us for all the antics we got up to in the bedroom.

He continued: "Last night I missed the entrance to the house and popped the car into the ditch. I am very pleased we used the old one and not the new one to go to the bar last night."

It was a wonderful opportunity to release my inner laughter so I did and the other two joined in, and we freed the tension inside us.

Louis invited us to sink into the comfortable lounge chairs and Nicole told us what a mess her clothes were in and asked if ours were also dirty and grubby. She also thanked us for lifting her out of the car so gently – evidently, she remembered that part.

Auguste was very courteous and beamed. "You were very little trouble because when we lifted you out, you were as light as a feather."

She rather liked this reply and blushed a little, as well as giving him an old fashioned girlie flirtatious glance.

It suddenly dawned on me that before we had left the bedroom last night, we had covered the pair up, but we had forgotten to put the trousers of Louis back on, therefore it was likely, he knew that we knew, he was wearing frilly knickers. It seemed there was possibly more to this whole affair. It was at this point, a tiny thought flashed across my brain. Nicole also knew something more than she was saying. Had she been aware of what had gone on after we had plucked her out of the ditch, and furthermore had she enjoyed it? I had been round the park a few times myself, but this was a new one for me. My conclusion was if she knew, she was never going to tell anyone.

As the evening progressed, we chatted about the lovely champagne, the previous night's rugby result, and various other topics. Finally, Auguste relayed to us all the repairs he had carried out on the 2CV and it was now running perfectly. When he finished there was a brief pause, and Louis gave a stuttering cough, which provoked our attention.

He began. "We invited you all here this evening not only to thank you for last night but also to ask you if you can help us with a problem we have?" He stopped speaking and looked around trying to find any reaction, but there wasn't any, we were silent, so he resumed:

"Many years ago we bought a small place in Barcelona. It is on the first floor of an apartment block right in the centre of the city. We put it up for sale some time ago and it sold very quickly: this week we have finalised the deal."

Again, he looked around at all our faces, we remained silent, so he went on.

"The transaction included the furniture, but there is a trunk and a number of boxes with our personal effects, still in the apartment. We have agreed with the buyers to remove them before next week, and have tried very hard to find a firm to go and collect them, but, unfortunately, we can't find anyone and we are unable to go ourselves as the boxes and the trunk are too heavy for us to carry."

Jean-Claude looked at me, then to Auguste, but only received a silent pause.

Eventually, he spoke up. "What do you think? We can't go tomorrow because we have arranged to go into the forest; can you manage Saturday and Sunday, Matthew?"

I nodded, and he then turned to Auguste and asked him.

With great dismay, he wrinkled his nose. "Sorry, I can't come with you, I have already agreed to go to Toulouse over the weekend."

It seemed to be my turn to speak. "Wait a minute. This is all a bit sudden, we had better have words with Genevieve and Daphers before we make any definite plans."

"Good idea," agreed Jean-Claude. "It's a bit late to telephone tonight, we will ring in the morning and see what they say?"

At this juncture, Nicole burst forth enthusiastically: "It might be nice if the girls went as well. The exact date of the changeover is next Wednesday, so it would be all right if you all went to collect the boxes and trunk and stuff, then stayed in the apartment until Tuesday, if you want to?"

Jean-Claude and I looked at each other; from both our expressions I could see we found it rather appealing. Louis quickly poured more champagne into our glasses. He had obviously tried very hard to arrange transport, it seemed he was presently quite worried.

"Barcelona might be rather pleasant at this time of year," I said, taking a healthy gulp from my glass. Then turning to the couple, I enquired, "How much luggage and boxes are in the apartment to bring back?"

Louis and Nicole looked at each other; the silent glance prevailed for a little longer than was comfortable. Eventually, Louis mumbled, "Well, as far as we can remember there is about a full car boot load."

Nicole glanced at her husband with an expression on her face which revealed to me disagreement, although she didn't say anything. I wondered whether he had given a good estimate, or maybe there was more than he had said.

We drank another bottle of champagne and asked lots of questions about the apartment and its location in Barcelona. Jean-Claude and I became quite excited and showed a fair sign of enthusiasm and willingness to go.

When all the talking was done we sidled up to the front door, where arrangements were made to return the following evening to discuss a possible plan to recover their property from Spain, emphasising the word possible, not wanting to raise the hopes of Louis and Nicole too high. We said goodnight in the usual elaborate way, myself now getting used to the hug from Nicole and her chest, wondering if she did that to all her men friends.

Outside, the air was fresh with a wonderful sweet smell of trees. Our happy trio made its pleasant journey along the road, before pausing to say 'bonne nuit' to Auguste.

On arrival at the cottage, Jean-Claude and I strolled in the garden with the dogs, nothing much was said; we were possibly both pondering on the Barcelona situation. I ventured an idea to Jean-Claude.

"If Daphers would like to come here and join us tomorrow in the pick-up truck, all four of us could use it to go to Barcelona over the weekend. What do you think?"

His eyes brightened, and 'what a good idea' sign sprinkled his face. He didn't say anything for a moment, then gently lifted his finger in a friendly genial fashion.

"I had completely forgotten about your pick-up truck, with its four seats and extra space in the back. We could all go in it, and we can transport all the boxes and things."

It did seem to fit the situation. Then, thinking maybe the night air and the booze were getting through to us, I smiled and suggested we sleep on it and discuss it in the morning before we rang the girls.

This was agreed, and we entered the lovely cottage, where we both had our own way of keeping warm. Mine was putting on pyjamas and a dressing gown and getting into bed with my socks on. The additional clothing did its job, for sleep came easily with a wonderful thought of seeing Daphers very soon.

A dog barking stirred me from my slumbers. The bed was warm and cosy, and really comfortable and kept saying, 'stay here with me momentarily'; which I did and mulled over yesterday and wondered about today.

After mulling and wondering, my next step was jumping out of bed and dressing, followed by sitting at the breakfast table in the kitchen with hot coffee and toast.

"Right," said Jean-Claude. "Who is going to telephone first, and what are we to say?"

"I'll go first and find out if Daphers can drop everything and drive down here today," adding, "she will have to arrange for our neighbour to look after Bulldog."

Jean-Claude contemplated what I had said over a piece of cake.

"Yes, you go first then. The whole outcome of the day and inevitably the weekend will depend on what Daphers says."

# Chapter Sixteen

I rang the number, and after the usual greetings, put forward our plan of campaign. There was a long pause at the other end of the telephone; I'm sure I could hear her thinking.

I waited patiently until she declared: "I do like the idea of going to Barcelona for the weekend and it would be very nice to go with Jean-Claude and Genevieve. Can I ring you back? Someone has to come and look after, and feed, Bulldog."

"Yes, but don't take too long please, we have other arrangements to make and everything depends on what you say."

"Ail right I'll be as quick as I can."

It wasn't long before the telephone rang, Jean-Claude waved for me to answer it.

"Hello," I said.

Daphers immediately blurted out; "I've succeeded in getting someone to feed Bulldog, so

I can come down in the pick-up today, but I have one proviso: you drive it down to Barcelona."

I was quick to reply. "It's a deal, can you be here for about five?"

There was a pause from the other end of the phone. "I'm sure I can."

"We need to make arrangements with Genevieve, can you wait by the phone and we will ring you back?"

"Yes," was the reply and she was gone.

I handed the phone to Jean-Claude and he rang the number for Genevieve. Listening to the one-sided conversation wasn't easy; after a while, he looked over at me. "Genevieve would like to come down here and go to Barcelona with us, but she needs to be picked up. Is there a chance Daphers can pick her up on her way down here?"

"I'm sure she can."

We telephoned Daphers again, and she replied, "Give me Genevieve's number and leave it to us, we will arrange everything."

Thinking this a brilliant suggestion, I duly did as she asked and left her to it. Jean-Claude couldn't resist a shake of my hand for a job well done. We both sat for a moment in thought.

"Don't forget," he said. "You, I, Auguste and Christian are going up the mountain this morning, Christian is sure he saw a 'sanglier' yesterday."

The mere mention of the word 'wild boar' created great excitement in him.

I sat and contemplated the situation. More mountaineering is going to test my fitness – if I can do this, it is possible for me to do anything. I had recently learned about guns, woods, and walking along strange paths, all these little things seemed to be testing me and giving me confidence and strength to go forward to do what I was trying to do.

We cleared the breakfast things and Jean-Claude prepared for the arrival of Auguste and Christian by placing four stubby tumblers on the table, alongside a bottle of whisky.

The others arrived with jubilant greetings, Christian talked about the wild boar, and Auguste about the night before and champagne. Eventually, Jean-Claude very politely held up his hand and poured whisky into the four tumblers. They looked over-generous measures to me, but for a full day up the mountains, perhaps they were required.

We raised the glasses in the air and like four musketeers clinked them, then emptied them. Afterwards, we noisily set them down on the table with a loud crash. The whisky was a little early in the morning for me and gave my insides a bit of a shock.

The weapons we were taking were placed in the corner of the room. I eyed them up, stood back and waited for instructions; I was a stranger to these regular activities.

Jean-Claude piped up. "Christian, you have your two-two rifle, Auguste, you have your three-o-three rifle. I'll take the shotgun and you can have the crossbow, Matthew," and he handed it to me.

The crossbow was fairly heavy and immediately appeared to me to be a lethal-looking weapon. Jean Claude gave it to me because it wasn't necessary to have a licence to own one in France, which was surprising. After all, it looked as though it could kill somebody with ease. I took hold of it by the wooden stock and checked it over. The front part of the crossbow was similar to a longbow used by Robin Hood, only this bow was shorter and made of steel. A cord was tied tight between each end of the bow, and the stock had a groove running down the centre to keep the arrow or the bolt in place. I decided it should be treated with the utmost respect and found it necessary to ask:

"Is it possible for me to fire this before we go into the forest?"

"Of course you can, we'll have a try in the garden," said Christian.

We were dressed in a similar fashion, although Auguste's style had a more military flavour.

They all donned their pink caps, then, with an attempted sleight-of-hand Christian plucked a pink cap from his rucksack. I saw it out of the corner of my eye and beamed. He indicated to all, he wanted to make a speech and raised his head.

"On this special occasion, I would like to present you, Matthew, with a cap, and invite you to join us, as an honorary member of the 'Chasse'."

I bowed my head forward and he slipped the back of the cap in place at the nape of my neck, and holding it there, pulled the peak forward into the perfect position. We all cheered and patted each other on the back like a tribe of teenagers.

It really did feel very, very, good.

We shouldered our rucksacks, guns and me my crossbow, which in French is called an 'arbalet', and we fumbled, nudged, and squeezed ourselves through the rear door and outside. The dogs joined us immediately, walking between us, doing doggy things, but with a sense of hope of more to come.

While we were all congregated in the rear garden, Jean-Claude produced a large, overripe watermelon from somewhere and set it on a tree stump, facing directly into the forest. Christian, obviously the expert with a crossbow, stepped forward and spoke in a very serious manner:

"Weapons like this are very dangerous over short distances, so it is best not to put the arrow in the groove until you are ready to fire: I shall demonstrate."

I listened to every word. At the very front of the weapon was a large, metal hook, shaped like a stirrup. He placed his foot into this and, using a great deal of force and both hands pulled the thick cord back, drawing it into the notch of the trigger mechanism, clicking it safely in position.

I watched intently.

Then, without the arrow in place, he pointed the crossbow at the watermelon and pulled the trigger releasing the cord, there was a loud twang as the cord gave up its energy.

He then handed the crossbow to me.

"You load it this time," he said.

I wasn't exactly afraid of it, but I was certainly extremely respectful. Everybody watched.

Using my foot in the same way as Christian, I started to pull the cord back but found it surprisingly difficult as it needed a great deal of effort. Eventually, I succeeded and managed to fit it snugly behind the notch of the trigger.

Christian watched me. "Now put your finger on the trigger and pull it without inserting the arrow."

I lifted the crossbow chest high and pulled the trigger. I felt and heard the thud of the cord this time and forcefully remarked, "This is a powerful piece of equipment."

He eyed me up. "Yes," he said. "Now pull the cord back again, but don't pull the trigger this time."

I put my foot in the stirrup and pulled the cord back into the notch of the trigger.

He then gave me a very stern instruction: "From now on, you must keep the crossbow pointing towards the target."

"I will," I replied without looking at him, my eyes fixed on the crossbow and the melon.

He said: "Now carefully put this arrow in place," and he forced the arrow with a steel razor-sharp tip into my clenched hand.

"I've given it to you in your right hand because that is your trigger hand and I don't want you pulling the trigger as you insert the arrow and whipping off the odd finger."

I didn't like the sound of that at all. It was possible to support the weapon with one hand only, but not for a long time, so tensioning the muscles in my left arm to support it was necessary to free my right hand.

I adjusted the grip of the arrow in my fingers, and in a slightly gingerly fashion slipped the lethal projectile into its groove.

Christian put his hand on my arm. "Aim at the melon and fire."

Bracing myself in readiness and returning my hand to the stock of the crossbow, I inserted my finger onto the trigger then fired. The whole thing shuddered in my hands, and within an instant, the arrow entered the melon and we all saw it split and burst open, the red juices inside violently squirting out. It quite took my breath away. At that moment I thought, 'What a silently deadly dangerous weapon this is.'

One of the others said: "Merde." Somebody else said: "Mon Dieu."

We all went and circumnavigated the tree stump, and could see the melon was in a mess and ripped to pieces.

Christian pulled and tugged at the arrow, eventually retrieving it out of the back of the melon. He gave it to me and raised both eyebrows.

"It's a deadly missile in the wrong hands, it would easily kill a man, be very careful with it."

While putting the arrow back with the others in my rucksack, I couldn't stop myself from thinking what a wonderful silent killer this piece of equipment would be if it was ever used in earnest. Nobody would hear a sound when it was fired, even the recipient wouldn't even hear the twang, because it would be too late. There was one other question lurking in my mind – 'would I be brave enough to use it?' The answer was, yes I would, under exceptional circumstances, undoubtedly, but only on the right people. The other thought lurking in my mind: we would need two crossbows.

# Chapter Seventeen

The creak of the garden gate brought me back to the present and I watched the dogs as they charged through excitedly, then run up the path for a distance, turn, stop, and stare back at us. We four followed and caught them up in our own time.

Christian took the lead, after came Jean-Claude, then me, with Auguste acting as tail-end-Charlie. This happy band strode forward at a canny pace, sometimes stretched out, sometimes bunched up. I was aware of the possibility of getting lost in this overgrown forest, so somewhere in the middle of this line was the perfect position for me. It was such an exciting place, different amounts of sunshine and rain gave each tree its character, size, and colour. The trouble was, there was such an abundant number of beautiful trees of a similar type, even the most experienced walker could possibly get lost. I just loved trees and most of them had the ability to speak to me. Some trees said a soft 'hello' as I went by, encouraging me to reply and say 'hello' back. Others were massive trees with great wide trunks and wide thick branches jutting out from all parts, these were grandfather and grandmother trees proudly advising, "hello, go carefully," saying it gently and elegantly without making a fuss. I could see younger, not yet fully grown trees, their leaves on a kind of swivel, twisting and turning in the slightest breeze, their branches not yet sure which way to go.

Our little convoy of people plodded on, through gaps between bushes randomly growing by the chance of light. A lot of these bushes reminded me of soldiers standing in ranks in the stand-easy position, waiting and waiting for some sort of instruction.

We ambled further along forming temporary paths from our heavy footsteps. The equipment I was carrying was not light, and I soon felt a drop of sweat on my forehead.

As we entered a clearing Christian stopped, and placed his binoculars to his eyes. The dogs became suddenly excited and Jean-Claude said, "Stay." But the instruction was too late, the dogs were already running off at full speed away from us. In the beginning, they followed a straight path, then suddenly they veered to the left. Auguste, who was directly behind me, must have seen the wild boar, for he raised and readied his rifle. All this happened in no more than a split second.

The wild boar being at a distance possibly didn't detect anything for it didn't move, maybe it was a bit deaf. It may have been the noise the dogs made that set the animal into action for it started to run. What made the wild boar move even faster was the loud bang the rifle bolt made hitting the back of the bullet inside the gun of Auguste. It had only managed another thirty or forty yards before Auguste fired again, but its speed was so great he missed; somebody swore in French, it might have been Christian. I could see the boar now crashing through the undergrowth and zigzagging along different paths, then it veered out into the open. The dogs were in full chase after it, the bigger dog in front, and the small one behind, doing its best, ears back, one thought in mind.

The four of us ran up quite a large slope, where the sky in front opened up, revealing the whole picture. The wild boar had a mighty lead, but the two dogs behind were catching up very quickly. For me, the spectacle was quite exciting, but also quite shocking, because at that moment my heart went out to the boar, which only seconds earlier had been enjoying a nice day out and a lovely lunch.

Auguste put his rifle to his shoulder again, but Jean-Claude quickly stopped him from firing by holding up his hand and pointing to the cliff edge. "It's heading for the drop," he yelled.

Then, in an even more excited but very concerned way, he repeated the same phrase. "It's heading for the drop."

'The drop' was the name they gave to the cliff face, which presently was not far in front of the boar, now running at a frightening pace with the dogs behind in full pursuit. We couldn't see the cliff edge itself, because of the low-lying bushes around the top of it, but we could easily make out the beast bulldozing its way into the mass of greenery, and the dogs all the time closing up behind, gaining at every stride. They were all so far away from us now, we only saw them intermittently crashing through the undergrowth, the boar increasing speed, possibly in a blind panic, getting nearer and nearer to the top of the cliff. I felt like shouting to the animal, 'put the brakes on or you'll go straight over the drop'. Next, we caught a glimpse of it, then to my dismay, it disappeared through the dense bushes very close to the edge.

I gasped, and put my hand to my mouth horrified, then felt embarrassed as I was the only one to do so – none of the others felt sorry for the fate of the poor animal.

Jean-Claude had his binoculars trained on the rapid turbulent upheaval at the top of the cliff, then suddenly snapped them down to his side, and let out a bewildering cry.

"The dogs, the dogs, my beautiful dogs, they've gone over the drop, they've gone over, oh no, oh no."

He put his hands to his face and covered both eyes in a gesture of disbelief. I put my arm around him, but there was no consoling him; he bent his head forward and slowly sank to his knees in despair. We all stepped back not knowing what to do, feeling quite helpless looking at each other, then looking at the cliff edge, then back at Jean-Claude grieving. He stayed on his knees for a long while and repeated.

"They've gone, they've gone."

Watching him suffer was awful but what could we do?

We stood like statues, four grown men, one kneeling on the ground with his face stricken in mental torture, the others trying their best to console him. Eventually, Auguste circled round behind him and put his arm around his friend.

"Let's make our way to the bottom of the cliff and see what's happened."

# Chapter Eighteen

Everything felt very awkward. Christian, Jean-Claude's oldest friend, moved towards him and comforted him, Jean-Claude made a gesture of response whilst continuing to make noises of despondency, occasionally crying out:

"My poor dogs, my poor dogs."

Fearing the worst and trying to come to terms with it, he slowly raised himself off the ground and put his head on the shoulder of Christian, and for a moment all went quiet.

This little moment of silence was broken by something moving a long way off to our left. We all looked up and glared in the direction of the commotion. Jean-Claude put his binoculars to his eyes and said:

"It's not possible."

It took a significant amount of time for him to believe exactly what was happening. Within seconds, in the distance, we saw both dogs scampering towards us. Jean-Claude kept his binoculars trained on them, and when they arrived he was jubilant. He hugged them, patted them, held one in each arm to his face, told them what good boys they were. They, in turn, loved it, although not absolutely sure why they were the centre of attention, it didn't matter, they just loved it.

The three of us watched this jubilation with bright shiny smiles, enjoying the euphoria. For me it was one of those tingling moments never to be forgotten. We were all so glad the dogs had returned, and within a short space of time, we started to gather ourselves together.

"What about the wild boar?" asked Christian.

For a brief moment, we had all forgotten about it.

"Do you think it went over the edge?"

He directed his binoculars to the edge of the cliff, peering from side to side, following the path the wild boar had taken. He pointed into the distance.

"I think it went over near that single pine tree; we need to take a look."

My French language skills had improved during these last few days, as very rarely did I not understand what was being said, even by Christian. He slung his rucksack over his shoulder and invited us all to join him in the search. Jean-Claude was willing and the dogs looked very keen, but my lack of eagerness must have been conveyed in my face, for Auguste quietly said:

"I'll stay here with Matthew. You two go, we'll still be here when you get back," and he winked in my direction.

We watched as the other two disappeared through the bushes. Being the oldest of the group, I was secretly pleased with this outcome and suspected Auguste shared my feelings.

We two walked on a little way and found a couple of old tree stumps. I took off my topcoat, folded it to protect the inside, placed it over one of the stumps to act as a cushion and sat on it. Auguste did a similar thing, and together we opened our rucksacks, me bringing out wine and baguettes, he bringing out bread, wine, cheese, and thick glass tumblers which appeared to be half-jam-jars.

He held out the glasses, I uncorked the wine, and we filled them with the excellent Bordeaux red.

"Cheers!" I said.

"Santé!" said Auguste.

I settled for my baguette, while he made inroads into his bread and cheese. Auguste and I had not known each other very long, only a couple of days, but during that period we had warmed to each other. Although from different backgrounds, in some ways we had the same adventuresome character.

I could still hear the other half of our party stumbling along, the sound they made getting fainter and fainter.

It was a very fine wine, and we sat and appreciated the quality.

Eventually, as I hoped he would, he looked over at me and in slow clear French, probably because it was the first time we had spoken without the others present, he enquired:

"I hear you are a marine man, did you always like ships?"

His question was said in a distinctly thoughtful manner, using a strong Southern French accent, which was easy for me to understand, and very inviting for me to answer.

"Yes, I lived in and around Portsmouth during my boyhood, the harbour in those days was always filled with ships. For a young boy, it was a very adventurous place, especially during the war."

I am not at all sure what provoked me to add the last phrase, it just popped out. Maybe I was hoping inadvertently it would lead to further conversation.

There was a long pause, after which he said: "The landings on the beaches in France in nineteen forty-four left from Portsmouth, didn't they?"

"Yes some of them," I said. "Every type of ship imaginable was berthed or anchored in the waters off the south coast of England. All the streets were filled with tanks and lorries. My dad was away fighting in Italy. My mum and I looked after the soldiers in the vehicles parked on the roads. We ferried them cups of tea – they had enough food, it was tea they wanted."

I looked across at him, wondering whether he wished for me to continue. From his facial expression he did, so I went on:

"Then one day all the vehicles started to move. I followed them on my bicycle down to the harbour. A lot of ships were very busy preparing to leave, and all the military and dock workers were loading other vessels with every possible cargo."

He was listening intently without saying a word.

"Every day I rode down to the harbour and watched this great armada gather. On my arrival one morning, I saw that all of the ships had sailed during darkness, and later found out 'D' Day had started. We didn't realise until after, the importance of that day."

I was almost sure he wanted to say something, so to encourage him I simply waited.

He was normally a jovial man, but on this occasion he leaned forward, slowly putting his elbows on his knees, and spoke earnestly.

"I remember the war. I had a bicycle like you and wanted to be part of it all, mostly I wanted to be in the French Resistance, but they said I was too young to carry a rifle, so they gave me the job of carrying messages and things. My bicycle took me everywhere and we saw many incidents we were not supposed to see."

I wanted to enquire what 'things' were and why he said 'we' and what sort of 'incidents' he saw, but I kept quiet realising he wanted to go on. He stared at the ground, then quietly and solemnly he lifted his head and stared at me.

"I lived in a village called Espalais here in the South, not far from Toulouse. The German 'SS' had taken over buildings for their headquarters on one side of the village not far away from where I lived. On the other side of the village, the terrifying German Gestapo had encamped themselves in a château."

I could see a glint of fear in his eye after he said it:

"Everyone was scared, having these cruel people living in the same place as us, pretending to like you one minute, then pushing you around with force the next. Being in a country occupied by such a brutal military force was difficult and very frightening."

He hesitated, before slowly starting to speak again.

"One terrible, terrible day, they killed my father." He paused. "They said it was by accident; they said it was a stray bullet; they told my mother my father was in the street during a raid by the Resistance and was shot in the crossfire."

He paused again to gather himself, the sadness in his face was heart-breaking.

"If they hadn't invaded us, he wouldn't have died."

It was a simple statement, saying it affected him and I watched him swallow hard. He took his time, before slowly continuing in a voice vibrating with emotion.

"After we buried my father, I was more resolute than before in my efforts to help the resistance. It must have been on the day when the ships left England and landed in the North of France, for the Germans around us began to panic; under normal circumstances, they were dangerous enough, but when they were panicking, they were even worse."

He hesitated a moment to catch his breath.

"Not far from the village they began to load all the vehicles and every piece of heavy armour they could find onto the railway trucks stationed in the railway sidings, presumably getting the whole trainload ready for transportation. It became clear they were having major problems somewhere because their attitude changed from one of indifferent arrogance to one of fearful brutality. The Resistance men from the area all went to Montauban, which was the main distribution point for the railways. The idea was for them to cause as much chaos as possible, by trying to divert the trains and railway trucks in the wrong directions."

He stopped again, took a deep breath and put his hand to his forehead as if he was going to break down. I waited, and he slowly recovered himself.

"In the sidings not far away, the Germans spent days and nights loading one particular train with tanks, armoured cars, big guns and passenger trucks to carry the soldiers. It was obvious this trainload was primed, prepared and ready to leave. Something significant was happening elsewhere in the country, we learned later about the landings in northern France."

He stumbled for a moment with his memories and his thoughts, but eventually found them and went on:

"I had a friend, Jacques, who also had a bicycle, he was the same age as me, and like me, he was too young to join the Resistance. All the men had left for Montauban, so Jacques and I got together, and with nothing or nobody to help us, we decided to devise a plan to divert the train, or find some way to stop it. Even if we only delayed it for a few days, we thought it would be helping, delaying it even longer we thought would be even better."

At this juncture he became agitated, and his speech quickened to a rate where his complete concentration was required.

"Every day we watched the progress the Germans were making from a hiding place in the wood, and could tell they were ready to go for they put the steam train in position at the front. After cycling home on the day, we stopped before the village and arranged to meet early the next morning on the edge of the wood in a thicket we used as a hideout, it was next to where the points changed from a single line to a double line. One line went to Toulouse and south, the other line went to Montauban and then up to the north of France. We decided if we could jam the points in some way on the railway lines, we could stop the train from going."

Auguste halted again, then threw his hands forward in a helpless fashion and stared directly into my face. "It sounds crazy now I say it, two boys caught up in a war, trying to stop a train full of Nazi soldiers and their deadly weapons of war."

After saying those words, he lowered his head and stared at the ground. When he was ready, he raised himself.

"The next morning on the way to the rendezvous with Jacques, I was stopped by German soldiers at a crossroad, they confronted me with their usual questions. Under normal circumstances, I answered the questions and went on my way, but on this occasion, they were over-aggressive, and pitifully I became frightened. They must have sensed I was up to something because, for some reason, one of their number pointed his rifle directly at me. They held me there and asked me lots of questions. It absolutely terrified me."

I could see from Auguste's facial features he was reliving the moment. I watched him slowly and deliberately recover himself – he did this by physically lifting his chin much higher than was customary. He put his hand to his throat and with a trembling voice he went on.

"As I stood shaking in front of the soldier, there was a shout from an officer sitting in an armoured car by the roadside. I didn't understand what he said, but suddenly they all ran and jumped into their vehicles and sped off down the road, leaving me standing there bewildered, a lonely bystander."

He stopped speaking and shuffled himself about in his seat. I didn't move, being totally transfixed on what he was saying.

"All the Germans headed off in the direction I intended to go, so I followed on my bicycle, diverting into the wood on a short cut as soon as I could. As I got nearer to the rendezvous point where I'd agreed to meet up with Jacques, the path became less well used and very rough, forcing me to slow down. As I approached our meeting place I became aware of some unfamiliar sounds and was unable to distinguish what they were. I hid my bicycle and searched for Jacques. I couldn't find him or his bicycle and I started to panic, I didn't know what to do."

Auguste sat in front of me and gripped both his hands very tightly, rubbing them together over and over again in an agitated and distraught manner; he struggled on.

"Finally I thought maybe he hadn't arrived yet or he had been stopped like me, or worse still was injured. The thought really upset me. The noise grew louder from the direction of the railway track so I crept along as quietly as I could towards the sound. As I approached closer I could hear German voices and much louder banging noises. The bushes in front of me were very close to the trackside where all the Germans were. I secreted myself into a position where I was able to see everything."

Auguste stopped speaking and sat back on his haunches, took a deep breath, lifted his head and looked straight at me.

"In front of me was chaos, total devastation, and destruction. The train we had planned to stop was lying tumbled over on the railway lines, with the first five trucks behind the train lying on their side behind. Two of the personnel carrying passenger trucks behind them were lying on top of one another, all crushed and bashed in. Trucks loaded with the very large guns and heavy vehicles, were now scattered all over the ground at strange angles. Steam was pumping out of the train and the cab was throwing flames and clouds of smoke out everywhere, a fire was starting to spread along the line to the petrol of the vehicles."

He stopped speaking and I could see he was reliving the memory. With determination he forced himself to continue:

"I have never seen such chaos. Bodies of German soldiers were lying everywhere, others were being lifted out of the trucks and laid on the ground. Many of them were dazed, others were in shock simply standing about viewing the carnage before them, unable to move. German officers were scurrying around barking orders; it was a sight I will never forget. An armoured car and a lorry approached down the other end of the track, and I saw it was the soldiers who had interrogated me at the cross-roads. I began to feel afraid and started to think again about Jacques, and scoured the area with my eyes trying to find my pal or his bicycle but I couldn't see any sign of him. I desperately scrutinized everything, including the bushes on the other side of the track, but it was to no avail, there was no sign of Jacques. Suddenly it struck me, my position in the wood was very vulnerable, if the Germans caught me now, I was going to be in terrible trouble, and they would interrogate all my family. I crept back to my bicycle and pedalled home, keeping to the woods, which also meant occasionally I had to push my bicycle across the fields. I arrived home and sat in the garden on the bench, and tried really hard to contemplate what had happened. My mother saw me and came out of the house, kissed me and asked if I was all right; I replied that I was. She asked if I had been doing messages for the Resistance, I fibbed and said that I had."

Suddenly he screwed his face up, as men do when they are trying not to cry.

"Jacques went missing that day."

Again he struggled for words but was determined to continue.

"I have never told anybody before about our plan to try and stop the train. There was always the risk if I told somebody, they would tell others, and then a possibility the Nazis would hear, and reprisals to our families would occur. Some folk who were so frightened they would tell on anybody."

He raised his head and looked at me and I could see the fear and anxiety in his eyes. I watched and eventually he said:

"It was such a difficult time. The situation up in the north of France must have deteriorated, for the Germans turned really nasty, and it became necessary to avoid them at all cost. Fearfulness could be seen in the faces of one or two of the more decent soldiers, maybe they knew it was the beginning of defeat. The Germans retrieved as many vehicles as they could without righting the train or the trucks, which they left sprawled all over the ground."

At this point, I wanted to console him and embrace him but could see he wanted to be left alone. The fear in his eyes disappeared and he then spoke with relative calmness:

"The villagers searched everywhere for Jacques, and I looked for him in all our secret places but couldn't find any sign of him. He hadn't used his bicycle to go to our rendezvous, it was still at his home. They asked me if I knew where he was; I said I didn't know, which was true."

He now waited and took time out to compose himself.

"Eventually, a crane was brought from Toulouse and the train was lifted and moved. The workers found Jacques underneath the steam train; he was hardly recognisable."

This was now Auguste's worst moment.

We sat in silence for a long time. When he was ready to speak again, he steadied himself and with a very heavy heart gently whispered.

"It is the first time I have told this to anyone. I felt it right to tell you because at that time you and I were youths fighting a common enemy, the only difference, you were on the other side of the water. We were both trying our best in very difficult situations.

I put out my hand and said: "Your secret will always be safe with me."

He clasped my hand and looked me in the eye.

"It was a long time ago, he was my best pal."

I filled his glass with wine and drained the bottle into mine. We raised our jam jars in mutual respect, and drank in an acknowledged silence.

# Chapter Nineteen

I left him with his thoughts and walked along up the slope to the top of the clearing, and stared at the blue sky. He had kept all those secrets to himself for all those years. I had time to reflect on Auguste and think what a wonderful man to have in a situation when it was necessary to keep your nerve, and also to keep a secret.

My mind, because of what he spoke about, switched once more to those two dreadful brothers. I had somehow already persuaded myself they were the ones, and a plan was formulating in my brain. At first, it was only a seed, but now it was growing furiously into a sapling and an idea of what I wanted to do was taking shape, but it needed a lot more scheming and plotting; the one thing I had in abundance was Passionate determination.

My thoughts strayed to the deadly crossbow, 'the silent killer'. Daphers and I would have to be the ones to pull the triggers, and it must be at the same time, I think we would require assistance. We would need to be quite close to make sure the job was done properly, also it would be nice to have a strong possibility of escape.

Hearing a rustle of leaves being scuffled underfoot, I caught a glimpse of the other two coming through the trees, which brought me back to reality. I turned and walked down the slope to Auguste. I was pleased to find him now fully recovered.

As we were collecting our things together, the dogs returned and scampered around us, these were soon followed by Jean-Claude and Christian.

I enquired. "Any sign of the wild boar?"

"No," he replied.

I was silently relieved.

We hoisted our rucksacks back on our shoulders, and assembled ourselves into the same convoy as for our passage up the mountain and set off at an enthusiastic pace on our return journey. For me, it couldn't end quickly enough, for I was so looking forward to seeing Daphers. Much to my relief, it wasn't long before I spotted our truck in the little garden of the cottage. The dogs made their presence felt first of all, by barking on arrival. The ladies must have heard for we had the pleasure of seeing them appear through the rear door. We made our way past the wooden gate, and I introduced Daphers to Christian and Auguste.

The two men didn't stay very long, and as they left, Auguste remarked:

"Looking forward to hearing about your expedition to Barcelona when you get back." I wondered whether that was a friendly 'keep in touch' request.

Once inside the house, Daphers and I had a big cuddle. Coffee and sweet biscuits were set on the table, and we all sat around listening to each other's events of the day. It turned out, left to their own devices, the girls had sorted themselves out more than amicably and enjoyed the journey down in the pick-up.

We were discussing the next day's trip to Barcelona when the phone rang. Jean-Claude lifted the receiver, listened and after a brief conversation, he said. "Oui, merci," and spoke to us all.

"That was Louis on the phone reminding us to go at six o'clock tonight for dinner. I have accepted the invitation, and I have told them we have all agreed to go to Barcelona and retrieve the remaining luggage for them. He was delighted; I think they were quite worried about it."

Both girls were enthusiastic and agreed, saying, we should start getting ready and demanded to shower first. Jean-Claude built the fire up and turned on as many heating appliances as he could; it wasn't all that cold, but the mountain freshness had appeared again.

During a quiet period, Daphers and I had a private moment and she told me signatures for the house sale are required on Monday afternoon and said we must return at the latest Monday lunchtime, which meant we must leave here early Monday morning.

I asked her, "Have they agreed to take the heavy furniture?"

"Yes, there is no problem there."

"What about the tractor?"

"That's been agreed as well."

"Wonderful, let's enjoy the trip before we tell the others. If we leave Barcelona late afternoon Sunday, we can easily be back here by nightfall."

"We'll tell them Sunday morning. OK?"

"OK."

Everyone was ready on time for dinner, which was quite miraculous. No one had prepared for such an event, nevertheless, we did our best with the clothes we had, and both ladies looked beautiful. Before leaving the cottage, discussions and decisions were made on a plan of campaign for the weekend.

It was only a short walk to the house of Louis and Nicole, and after elaborate greetings and an aperitif, we ate in the charming dining-room and drank generous volumes of champagne. They gave us all the details of where the apartment was situated in the city, also the total layout of the property and said, as they had sold the property furnished, we could make ourselves as comfortable as possible and stay overnight, or even more. They liked the idea of us taking the pick-up truck – I sensed from this, there might be more personal belongings to come back than they had initially indicated. The keys to the apartment were handed over and advice to take care during our stay in Barcelona.

Jean-Claude pondered this, then remarked:

"I've heard rumours also, and some of them not very nice," adding, "we will try our best to take special care."

The evening ended in the usual kisses and 'bonne nuit'.

The four of us walked back to the cottage full of chat about the evening and the trip to be undertaken the next day. After arriving, tired but delighted, Daphers and I were soon cuddling in the little bed in the little cottage and in next to no time and were very quickly fast asleep.

After a well laid out breakfast, and the packing of small holdalls, we were all ready to leave. Jean-Claude arranged for the dogs to be looked after and fed, and soon we were on our way to Barcelona.

The drive there was uneventful, and our 'sat-nav' took us virtually to the door. Parking was difficult because the pick-up is longer than an ordinary car. It was necessary to tour around the small side-streets in search of space until we finally found a successful spot. Remembering what was said yesterday, I locked the car and made sure nothing was on view inside. It was a fair walk to the apartment entrance and would be a notable distance for the packages and boxes to travel. The apartment itself was reached by way of the lift and was as they described. It consisted of a large lounge, a nice-sized kitchen and a couple of good-sized bedrooms. The reason for our journey was neatly stored in cardboard boxes a trunk and suitcases, and stacked in the corner of the lounge in a discreet manner.

After choosing bedrooms, we all decided to make a minor tour of Barcelona to see what we could discover. The apartment was not far from a large square which had plenty of choice for refreshment, and we noted an acceptable restaurant for the evening. On our return walk, Daphers purchased supplies for the following morning, then the ladies both spotted a small market and with considerable excitement bought girlie things.

We showered and changed for the evening, and ate in the designated restaurant. The Spanish proprietor was a genial fellow, who told us the following day was special, the square in the afternoon would be filled with dancing and laughter and entertainment, and we mustn't miss it. He spoke in English with a little French thrown in, which caused respectful amusement among us. The evening terminated without a night-cap.

There was excitement in the air the following morning. The girls laid the table for breakfast, strong coffee and the usual patisseries, only this time the best Spain could offer.

Daphers and I thought it right at this juncture to inform Jean-Claude and Genevieve of the need for us to return to our home in the Loire for Monday lunchtime, and therefore it would be necessary to leave Barcelona for Eeee sometime late in the afternoon. They thought this most acceptable and were in full agreement.

Jean-Claude asked the question: "When do you think we should take the boxes down to the car?"

I replied, "Yes I've been thinking about that myself, it will probably take several trips. We have a cover for the back of the truck so the boxes won't be in view, but I think we should leave it until we are ready to go. The area where we are parked looks a bit suspicious to me."

Jean-Claude nodded his agreement.

All four of us left the apartment and walked the streets of Barcelona. It was the first time

Daphers and I had visited this wonderful city and very soon we were appreciating the unusual architecture of Gaudi's stunning and magnificent 'Expiatori Sagrada Familia' with its gargoyles of candy and impudent faces hidden away in the brickwork. 'Parc Gueli' popped up with his buildings made like gingerbread houses, with their rounded contours of melted marzipan. It was a struggle for me as a man, who had been brought up in my younger days with pantomime, not to muse on the possibility of a relationship between this architect and writers of fairy tales.

A saunter round by the Gothic Cathedral brought a different vibrancy because of the scent from candles and incense. Walking a little further we were delighted by the smell of freshly baked bread, accompanied by the sweet aroma of doughnuts, which encouraged us to choose a restaurant to further taste wine and Spanish fare. As we drank our coffee, we were alerted by the faint sound of music a distance away; this delighted us all and caused a tapping of our feet and a decision to have an after-lunch stroll.

We headed along a very wide road, amassed with people walking to the city square. Suddenly a child's squeal of glee turned all our heads towards a crowd encircling a golden cowboy. To the mature eye, it was obviously human, but to the eye of the innocent, it was a statue of solid gold. The introduction of a coin into the Stetson hat on the ground by the feet of this automaton produced a movement of his hand towards his hip and his Colt 45. This action was accompanied by a click of the tongue and a wink of the eye, all executed with robotic automated precision. The cowboy's hand remained steadfastly poised over the holster in such a way as to give the indication the gun was ready to be drawn. For the child, it created a total and utter eye-opening surprise. The pose of the cowboy was held for just a moment until another coin was dropped into his hat, and then he gave a tiny indication of a bow of thanks, followed by the automaton's return to solid gold.

The girls and boys in attendance stared, laughed, clapped and jumped up and down in adoration, the crowd looking on showing their approval and respect with a smattering of applause. It was a simple spectacle done with great quality.

I turned to my wife and instantly saw the pleasure in her eyes as she watched the children. I also saw the sadness and the empty loneliness created by the loss we had endured long ago, and the possibility of grandchildren having been snatched so violently from our world. It was still there despite the long weaving journey our lives had taken. I placed my arm around her in mutual, wordless understanding, not at all surprised to see these emotions so easily revealed. We were joined in thought, desire, love, and intent for one another.

We continued our walk and finally made our entrance into the square. A band of folkloric musicians were playing a well-rehearsed piece and local people were already dancing together in an immense circle. The dance was sedate and easy to learn, and our little complement were soon holding hands with unknown delightful people, all stepping backward, forwards and sideways, swaying to and fro with the music. We could have stayed for longer, but we had to return to Eeee; a wave from Jean-Claude indicated it was time to go.

# Chapter Twenty

Our little group collected itself and with reluctance made its way back to the apartment. Once inside, over a cup of coffee, we involved ourselves in a short discussion on the best way of getting the boxes and luggage down to the pick-up. It was decided the men should carry the trunk, along with a box and a holdall, and the girls a box each.

Our modest caravan made cumbersome progress via the lift to the street, walked a short distance, and after turning a couple of corners arrived at the pick-up truck.

I immediately felt uncomfortable, finding the street overly desolate. The others didn't seem to notice anything odd; probably it was my maritime days taking over. Another car was parked at the far end of the street, but ours was the only one with right-hand drive and English number plates.

I pulled the cover away and we lifted the trunk and boxes we had brought into the back of the truck.

Jean-Claude looked about, beginning to receive a sense of unease himself. "Have we to put the holdalls into the back as well?"

"No, let's lock them up in the cab," I replied. "Can you, Genevieve and Daphers manage the other cases? I'll stay with the truck."

"Yes," they said and started back to the apartment.

When the other three returned loaded with more items, Jean-Claude remarked, "There are some boxes left, Genevieve and I must make one more journey."

"Can you lock the apartment up when you leave? Daphers and I will stay here and slip a rope across all these boxes to tie them down."

"Yes," he said, and they both set off once more.

I tied the rope around a hook on the sidewall in the back of the truck and passed it over the boxes, walked across to the centre of the road, pulled it tight and tied it to a hook opposite, then passed the rope back to Daphers, who was standing on the pavement. She, in turn, tied it around a hook on her side and passed it back to me and I tied it off.

Immediately I finished doing this, a scuffling noise began a little way off behind me and the sound of running feet. Suddenly somewhere from my left, two men appeared advancing towards us at pace, one heading towards me, the other hurtling towards my wife. The main thought in my brain was how to get round to protect Daphers, but my movements were suddenly interrupted by a hand violently grabbing my left arm, and another hand from the same body expertly attempting to enter my pocket. Shock, anger, and instinct within me took over, and I grasped the violently offensive arm, and pulled it with all my angered strength into the side of the truck, then kneed the owner of the arm heavily in the groin. A gargoyled expression instantly appeared on the robber's face, indicating he had received a certain amount of pain somewhere in the lower region. As a defensive ploy, he threw his arms in the air and pushed me away, escaping my grasp, and with a lopsided unhealthy looking limp hobbled away up the street, completely forgetting about my wallet.

The other robber looked more wiry than his limping mate and was tussling with Daphers. She was putting up a devil of a fight, thrashing her arms about with her fists clenched trying to defend herself. The red mist appeared in my eyes, and with gritted teeth, I tore round to the other side of the truck, grabbed the robber by his shirt and pulled as hard as I could. He turned, faced me and ripped his shirt from my grasp, then heaved and pushed me fiercely away making me stumble backward. With surprising speed, he ran off in the same direction as his mate, clutching Dapher's handbag.

I took her in my arms and hugged and hugged her. "Are you all right?"

She was trembling. "Yes," she said.

"Oh, that's good, how did he get your handbag? It was over your shoulder."

"He cut the strap with a knife," she said.

"Oh dear, oh dear, I'm sorry; I should have protected you better."

We hugged again so tightly until her shaking calmed. It took quite some time. The hug also helped me, to steady myself.

I held her at arm's length. "Were all your valuables in the handbag?"

She looked at me and smiled. "No, it was the one I bought in the market yesterday; only my lipstick, mirror and a handkerchief were in it, nothing else."

"That's a relief," I said and opened the passenger door of the truck and helped her safely onto the seat and stood for a moment by the open door. I took her hand; she smiled at me deliberately and shook her head.

"I don't think the colour of the handbag would suit him, he had such a sallow complexion for a Spaniard."

I could not stop a smile. What a woman. Was there any other man more proud than I? She had suffered a terrible assault and yet she could turn it into amusement. What a woman!

I wandered to the back of the truck, pausing at the tailgate to reflect on the violence that had just occurred, thinking that the incident had been very nasty, and how surprised I was at my reaction. From the moment the thief grabbed my arm, my immediate response was one of complete unafraid commitment. The thieves probably thought two old people were easy targets and I was so delighted to think about how wrong they were. It was at that moment my mind was made up, I was strong enough and along with Daphers, saw we could take on anything or anybody. I knew there and then, it was time to finalise some sort of plan and revisit England and create some justice in this tiny little world of ours.

Jean-Claude and Genevieve arrived back carrying the remaining boxes. He saw my serious expression and raised an eyebrow in a concerned way: "Is everything alright?"

"It is now," I replied and moved the cover across to allow him to place the remaining boxes into the back of the truck. Genevieve also noticed something was wrong and immediately went to see Daphers in the cab.

"Are you all right, Daphne?" she enquired.

"Yes I think so," she said and commenced to relay what had happened to us. They were both soon joined by Jean-Claude, who listened in silence.

After securing the boxes, I went and sat in the driver's seat in time to hear the end of the account of the robbery.

Jean-Claude reacted instantly. "Are you going to contact the police? One of the robbers used a knife."

Daphers paused and thought for a moment, then said, "He only used it to cut the strap on my bag, and I don't think I would be able to give a full description of the thieves to the police."

She looked at me. "Would you be able to identify them again, Matthew?"

"No," I said. "If we go to the police, we will be there for ages, maybe all night. Also we are bound to have a language problem, and anyway it's probably a common occurrence. I think we should swallow hard and head off back to Eeee. What do you say, love?"

"Yes, if everyone is in agreement, I think we should go home."

We all nodded, I started the car, and we all belted up and settled down.

# Chapter Twenty-One

During the journey, we spoke in depth about the robbery and carried on the conversation about the pros and cons of not going to the police.

Jean-Claude commented, "It is too late now anyway," and pointed to the passing sign which read: 'You Are Entering France'. The subject was left behind, and in its place, we reminisced about the beauty of Barcelona, rather than the criminal dregs that sometimes hounded the streets.

When this topic of conversation was exhausted, Genevieve suddenly came out with a question she had obviously wanted to ask for a while:

"Where are you both going to live, when your house is finally sold?"

I too had been thinking about this off and on for some time and had one or two ideas. We needed a place where we could drive over to England, but also a place where we could hide away and get forgotten in mountainous forests.

Daphers answered Genevieve and explained the complication of our circumstance. "We have agreed to sell all of the heavy furniture to the buyers; anything left over we are giving to our neighbours to sell as they please. Over the years they gave us great friendship and when our French needed improving, they were very patient and very kind."

I suddenly, annoyingly interrupted: "All our personal effects are to go into storage until we need them."

"Yes, yes," broke in Genevieve, "that's all right, but where are you actually going to live? Maybe somewhere like Eeee might be nice?"

I glanced at Jean-Claude, and he looked back at me. He must have noticed my inquisitive expression, for we had one of those silences, which were uncommon between us.

Then he asked: "What do you think, Matthew, where would you like to live?"

My plan for these two dreadful men in England was coming more and more to the forefront of my mind. I knew now it would probably require more than just Daphers and myself to deal with them. It would be handy to have a man preferably skilled with his hands on our side, who recognised the importance of keeping silent. I knew a man of that quality, who very conveniently lived in Eeee. So, answering Jean-Claude, but enjoying and relishing Genevieve's sentiments, I added:

"We will see if we can find somewhere in Eeee to live for a while. What do you think Daphne?"

Unable to see her face as she was in the back of the pick-up, I suspected it would be shaped in curiosity and surprise. She remarked, "I think it would be lovely if we could find a nice house to live in for a little while. We don't have a long time to find one, I will make some enquiries when we get back."

This prompted Genevieve to join the conversation. "Leave it to me," she said, just like that.

The mirror informed me they gave each other an enormous hug, and thereafter all of the car was filled with excited chatter.

We arrived in Eeee and parked in the drive of the lovely cottage. The girls rustled up something to eat, we opened a bottle of wine, and it wasn't long before all of us were tucked up in bed.

It was an opportunity for me to ask Daphers what all the chattering was about, and what the outcome was. She did make a valiant attempt at a reply, only to find sleep winning the contest.

Over early breakfast the following morning, we discussed a possible time to drop the cargo of boxes off to Louis and Nicole. This instantly caused Genevieve to scuttle off to the phone, dial a number and after some hectic chatter, immediately nod to Daphers, who smiled appealingly in appreciation. I couldn't help feeling there was a conspiracy afoot.

"It's all arranged," she said, "we can go now. You boys are to empty the truck, Daphers and I have things to discuss with Nicole." More smiles glowed on both their faces. It was obvious they were thoroughly enjoying this confidential private liaison.

The drive to Louis and Nicole's house was short. I reversed the pick-up truck through the gates, down the drive and parked outside their garage. Both he and Nicole came out of the house and greeted us. Nicole took charge of the ladies, who couldn't wait to commence discussions, and in total excitement disappeared through the front door.

Upon discharging all the cargo into the garage, invitations for us to join everyone for coffee immediately followed, but first it was necessary for me to have a word with the two men.

"Daphers and I must be getting back to the Loire because we have to finalise the signing of the house this afternoon!"

Then turning to Jean-Claude, I asked. "Can you find a place to park our other car? I have a feeling we will be coming back here quite soon."

"Sure," he said and took the keys from me.

At this point, we were joined by the ladies. "Time we were going home, Matthew, well home for another day or two," exclaimed Daphers.

My face was smiling, this time it was a partial smile of curiosity.

She saw it and knew what it was. "I'll tell you on the journey home," she chirped.

We collected our remaining belongings from the little cottage, leaving all the wine as a 'thank you,' and with many hugs and kisses departed down the road to the Loire.

# Chapter Twenty-two

At the beginning of our journey, we studied the road system and the directions around the approaches of Toulouse, but once we were free of the city we joined the French motorway system and driving became very much easier. By then, it was time for me to listen to where we were going to lay our heads over the next few weeks. I indicated this to Daphers by placing my hand on her knee and giving it a slight squeeze.

"How did you do on the accommodation front?"

She acknowledged this question by taking a deep intake of breath.

"Nicole was very helpful and explained that there was a choice of two places for rental in Eeee. One, which is in the form of a 'chambre d'hote' in the middle of the village, and the other a small cottage style house on one level in its own grounds, not far from Auguste, and owned by Louis and Nicole."

I interrupted as usual. "The second one sounds very good, also near Auguste sounds even better."

She narrowed her eyes and peered at me sideways.

Taking that to be a bit of a reprimand, I went quickly on.

"Sorry, carry on, I'll try my best not to interrupt anymore."

After a pause and a grin, she continued.

"I've anticipated your reply and asked Nicole about the second house, and she said it had been used earlier in the year; however, it was now vacant and she sort of insisted we use it. She said we could have it for as long as we like, and is arranging for it to be cleaned and readied for when we get back. I've told her that would be lovely."

I butted in again: "What do you think 'readied' means?"

She smiled. "Readied is as near a translation as I can get. I think it means seeing to the heating, water, gardening, and laundry. I am sure that's what she meant, oh, and by the way, we have a problem, she won't take any payment for the first few months as bringing back the boxes from Spain was enough."

I took my eyes off the road for a second. "If it gets too embarrassing, we will pay them in bottles of champagne or wine or something else; we must have a think about it."

Daphers responded, "I agree, but let's have a look at the house first, and if we like it we can live in it and then sort out the problem of payment when it arises."

We motored on for a while both saying very little, and I began thinking it was time to tell my wife about my plan to try and find out more about these two brothers in England. I realised I couldn't say very much because I didn't know very much, also I didn't really know how to approach the subject, so not being very good at approaching things indirectly, I just came out with it.

"We need to go to England again as soon as it's convenient; we need to gather more information."

She glanced at me sideways with one of those glances I have come to know so well, and she handed me a mint.

"When are you going to tell me what all this is about?"

"I'm afraid you will just have to trust me, love. I will tell you more when I know more. We need to arrange ferries, car hire, and a B & B. It would be very nice if we could go as soon as possible. We could arrange it all when we have settled the house sale and everything else."

She didn't seem too happy but saw she was not going to get any more information, so she just settled back in her seat.

We continued down the motorway toll road, then negotiated the smaller roads and finally came to rest outside the drive of our house. Daphers got out of the car and opened the gates. When she climbed back in she said disappointedly:

"There is no sign of Bulldog."

"Maybe he's on the veranda, sitting there waiting," I replied, putting the car into first gear and slowly sauntering down the drive. We both glanced from side to side hoping to spot the slightly ugly, yet appealingly delightful little face. But it was to no avail, he was nowhere to be seen. We maintained our search by shouting and looking, but he didn't appear to be about.

Our appointment with the French solicitor had to be kept, and we went to his office and signed the house away. All parties are required to be present in France at the signing, and the money is handed over at the time, in this instance a cheque.

The Major and his partner Madeleine came back to the house with us and arrangements previously agreed by Daphers were carried out. Because it now seemed we were going to live in a fully furnished rented cottage, most of the light furniture and many of the other items would now not be needed. Daphers and I had a discussion and came to the conclusion nothing was of sentimental value, and by selling them we would save on storage, so we offered them all at a knockdown price to the new owners. As they were living in furnished accommodation it didn't take long for them to agree and an additional cheque was written out by them. At this point, a bottle of champagne was opened and four glasses now belonging to the new owners were produced, a toast was made, sealing the whole deal. The only items remaining in the house belonging to us now were all the boxed and suitcases put to one side.

After the Major and Madeleine departed, we searched again for Bulldog, but our search was not at all fruitful.

We sat on the veranda finishing the champagne, wondering about our next move when our neighbour Marcel appeared at the top of the drive, we waved and he quickly joined us. After general chit chat, I enquired: "Have you seen Bulldog?"

"No, sorry, not for a while."

Further movement at the gates caused me to turn in time to see a van chug its way down the drive towards us. It came to rest opposite to where we were sitting on the veranda and Albert struggled his way out of the driver's seat. After the usual greetings, he asked the question:

"Have you lost somebody?"

"Yes," came the spontaneous reply from us all.

"Come and have a look inside my van," he said.

We all walked round to the front window of his van, and he pointed inside. There, curled up on the passenger seat with eyes wide open staring up at us, was the unmistakable face of Bulldog.

Albert shook his head. "He has been camped out with me for the last few days; if he's not in the house, he's in the van. What do you make of that?"

Then with a slight hesitation, he continued: "I have come to return him home." He had a watchful submissive look on his face, also, what could only be described for a man of his character, a sorrowful expression.

Daphers was delighted to see Bulldog and she scurried round to the other side of the van, opened the door, reached in stroked him and said, "There you are, Bulldog." It was obvious she had become very fond of this gentle, friendly pussycat.

It was a difficult situation, but a possible solution suddenly dawned on me.

"Daphers," I whispered in English as gently as I could. "I don't think Bulldog wants to stay here; it looks like he has found a new home."

I saw the despair in her eyes. Knowing she had grown to love this delightful little creature, I further explained:

"We are leaving this house in a few days and we have things to do. It would be very difficult to take him with us, maybe it is best we should ask Albert to look after him."

The realisation swept across her face as she saw, under the circumstances, this would probably be the best solution. She opened the passenger door wide and slowly and gently picked up Bulldog, gave him a kiss on his little head and a really big hug, then placed him back on the front seat of the van.

She then turned to Albert and in her best French explained: "We have sold this house and are leaving in a few days. Can you look after him from now on? He seems to have found his home with you."

Albert beamed with a smile of pure delight.

"He and I have become really good pals, I am sure we will get on very well. I will keep him safe."

"Thanks very much," responded Daphers. "I'll go and get all his food for you and all the other stuff." She returned with bags and more bags. Albert opened the back of his van, and they both nestled all Bulldog's gear in amongst all the other equipment.

Having no knowledge of the English language, before he went, he asked the question: "What is this Bulldog?"

"It's his name," said Daphers.

Albert repeated it with difficulty. "Bulldog," and swung himself in one movement into the driver's seat. We all stood and watched Bulldog up the drive.

# Chapter Twenty-Three

Daphers gave a little wave as the van disappeared through the gates and headed off to his new home. I could see she was struggling to maintain her composure, so I put my arm around her and applied a really strong, extended cuddle, accompanied by a kiss on the forehead.

Marcel viewed things from a few steps away and waited.

"I'm glad you have found a home for Bulldog; he was a lovely cat." The word Bulldog was not easy for the French to say, but he had managed to make it recognisable.

After asserting himself, he ventured.

"Marie and I would like you both to come round tomorrow night and join us for dinner, she has started preparing your favourite, Matthew."

This was too good to miss on two counts: one, we didn't have much in the fridge and two, Marie served the best 'Cous Cous' in France.

"We would love to come, what do you think? About the usual time?"

He strode off down the drive, waving as he went out the gates.

When the two of us were left alone Daphers began thinking again about Bulldog, and couldn't hold back the tears. I held her in my arms.

Eventually, she said, "He's gone to a really good home, and it would have been impossible to take him with us, wouldn't it?"

"Yes, it would," I said.

"He was such a lovely, gentle creature, I am going to miss him." She paused, then continued: "I'm sure Albert will look after him; am I being silly?"

"Certainly not," I replied. "I shall miss him too, especially his companionship in the mornings when we stood on this veranda admiring the view, and he would stroll up and sit beside me, admiring the view with me. He always sat in an upright position, as if to say, 'what a pleasant sight'. At peace with himself. It always made me smile and gave me a feeling of calmed contentment; I shall miss him as much as you."

She picked up the bottle of Ricard. "Would you like another?"

"No thanks, love, it's time we were in bed."

We tidied the glasses and jumped into bed, but before we went to sleep, I took her hand and quietly said:

"I'm collecting cash, Pounds, and Euros, I think they might be useful later on. If you get the chance, can you see if you can squeeze some into your purse?"

She replied in a sleepy tone before she fell asleep.

"All right, if I get the chance!"

We both slept very well as usual. Daphers woke early, sneaked out of bed, took her shower, made some tea, then returned to the bedroom and presented me with a cup. She sat down beside me, and with inquisitive eyes looked at me.

"What was that you whispered in my ear last night, about collecting cash?"

It was a chance gesture on my part, and deliberately said at that time in the hope she might regard it as not being important, and put it to the back of her mind. Obviously, I was mistaken.

My feeble response was, "Well, it might be useful later on."

"Yes, I heard that bit. Are you going to elaborate a little more for me, maybe let me in on your secret?"

Another lame reply came out.

"I hope you don't mind my not giving you any more information. There is a good deal of thinking and an awful lot of planning needed before I can give you any further details of what we are going to do."

I gave her a kiss on the forehead, then in the momentary lull in conversation added, "We need to go to England soon, will you help organise it with me?"

"Yes, of course, I'll go and make some tea."

When we sat at the table, Daphers asked:

"What would you like me to do?"

"Well," I said, "we need to arrange the ferry, car-hire, parking at Calais and book that hotel in England again. Can you do the hotel? I'll arrange the car-hire and the ferry."

She glanced at me curiously. "Why are we hiring a car? Why are we not using our pick-up truck? After all, it is a right-hand drive?"

"When we go this time, I think it might be a good idea not to use the pick-up truck, not to show it about the place. It would be nice if we could go and come back without being seen, you know hopefully totally unnoticed."

After finishing the sentence, I glanced sideways at her, to see what sort of an expression she had on her face; it was an understanding one, so I continued.

"I would like us to stay in the same hotel as before, then drive and hunt about around the villages and the woods in that area, where I went with the guys; you know, on that day when you practised on the organ for the wedding in the church. It would be good if we could find the cul-de-sac road near the wood with the houses on either side. I only have a vague idea where it is. We need to find somewhere out of the way, which is unobtrusive; a cottage, or a house, somewhere for us to stay and find out more information about the houses."

Dashers immediately said, "What cul-de-sac road?"

"We have to find houses in a cul-de-sac with a wood at the end, it's in a village amongst other villages. I have an idea of the area but only an idea."

She looked at me. "I'm not going to get any more, am I?"

"No, I'm afraid not, love, only because I don't know anymore."

Stopping and thinking to myself, what I am doing is a long shot, but I knew we simply had to start somewhere. "It would be nice if we were to sail over to the UK, stay for a while, find something, anything really, then sail back with as little fuss as possible."

I realised the whole thing didn't make a lot of sense, but still, she took my hand and looked at me and spoke softly.

"I understand there is something you want to do, maybe even must do. I also know it is to do with that village. Can you not share it with me? How about spilling some of the beans?"

She half-smiled. "I am getting rather anxious."

"The trouble is, love, I have no real beans to spill, everything depends on our next trip over the water back to England, and what we find."

I paused, scratched the back of my head, brushed my hair back with my hands and made a face.

"As soon as the picture becomes clearer, I will let you know; at the moment it is just a blurred Picasso print of a print."

"Oh well, I've always thought most of your ideas to be pretty good, so I will have to trust you again, but you are skating on thin ice."

"The only thing I have at the moment is my absolute determination; I haven't got anything else."

At that I winked and ducked into our little office, picked up the phone and arranged the ferry and the parking of the pick-up. Luckily the parking included the transportation to the ferry. More fiddling with the phone produced a hire-car in England with a firm we had used before.

I found Daphers packing her rucksack, and whispered in her ear, "I've done my arranging on the phone – can you do the hotel?"

She looked up and replied, "Yes, of course, can you pack your rucksack?"

She paused, then politely asked: "Do you know how long we are going to be there? I am sure I haven't packed enough, and my rucksack is full. If you have any room left in yours, can you take more of everything of mine?"

Sometimes women say things men can't immediately make sense of; this was such an occasion. I had learned from past experience to pretend to understand and reply, and then hope the reply is good.

"Yes, you'll need one or two extra jumpers and some very strong walking shoes to travel in, and also both pairs of binoculars."

"Why are you taking the binoculars?" she quizzed.

Something told me we would need binoculars on this trip, but because I had nothing sound to say, nothing positive about what we intended to do, the best answer I could come up with was:

"Just in case."

"Just in case of what?" she said.

I thought, 'heck this is going to go on forever, so best refer back to the Navy days'.

"Just in case I see some interesting ships when we go across the Channel on the ferry; you know to watch them, to see them clearer."

She laughed. "That is the most feeble excuse I have ever heard."

"That's the best you're going to get!" And I made my escape into the lounge, and settled on the sofa for probably the last time with my face buried in a newspaper.

# Chapter Twenty-Four

Daphers woke me with a cup of tea and told me it was time to get ready for dinner. It was not a dressing up occasion, so I donned a smart shirt and trousers. She dressed in a bright blouse and slacks and looked beautiful.

"Have we got the wine and the flowers?" I asked.

"Yes," she replied. "Do you realise this will probably be the last evening we will spend in this delightful village, apart from maybe coming back for our stuff? Let's make absolutely sure we enjoy it."

"Better take another bottle of wine then; I'll carry these, you take the flowers."

We took the short walk along the lane to Marcel and Marie's, entered the drive and knocked on the door. It just so happened the French doors opened directly into the dining room. Marcel and Marie invited us in, and as they did so, we were confronted by the shouting and waving of all of our friends who lived in the village, and the table set for a celebration.

We ate, we drank, we listened to jokes, some of which we didn't understand and we had a scrumptious time. All the presents we received were marvellous.

At the end of the evening, a speech was called for, so in my best French, I thanked everybody for their presents, but most of all for their friendship, which brought an enormous cheer.

On finally leaving, we kissed or shook hands with everyone, then cried with everyone, and wobbled back for the last time to our house.

We were pleased we had agreed to leave the bed for our buyers, it was far too heavy to move, and anyway, we always slept in it so gracefully.

The following day we were presented with a very fine morning and no hangover. The four very large suitcases, the chests, and the trunks containing our clothes and all the personal stuff we wanted to take to Eeee were loaded into the back of the truck.

Daphers asked: "Will the truck be all right when it is parked with only that big plastic cover over it at the back?"

"Yes, I've checked it is in a secure parking area, I'll also make sure to tie everything down good and tight."

After checking all the rooms inside the house in case we had forgotten anything, we sat in the chairs on the veranda with our rucksacks at our feet and waited for the estate agent to make an appearance. It was agreed he would attend to read the meters and pass the keys on to the new owners.

After he arrived, Daphers placed all the rucksacks onto the back seat of the pick-up truck. I jumped into the driver's seat and we drove through the gates, both turning at the last moment to wave goodbye to our delightful charming house.

As we entered the motorway, my thoughts focused on what we were hoping to find in that village in England. Whatever we found, would determine what we were eventually going to do. First of all, we had to be certain we were doing the right thing, to the right people, not what we thought to be the right thing to the right people, and end up doing the wrong thing to the wrong people. In the next few days or maybe a week we would know.

As I was thinking, Daphers spoke up. "I forgot to tell you, I couldn't get the same hotel as last time, so I have booked us into a B&B in another village close by, is that OK?"

"Yes, it will probably be even better than the hotel, hopefully, more discreet." Then I gave her the thumbs up in acknowledgement and a great big smile, followed by:

"Are you happy with what we are doing?"

She paused. "Yes, I am. No matter what happens, we have sold the house, we had no one to leave it to, and now we have more money to spend however we like. If things don't go according to plan, we can always return to Eeee and live there forever."

The journey continued contentedly without incident and we arrived at the port and parked at the arranged place. A driver delivered us to the ferry and we boarded by walking up the gangway, with our rucksacks slung over our shoulders.

The crossing was short, and after a snack, we sat and surveyed the passing ships.

Daphers closed her eyes and went to sleep.

I knew at some point in the next few days I would have to tell Daphers what all this activity was about. Why we were doing what we were doing. I must choose the right time – it was so, so, important.

# Chapter Twenty-Five

Watching the mist of the sea spray showering the bows of the ships, my mind wandered back to how different it must have been two hundred and fifty years ago when men sailed in wooden galleons trying to discover unknown lands thousands of miles away, the wind their only source of power. Sadly not always blowing in the right direction. My heart went out to those unbelievably brave men, every day fighting for their lives, wondering what was over the horizon; inquisitiveness driving them forward.

This led me to think it was time I told Daphers why we had sold the house and why we were going on these escapades. The right moment was very important.

My reflections and thoughts were disturbed when I saw land approaching and gently woke her.

"I think we are about here."

She shuffled, blinked and saw we were close to England.

"That was a very short passage, we'll have to get ready to disembark."

The ferry docked and we alighted down the gangway, then walked the short distance to collect the hire car. Our portable 'sat-nav' was a useful tool for finding the new Bed and Breakfast, which was some distance from where we wanted to be, but it didn't matter. After we settled into our room we took the opportunity to study the maps bought on the ferry and compared them with the ones we found at the B&B. Together they gave us information about the area. On the best map I marked the village where I thought we wanted to be; it looked more like a small town. It was so important to find the road of these two brothers, but I couldn't find it anywhere on the map, because the whole area was surrounded by an enormous wood, well more like a forest, which seemed to completely enclose the village. To find this road we needed to search the village and the wood on foot, but imperative under no circumstances to be seen by anybody.

My idea was to park the car somewhere around the wood and under the pretence of maybe bird watching try to find a place for us to hide or shelter, so we could spy on the specific road and possibly the houses of the two brothers. It was absolutely essential to keep as far away from the road as possible – under no circumstances were we to be discovered. It was all a bit of a long shot but we had now come this far and I definitely felt we were getting nearer and nearer to our quarry.

Daphers took my thoughts away and enquired: "You've been studying this map for a long time; what are you looking for?"

"Right now, I'm not exactly sure," I said. "I'm hoping when I see it I'll know."

"Are you sure you'll see it, what if we don't see it?"

"Well, we keep looking until we do."

That sounded a bit brusque, so I added; "Walking around these woods will be very pleasant anyway, and we have brought the binoculars, so we could possibly do a little bird watching."

She responded immediately. "Oh, I like that, what a good idea! If you had said that before I would have brought a book. I'll see if I've got a couple of writing pads or something in my handbag. We could collect and write down the birds we see and name them if we can."

She went off and started searching her handbag and rucksack, eventually finding something that resembled a notepad, some other paper and a couple of pencils.

She returned to the map and showed more interest than previously. "Where do you think we ought to start?"

I wanted to circumnavigate the village in a clockwise direction, beginning in the west, so I suggested in an enquiring way:

"How about we park the car somewhere near there?" pointing to the left of the village on the map. "That will enable us to look right round all that section of the wood."

Daphers agreed and marked the map with a pencil.

"So we start tomorrow," she said. "The weather forecast says it is going to be good for the next couple of days. We could leave straight away after breakfast."

She pondered this for a few seconds then put her fingers to her lips. "We'll need some sandwiches for lunch. I wonder if the landlady will give us a flask of coffee? It's a fair distance to the village, so there must be a shop or a supermarket we can use on the way."

Putting my arm around her I replied, "You seem to have taken over, it will be nice to be under your guidance during this bird-watching holiday, I think I'll just follow along in your wake."

She smiled. "I think our next step is to have a shower and go to bed."

"What a good plan," I said.

Sleeping was no problem at all for either of us.

We breakfasted on kippers, and Daphne asked about the flask but it wasn't forthcoming, only apologies. So with rucksacks packed and binoculars around our necks, we ventured to the first section of the wood, calling on the way at a store where we purchased all necessary provisions.

Finding and parking in our chosen place, or very close, was fairly easy and we embarked on our ornithological expedition. In the beginning, we kept to the outskirts, but soon we were walking through the wood itself. Apart from the odd bird, we didn't see a soul. When it was time for lunch, we found a nice spot in the sunshine and sat down on some large stones.

In the quiet of the surrounding trees, I felt it was now the right time to broach the subject of why we were here, and so began to speak in a very gentle manner.

"It is time I told you why we are here." And I softly took her hand.

"We have come over to England to find those two brutal brothers who created that awful, dreadful, dreadful tragedy in our lives."

I struggled to go on but managed.

"This is the first step to try and find the houses they live in."

It wasn't necessary for me to explain any further because I could see by her face she understood exactly what I was saying. She stood up, I followed, and she gripped my arms, and stared into my eyes. I watched her face fiercely sadden into a reflection of years before and saw a tear spill from her eye. We remained standing like statues not moving, it was some time before her expression changed and her face slowly returned to as it had been. We put our arms around each other and hugged each other with all the force we could muster. The memory was still with us and we both shed a tear quietly and knowingly.

"Are you with me?" I said.

She replied, "Are we going to do something about it?"

"Yes, we are."

"Then, of course, I am with you. I am with you all the way; it is time somebody did something about it, and I think we are that somebody."

She paused and stared at me. "One thing, we must be sure we get everything right, no mistakes, it was a long time ago. Throughout whatever we are going to do, always remember I am with you all the way, right to the very end."

She had now put me in a position where all the half plans I had been making over the past months, suddenly had a chance of becoming reality. It also abruptly dawned on me what a big moment this was, because her enthusiasm not only re-enforced my determination, it gave me a renewed spirit and passion to do what was now essential.

I looked at her. "One thing, we must be completely and utterly sure it is them."

"Yes," she said, "we must be absolutely sure."

Before we set off again, I took her hand. "We need to find somewhere to spy on these two, an old shed or a barn, anything where we can see as much as possible. We'll circle round between those two big trees and try skirting along behind those houses, but keeping them at a very good distance."

We walked and watched and searched, but it was all to no avail, not even the smallest shelter revealed itself and we finally arrived back at our hire-car, a little disappointed, but full of enthusiasm for our evening meal. We wasted no time at all reaching our B & B, and dinner was spent discussing the day and what to do the following day.

Sleep was good. After breakfast, we parked the car in a new spot, walked a new route and turned up much the same as the first day, so we returned to the B & B with the hope that our luck would improve the next day.

# Chapter Twenty-Six

The following morning we took to meandering through the forest and the woods, wearing our binoculars around our necks, still under the pretence of bird watching, trying our best to look the part. Our little books by now were filled with scribbles, sketches, and names of birds we spotted perched or flying in and around the trees. It started as a bit of nonsense in the beginning, but as time passed we began to take more interest in all of these individual delightful creatures, and some of the drawings became reasonably recognisable. This could have been because of the knowledge we accumulated, or maybe the improvement in our artistic flair. The names given were possibly not correct, but by doing this, our interest was maintained and put a smile on our face. The more time we spent in the woods, the more we enjoyed it, but my constant awareness of the resolute importance of finding a discreet place, out of the way, yet in sight of our quarry, was never far from my mind. A good base to spy on the brothers' road was essential to our plan. This was really my one and only aim.

As time passed I began to get a little anxious and repeatedly reminded myself to remain patient, thinking it best to keep calm and not to make our presence in the village too obvious. The rule was never to go close to any of the houses, and to stick to the woods as much as possible, avoiding any contact with people as best we could, always remembering the need to find somewhere to gain further information about these two brothers.

From our rambling, we learned that the village was old and quite large, but compact with a main road which wasn't very busy leading through and out to the nearest town. As normal for the countryside, there were lanes and streets with houses on both sides constructed at different times over the centuries, and therefore of different designs, all with different sized front and rear gardens. Some of the roads led off at right angles, then turned at right angles. There were one or two cul-de-sacs with various semi-detached houses on one side and rows of terraced houses on the other. It was a village where houses were built, lived in, left, knocked down and rebuilt again, a typical old English village although we thought this village to be the size of a town – there were bits and pieces of it everywhere.

On the outskirts of the village, along another road, was a general store and a very old church including the inevitable graveyard, a town hall, a garage, and other shops. All this was surrounded by woods, or the occasional small paddock on the outskirts fenced off for horses.

In the beginning, we tried to do everything methodically, by going around the village in one direction, closely maintaining our bearings by sticking to paths. Unfortunately, there were a couple of occasions where we strayed out too far, and to our dismay temporarily got lost. This gave us some concern because our plan was to always keep ourselves to ourselves and not become known to anyone.

On the third night we didn't sleep very well and woke at first light, then without breakfast left the B & B early, and with the aid of our trusted map, parked the car this time in a partially fenced excuse of a car park, with no sign, only overgrown grass, and weeds. Opening the boot, we shouldered our rucksacks and set off, first looking and surveying the area around us, occasionally viewing the high branches of the trees, trying to find a clue as to where the particular road of interest would be, always aware of not getting too close. It was also forever necessary to glance forward along the ground from time to time, so as not to trip on a stump of a tree or fall into a ditch; an accident now would be disastrous.

This section of wooded area around the village was exceptionally dense, and we began to climb a slope which was fairly steep; Daphers looked at me.

"Is it essential we go up here? It's awfully difficult."

I waved her on and we continued for a time, then stopped for breath. In front of us was nothing but very high trees and no path.

"Let's see if we can reach the top?"

Three-quarters of the way up the hill we saw the top of a couple of buildings. From a distance, they looked old and unused. Slowly we scrambled further up, wondering what they were and if anyone lived there. Our approach from the rear gave us a reasonable insight into the house itself. A far as I could see, it was not derelict, nor was it in the first flush of youth.

There was a main house on the right, and a large barn sort of building over to the left. The whole area was surrounded by untidy uncut grass, trees, and large uncut hedges. It is always a strange moment when walking in woods to find you are suddenly and possibly an intruder in someone else's back garden. The thought made me stop and take hold of my wife's arm.

"Dogs," I said.

"Where?" she asked.

"No," I said. "Maybe they have dogs, although I can't see or hear anything."

We both stopped and looked about for a while, just peering at the buildings, not quite knowing where to go or what to do. It seemed a good idea to do nothing, so we just stood there looking. The situation was a delicate one because it would not have been very helpful to be discovered in this out of the way part of the wood, standing there looking at the back of a house like a couple of gormless statues. Our only excuse for being there and possibly plausible explanation was bird watching, so, clutching my binoculars and my bird book, I readied myself with the phrase 'Oh, we are so sorry, we were bird watching and got lost.' Then wave my binoculars in the air. Slowly we edged ourselves forward, shuffling rather than stepping, both maintaining a watchful eye in all directions. By doing this and moving to my left, it was possible to get a better view of the rear of the house. I could see although not built on a very large ground area, was two storeys high with a very good roof.

Daphers and I cautiously made our way further and further round towards the front. Someone had made a half-hearted attempt at fashioning a drive, which was now overgrown by grass on either side.

# Chapter Twenty Seven

The house itself appeared to be desolate, with no visible sign of having been lived in for some time. Moving further round, we saw logs stacked up against the wall by the front door under a covered lean-to. On the ground, partially covered by the overgrown grassy section, were planks of wood long enough to be scaffolding planks, and by the side of the front door were the inevitable plant pots crookedly scattered about.

Daphers and I approached with caution and stood gazing at all before us, then advanced further until we were right in front of the house. If anybody lived there, they surely would see us now. She broke the silence.

"Maybe the owners have gone out for the day, or maybe they are inside out of sight, or maybe they are in the barn."

We turned around and looked at the barn, which was in a strange position because it was to the far left of the house.

"Let's take a look at the barn."

I took her hand and we walked along the meandering half gravelled path, then slowly drifted around the corner to the end of the barn where we found a very large closed and securely locked door, with an inserted small door.

Thinking it was wise at this point not to go any further, we wandered back to look at the front of the house, and my head turned to follow the track leading towards what looked like the entrance to the road. It was fairly obvious this house was mostly hidden from all prying village eyes, because of the overgrown trees and out of control hedges surrounding it.

Slowly we wandered and dithered about in an embarrassed manner, expecting something to happen, or someone to appear suddenly in front of us, saying:

'What do you want?' 'Bugger off' or worse.

I looked at the house again, trying my best to ascertain if anybody lived there, or if anybody had even visited in the last year. The whole place looked as if it had been unoccupied for quite a long time.

I let go of Daphers' hand and walked back around the corner to look at the barn doors, and tried to have a peep inside the barn through a crack, but it was far too dark to see anything. Behind the barn was another of those large hedges. I managed to find a space between a couple of branches and peered through. We were perched high on a hill, very nearly hidden from view. It was quite easy to see a road and houses a long way down, right at the bottom.

At this moment my heart skipped a beat! I questioned myself: 'Was this the road we were looking for?' Those houses down below on this side and the other side! Were they the houses we were looking for?

I was so excited my heart was pounding, it was difficult to keep control of myself. Fortunately, my head said:

'Matthew, hold your foot up a bit, wait and think for a moment. Is it wise at this stage to show too much emotion?'

It was not an easy task under the circumstances, because my brain was racing. By girding up a lot of concentration and standing ever so still, and breathing softly, I managed to restrain my emotions. Peering down again through the branches I thought, surely these must be the houses I had previously sighted from the road through the car window, on that bend, at a distance, on that day of the pub crawl, quite some time ago. Scanning both sides of the road made me more sure. This was definitely the place we had been trying to find. Keeping calm was very difficult. Down there, below, was awfully quiet, which seemed to help me.

To stop Daphers from detecting anything different in my thoughts, I turned and walked slowly to the centre of the overgrown front garden and looked at the house, staring at the upstairs windows.

Daphers joined me, and we both spotted the sign-post on the left-hand side near the entrance, where the drive-cum-gravel path went through an opening. It was leaning over towards the hedge, partially hidden by the leaves, and looked as though it was just about to fall over. It had probably been obscured like that for months or even years.

I walked over and held the leaves aside so I could see it better, and the sign fell over. I picked it up and propped it against the hedge. The sign, a rather grubby piece of hardboard, read, 'For Sale or Rent,' that's all, with a telephone number underneath. Still not sure whether the house was occupied, but gaining in confidence with each passing moment, I turned to Daphers.

"Look, this house is about perfect for what we want. Let's take the bull by the horns and just knock on the door, the worst we can get is somebody to tell us to shove off. All indications are the house has not been lived in for ages, and it looks like nobody has visited it for a long time."

She grinned and wrinkled her brow.

"OK, let's knock on the door."

I went over and gave the door a little tap, but there was no response.

Cautiously we tip-toed up to one of the front windows still expecting to be startled by a voice out of the blue, or a face, but there was no sign of life.

Through the window, I could see pieces of furniture, chairs and a fireplace. I tried knocking on the front door again, but there was still no reply.

Daphers nudged my elbow and said: "For my sake, knock on the door again one more time."

I turned towards the door and gave it another knock, waited for a moment, then uttered:

"There's nobody here, the place is empty."

At last, I was pretty sure the house was not occupied so I said, "Let's have a good look round."

We both wandered off in different directions, I went around behind the barn again and looked over the hedge. The ground between us and the road was mainly covered by very large bushes and trees.

I walked back to the front of the house and followed the half-gravelled path through the extended gap in the hedge, then meandered left down an incline and saw where I think the path joined the road.

On returning to the house it suddenly struck me: it wasn't vandalised in any way, no windows were broken, nothing was boarded up; in fact, it seemed as far as I could see completely intact but neglected and forgotten; it was most extraordinary.

Strolling back over to the sign and rubbing the wooden board revealed more of the telephone number. I dropped my rucksack on a nearby stone and pulled out my birdwatching book and jotted it down. Everything about this property was getting more and more interesting. I couldn't resist walking again to the place behind the barn, standing on my tiptoes and peering through the space in the hedge. Over the bushes and between the branches of the trees, I could see more of the houses below and was more and more sure, the road below was the road we were looking for. A bolt of further excitement appeared somewhere in my boots, made its way upwards and finally lodged itself in my brain. My immediate response was to shout out loud but fortunately my mouth didn't respond to my brain, and I kept quiet.

"Calm down, Matthew, calm down," I whispered to myself and wandered back along the path.

Daphers joined me and gripped my arm; she had an all-knowing smile on her face. It must have been my fidgeting or my quickness of walk or my eyes widening, or something, for she knew.

She kissed me and said: "This is the beginning, isn't it?" She had sensed it all.

"Yes," I said. "This is the beginning."

# Chapter Twenty-Eight

This house gave us everything we wanted. Forward thinking told me it may be possible to get a better view from the upstairs windows of the house.

It was so difficult to contain my excitement.

Daphers moved and squeezed my hand.

"Let's ring the number, see if we can rent it for a week, or even a few days. It says 'for sale or rent', it does look good, and you are so excited."

She followed this by saying: "Nothing ventured and nothing gained and all that business."

I took the mobile and tapped in the number, but was unable to get a signal.

"Look," I said, "I'll shoot down to the car, and try for a signal in the car park. If I can't get a signal there, I'll go into the village and drive around until I get one. What do you think?"

Daphers was in full agreement. "Yes, good idea, I'll have a scout around here while you're gone. I'll take a look over the hedge from time to time."

I was left shaking my head slowly from side to side, wondering how long she had known what I'd been doing.

After giving her a kiss, I set off through the wood, moving quickly but taking care not to stumble at this crucial time. There was no phone signal at the car, so I drove into the village, found a signal and poked in the number.

Ring-ring, ring-ring. I waited, ring-ring, ring ring.

Eventually, a female voice at the other end said "Hello," and stopped.

I had my 'spiel' ready, so quickly said, "Hello, my wife and I are up by the old house, on the hill near the village of Epscomont. We are ornithologists and have been up in the woods watching the birds, and we noticed a house up there for sale or rent. I have taken your number from the sign. We don't want to buy the house, but we would like to rent it for a few days, or a week. Have I got the right telephone number?"

Deciding I had said enough, I waited for a reply but only received a long silence.

Eventually, a woman's voice on the other end said, "Yes, you have the right number."

I waited, listening to the silence until the voice continued.

"It is my house; I have never rented it out before though." There was another hesitation. "Birdwatching you say?"

"Yes, that's right," I replied.

Not wanting to explain further, although wanting to encourage her, I asked:

"How much would it be to rent the house for a week? If you let me know now, we could visit you tomorrow, and give you the cash for a week's rent."

There was no response from the other end. I resisted speaking, which gave me a little more time to try and figure out what to say next. I thought I had waited for long enough and in the end, blurted forth:

"How about we give you three hundred pounds to rent it for the week, would that be all right?" Then stopped speaking, hoping I hadn't been too eager.

The immediate reply was, "You would have to take it as it is!"

"We just need it as a base, to watch the birds," I fibbed. "Is that settled then?"

"Yes," was the response, so I suggested we visit the following day at about two o'clock, with the money.

"Can the electricity be switched on?" I added.

"Yes, it is just a switch in the kitchen cupboard."

We had another delay, then. "You will need my address, I'm about twenty-five miles away; my name is Mrs Ramsbottom."

She gave me the address and I wrote it down, not forgetting the postcode, very important. She then said nothing and put the phone down without saying goodbye; strange but maybe that's the way it was.

I had plenty of time to think about things when driving back to the carpark in the wood, and when walking back up to the house.

On my arrival Daphers greeted me eagerly, wanting to know all that had happened, including the gist of the conversation. She listened, told me I was brilliant and gave me a kiss. It was noticeable from her enthusiasm that she was beginning to understand where I was going with this thing, and liked it.

After I asked if she had seen anything, she responded:

"I've had a good scout around, it's really interesting."

I wasn't sure what she meant by it but decided not to comment.

"It's time we went. Is there anything you want to check here before we leave?" she asked.

"Yes, I would like to take another look round, to get a mental picture in my mind of the place and the whole area."

I did just that, then we set off by the rear garden through the wood to the car, only this time going a different way, so as not to create a visible path. Again I admired the trees, the leaves had their different shade of green. It wouldn't be long before they would embrace us with their excitingly beautiful autumnal colour change, the annual wonderful natural spectacular.

The car park appeared sooner than anticipated, the hire-car the only one present in the overgrown grassy compound. With our gear dumped in the boot, we sat in the front seats of the car in a little private world of our own and looked at each other. My wife had a slightly furrowed brow but her face still managed to contain a smile. She was still the most beautiful girl in the world to me. It was not only physical beauty, but it was also her inner beauty. I joined her smile, so glad she was on my side.

She half-whispered, "Don't forget I am with you all the way. I'm not yet sure what you are planning, or what we are going to do, but remember I am with you all the way."

It was the beginning; I was sure I would always remember these poignant moments at a later date and talk of them. I started the car, put it into gear and manoeuvred onto the road.

On the way back to the B & B we talked about what we had seen, the possibilities and the probabilities. We timed the journey to our lodgings at approximately an hour and informed the landlady this would be our last night. After a shower, a change of clothes, a few drinks and a very pleasant supper, we both had a great sleep.

The following morning we breakfasted and settled the bill with cash. From now on we would try not to leave any obvious trace of our presence – the idea of a complete escape did appeal to me, so always paying for everything in cash was important.

After a search we eventually found a supermarket and bought quantities of shopping of every description, again paying cash. The previous evening had been spent talking over if there would be any crockery, cutlery, or a kettle in the house. We decided in the end against buying any of these things, hoping there would be some already there.

Further along the high street we found a bank and debated whether to extract another five hundred pounds from our French bank account. The ferry had already coughed up six hundred so we decided we had enough. Daphers was never happy carrying a lot of cash, and I was a little reluctant to use the bank, not wanting anybody to know where we were or who we were. Fortunately, the town, like the B&B, was a long way from the house so hopefully, nobody would remember us. Mrs Ramsbottom's postcode was introduced into the sat-nav system, and following gentle-voiced instructions, we set forth.

During the journey, I tried my best to keep as calm as possible, repeating in my mind how the conversation should go when meeting this lady. Was she going to be old or young, what was she going to be like? From our conversation on the phone, I assumed she would be old, possibly a woman settled in her ways, rather discontented and not very confident. My idea was for us to be in and out of the house as quickly as possible, most of all remembering to ask the most important questions.

# Chapter Twenty-Nine

After about two hours we arrived at the village of Brogdon with its houses built close together. The sat-nav directed us to the required street quite easily.

Daphers counted the numbers as we went along. "72, 74, 76. That's the one," she bellowed. It was quite obvious she was keen, not usually as excited as this.

The house was a brick-built semi-detached property with a small front garden, a wall then the pavement. I parked the car past the single gate entrance so that it could not be seen from the lounge window. Then I had a moment of just thinking; this business about keeping out of the way and unnoticed, was I taking it too far, was I trying too hard to keep us out of the limelight?

Did it matter? On reflection, I thought, I'm sure it did.

A nudge on my elbow made me turn slightly, and look at the raised eyebrows and the gentle smile of Daphers.

"Come on, let's go," she said.

We put on our woolly hats and wrapped our scarves around our neck in an attempt to persuade Mrs Ramsbottom we were serious birdwatchers; it was a silly way to try and acquire a modicum of disguise, but that's what we did.

After closing and locking the car, we opened the gate, walked down the very small path, rang the bell on the right-hand side of the door-frame and waited.

Eventually, Mrs Ramsbottom materialised at the front door. She appeared to be an elderly woman, although probably younger than us, making me wonder whether I should stoop a bit to look older. So, making the effort, I lowered my frame.

She wore a red cardigan, a dark blue skirt and some sort of stockings that terminated under the knee; also, on her face beside a little make-up, was a quizzical attempt at a smile. She wasn't wearing glasses, which for some reason I found quite pleasing.

We entered the hall and closed the front door behind us. I felt she was not totally happy about letting us in, and would have preferred to keep us on the door-step, but as there was private business to be dealt with, and money involved, prying eyes must be kept at bay.

A half-hearted wave from her indicated we should enter the room on the right. It turned out to be a normal old ladies' lounge, very pleasant with patterned wallpaper, and lots of ornaments, pictures, and photographs. Pleasingly it wasn't too warm, and removing woolly hats and scarves was not a necessity.

On refusing a seat, I immediately took out my wallet and counted three hundred pounds onto a nearby table, whilst politely saying:

"That's what we agreed, is that okay?"

She looked at the money, hesitated, then left it where it was, nervously replying:

"Yes, I have arranged for a man to put a new gas bottle and a wrench outside the back door."

Then added: "It has cost me twenty pounds."

She caught my eye, giving the immediate impression this was additional. I pulled another twenty pounds from the wallet, quite happy to oblige, and placed it on the pile. This time she took the money and handed me the keys, quickly adding:

"The electrical switch is up in the cupboard on the right as you enter through the kitchen door; as I said, it needs to be switched on."

A thought struck me: 'why had the man not fitted the gas bottle and connected it in place, then switched the electricity on while he was there?'

Something had been bothering me ever since we first found the house; I hesitated for a moment, before saying:

"Can I ask you something?"

She looked despondently and quizzically at me. "Yes," she said.

Slowly and cautiously I conveyed my thoughts:

"It looks as though the house has been empty for some time, but it seems in good condition for its age, and as far as I can see it hasn't been vandalised or anything."

"No," she said.

Giving her time and hoping for more information, I waited, but none came, so I found it necessary to probe further.

"It really is ideal for us, but we won't be in the house a lot of the time."

I stopped, hesitated, then slowly went on, "We are going to spend a fair amount of time away from it, walking in the woods."

This was, of course, a fib as our real intention was to stay and spy, but I had sensed something wasn't quite right with this house from the start and felt I had to pursue it.

She still didn't say anything and because of this, I pressed her even further.

"All our gear and the car will be left up there for most of the day – will everything be secure, whilst we are out?"

She said nothing, and I became even more suspicious, so I followed it with:

"I know it sounds like a silly question, but it is rather isolated and to some extent hidden away; is there something we should know?"

# Chapter Thirty

She looked at all the money in her hand, flicked her eyes at my wife, then at me, turned back to my wife again and fingered the lobe of her ear, obviously troubled by something.

For a split second, I thought she was going to hand all the money back to me.

Instead, she straightened up and with some reluctance blurted forth:

"I am sure you will find out anyway." She stopped after saying it, hesitated, waited and started again. "My sister lived in that house, and it is over a year now since she died in that house."

Now there was a long pause and she swallowed very hard.

"She died of a heart attack, but what has kept people away from the house all this time, is, she had leprosy."

She paused again, looked at us both and very quietly said:

"I understand that leprosy is not a very contagious decease, but everyone in the village knew she had it, and they are all scared stiff."

When I first heard her say this, it stunned me, and I glanced at Daphers. My wife's eyes were wide open and glued to mine obviously wanting to discuss things with me, but she couldn't in front of Mrs Ramsbottom. Between us, we didn't say anything, partly because we would have been heard.

I turned to Mrs Ramsbottom. "I can understand why all the villagers are terrified, probably general village gossip must have made it even worse. No wonder the house hasn't been sold. Has anybody been to see it?"

She responded by saying: "Nobody has even made an enquiry."

Anxiously and sadly she continued: "The only person to visit the house since then, is me and the man I paid to leave the gas bottle and he won't go inside."

If we had said we didn't want to stay in the house, she would have accepted it and given us the money back.

A strange silence fell about the room.

Daphers and I had talked about leprosy before. An old acquaintance of ours in France, Jean-

Pierre, had bought umpteen hectares of land, part of which, many years previously, had been a leper colony. Initially, we had questioned the intelligence of a man who would pay such a lot of money for a leper colony. I remembered the day we had found this out, gone home and investigated the possibility of contracting the disease from the fragments in the soil left all those years ago. We discovered it was only possible to become infected by direct contact via nasal mucous or bodily fluid. Our friend Jean-Pierre has had the land for a number of years and has had no ill effects.

Daphers broke the silence and whispered to me, "Do you remember Jean-Pierre, who bought all that land?"

"Yes, I was thinking about that too."

"I think this is all right, Matthew, let's give it a go. The house is in a great location and it won't make any difference to us."

Without replying, I turned to Mrs Ramsbottom. "We'll take the house for a week please."

She looked visibly relieved, and relaxed for the first time since our arrival.

She took the keys and handed them over to me, saying, "I haven't got your name."

"Our name is Peters, Mr and Mrs Peters." Rather surprised at my ease of telling a lie, I then went on:

"Oh, we may stay a week or we may leave earlier. If we do we will lock up everything, turn the gas and the electricity off and bring the keys back here. If you are not in, we will put them through the letterbox in the front door. Is that OK?"

We both received a rather gleeful nod of approval. On our departure we didn't shake hands, only said goodbye, and closed the front door on our way out, finding the whole thing, in the end, to be most agreeable.

Without looking back, we climbed into the car and with hats still on our heads and scarves still wrapped around our necks, we drove off. On the journey to the house, my thoughts turned back to leprosy. What if bits of me started falling off? There and then I decided to keep a keen eye on all parts, particularly the extremities, definitely not allowing things to get out of hand. One thing was for sure, we weren't going to be bored for a while. Thinking about the situation gave me one of the most exciting drives I had ever had in my life.

On approaching the woods near the house, we decided further investigation of the area was necessary, so we parked in the usual spot, away from the village, leaving all we had bought tucked in the boot.

A feeling of excitement was in the air as we walked up to the house, which, on this occasion, seemed to take us no time at all. Drawing closer I encountered both trepidation and excitement because I suddenly realised not only were we going to live here, we were going to spy from here. Our first sighting was the gas bottle and wrench outside the back door which was a good sign.

Daphers, seeming not to care about anything, took the keys from her pocket, and after a bit of fiddling found the right one, turned it in the lock and opened the back door. It was quite dark inside the house and there was a smell not of damp but a dusty, unused smell.

We walked through the kitchen into the lounge and saw a large ornate stone fireplace at one end, and an old oak table at the other. In between were a sofa and two easy chairs. The floor was covered by old rugs; the one in front of the fireplace, an old fashioned handmade rag rug had been at war with sparks from the fire, and lost. The ceiling was quite low and darkened by the smoke from the fire.

We returned to the kitchen, which was quite adequate. Testing both taps produced water, and an electric kettle was included at the end of one of the work surfaces. Daphers was already opening cupboard doors and investigating their contents; in doing so, she discovered the fuse box. I dived in and switched the electricity on. A light came on in the kitchen and I immediately switched it off again, thinking it might possibly be seen from the village, even though it wasn't dark yet. Another moment where the phrase, 'hold your foot up a bit, Matthew' should have been employed. Hopefully, I will remember about that sort of thing in the future.

Daphers stayed in the kitchen while I wandered around the rooms as if on holiday. But this wasn't a holiday, we were on a mission, purely and simply to discover whether the houses below down the big slope, were the houses of the two men we were seriously interested in.

The stairs at the end of the lounge going up were very steep, fortunately, a banister running along the right-hand side aided the ascension. Climbing up and down the stairs was very good exercise, but help was sometimes useful.

At the top, off the landing, were two bedrooms, one on the left and one on the right, and at the end a separate toilet next to the bathroom. My interest lay in the bedroom on the right, and on entering I crept along the wall and peered through the window. Joy of joys, in the distance, over the hedge and through the trees down below, I could see the roofs and the front of the far houses across the road. Excited, I retraced my steps and ventured into the left-hand bedroom. Again I crept along the wall to the window, where I could see the backs of the nearside houses and their gardens.

I took a moment to absorb what I had seen and immediately knew that this could not be better – after all this time searching, we had finally found exactly what we were looking for.

I went back downstairs, where Daphers was still busying away. I told her how perfect this house was for us, and with controlled excitement explained to her, 'the beginning had begun'.

We hugged and hugged without saying a word. Finally, we sat at the little table in the kitchen and decided to investigate the house further, giving our first priority to bringing the car up to the house and parking it in a safe place. Behind the barn wall was the obvious spot and won the vote.

We donned our scarves and hats.

Daphers said, "Why are we both going, why can't just one of us go?"

My quick reply tumbled out of my mouth. "I'm still not sure about this place, I can't leave you up here all by yourself."

The moment I said it, I knew it was a bit of a fib.

She half-smiled at me.

For years my wonderful wife had also been my greatest companion, and in some ways, she was far stronger than I when it came to dealing with strange or creepy situations; sometimes it was just good to have her by my side. When we were working in our garden in France, I often discovered snakes in the compost or under the log pile; they gave me the creeps. A shout from me on the other side of the lawn always attracted an enquiry from her, as to what was the matter. "A snake," I would bellow. She then brought over the necessary implement to deal with the scary creature. Gently she searched for it, and encouraged it onto whatever tool she had in hand, walked with it to the far end of the forest, placed it on the ground, then on her return never failed to ask me if I was all right.

The present moment was one of those times when I needed her back-up.

Without hesitation, she agreed to come with me, and we went outside, locking the back door behind us. There was a chill in the air, and the light was fading fast. Because of this, we decided to follow our path through the wood, keeping an eye on the position of the road. In time we could see it and assumed it was the road leading into and out of the village, I made a mental note to investigate it another time. We carried on along the path mainly made by us and before long we saw our car in the excuse of a car park, again the only one, thank goodness; let's hope this lack of birdwatchers continues.

We arranged ourselves in the front seats, knowing this was an important moment because we now had to drive the car up to the house, and not be noticed by anyone below in the village, we must try to be completely invisible from now on. With headlights on, I drove out of the car park, and along the road towards the village. By going steadily we easily found the sloping gravel path on the left leading up to the house. As I entered I switched off all the lights so we wouldn't be seen, and nosed the car up the hill to our 'spy house'. Then in the seriously fading light, managed to park the car beside the barn wall, so hiding it from prying eyes below.

# Chapter Thirty-One

During the short journey, we discussed maintaining a blackout system on all the windows of the house to keep ourselves hidden, hoping the curtains would be thick enough to help.

Daphers opened the front door and we were just able without a light to manoeuvre all the shopping and gear from the car boot into the house, with little fuss. The food and drink were amongst the biggest items to stow away; rucksacks and others were bundled inside quickly without any bother.

Once these chores were completed, we scurried round all the windows, drawing the curtains, which fortunately were made from an old-fashioned dense fabric with linings. These ensured the light from inside would be hidden, giving no sign to the outside world of habitation. Everything front, back, upstairs and downstairs, were tucked inside the window frames so tightly no light could escape. A thick blanket and a certain amount of fiddling eventually managed to eliminate the kitchen window completely.

The house was like the blackout during the Second World War.

I prepared the fire by using the paper and sticks by the fireplace but had no intention of using it. We had a large log fire in France, and I always had huge success in lighting any kind of fire, and once helped to light the boilers to create the steam which powered one of the mighty ships of my marine days.

Daphers came in from the kitchen with some tea.

"I don't think you should light the fire, the smoke will be seen down in the village. Let's warm ourselves up with a nice plunge of whisky in the tea!"

The tea and the whisky warmed us and encouraged us to discuss plans for the exciting days ahead. We talked over the importance of keeping a low profile and not being discovered in our hide-away, and the brightness from the electric lights. Daphers came forward and said she had seen a box of candles in the kitchen. We groped about in the cupboards and drawers for a while and eventually found a full box. I agreed they would be better than using the electric lights. Unable to find any candle holders and needing to move from room to room, I melted hot wax into the centre of a couple of squat coffee cups and stuck candles in. It was not very hygienic, but it was functional.

As it was getting cold and late the thought of sleep entered our heads, so we climbed the steep stairs, each with a candle, and after a search found two old electric fires in a wardrobe, I plugged one into a wall socket and hoped for the best. Slowly, as I watched, both bars produced an improving red glow, which gave me pleasant satisfaction. It soon manifested itself into a fiery heat and made me keep my eye on it for a while before plugging in the other one, which, fortunately, achieved the same result.

Daphers joined me in the bedroom, carrying an armful of sheets.

"They're a bit damp," she said scattering them along the side of the bed a good distance from the electric fires. She then disappeared and returned with blankets and did a similar thing with them. I rearranged the electric fires in front of them to take the dampness away, then we both returned downstairs for food, more tea, and whisky.

A pale moon allowed me to venture outside to check the blackout arrangements; it seemed very good, even with the candles in full glow. While standing in front of the house, my thoughts strayed to why at my age was I getting so excited by all this. Should I not be donning slippers, wearing a cardigan and sitting in front of the fire?

A satisfactory smile of determination appeared on my face, and that was enough.

Afterwards, a further stroll around the garden was nice, taking in the atmosphere and casting an enquiring eye over the hedge on to the road below. Lights were scattered to the left and darkness scattered to the right, but nothing else.

When I re-entered the house and joined my wife, the quizzical expression on her face was quite noticeable.

"It looks as though you have been enjoying yourself; sorry to spoil it, but we have no hot water," she said.

"Hopefully an immersion heater," I shouted, running up the stairs holding a candle. The bathroom was favourite, and on opening the only cupboard in the corner, I saw facing me on the wall a tank, with an old fashioned brown electrical switch beside it. The little lever was in the up position, I reversed it and went back downstairs.

"I've switched something on, hopefully, the immersion heater. We may have to wait till morning for any result."

The reply came, "There is no gas in the cooker either."

I had forgotten about that, my mind was on other things. I bowled the heavy gas bottle through the back door, then struggled to get it into position at the side of the cooker.

A wrestle and a grapple with the connection eventually gave me success, and finally on opening the valve to the cooker I managed with a bit of a fuss to get flames. Leaving the cooker door open gave us some warmth.

We sat at the table in the candlelight, joined hands, looked at each other and the loving smile arrived again on both our faces.

Daphers handed me a lighted coffee cup candle. We switched everything off and climbed the stairs together like Wee Willie Winkie and Wee Willie Winkie's Wife.

In the bedroom, the heaters had done their work – if anything, the room was too warm. We arranged the sheets, pillows and numerous blankets into their correct order for sleep and selected a non-showering routine for the evening, allowing only a quick wash and brush-up. Clean, crinkled night attire was unloaded from the rucksacks and slipped on. We slid gently into the bed, kissed, blew all the candles out in unison, and snuggled up.

After sleeping contentedly for a period, for no reason awoke with eyes wide open. Laying stock still in bed, I listened intently for any sort of noise, but there wasn't a noise; I wondered what had woken me. Then immediately dismissed the idea I had been disturbed by the old leprosy lady of the house, although just for a split second my thought turned; 'maybe, just maybe,' then, 'no let's not go down that road'. Staring into the darkness made me aware of my new surroundings and I asked myself:

'Is what we intend to do in the future dangerous? My reply to myself was, 'it is undoubtedly very dangerous, and will get progressively more dangerous as time passes. Am I worried about it? Absolutely not, just very determined'.

My thoughts dwindled away and the exhaustion of the previous day finally immersed me back into sleep.

I awoke the following morning with the light from 93 million miles away attempting to penetrate the curtains, thankfully without any success but giving just enough light to see without a candle.

Daphers entered the bedroom and announced, "The sun is shining, and I've made a cup of tea," then she jumped into bed, gave me a kiss and sat back. We chatted about the previous day and what we intended to do in the following week, then she swung her legs on to the floor, saying, "You were successful with the hot water, I'm going to have a shower," and went off to carry out those duties ladies carry out in the morning.

On her return to the bedroom, I ambiguously suggested:

"Let's cautiously open the curtains a minimal amount, just enough to see if we can see what we want to see."

Daphers replied with a nod. "Good idea, you do it and I'll go and make some toast and jam." She hesitated, then glanced at me and said:

"Don't worry, whatever I do, I will be most discreet," and she slipped away down the stairs.

After a quick look at the houses on the road below, I heard the call, went downstairs to the kitchen and through a small parting in the curtain looked from the back of the house out into the wood.

"It's lovely out there, but before I go out, I'll take the binoculars upstairs and see which pair needs to go in which bedroom."

"OK," she said and smiled.

I climbed the stairs, chose to take both pairs of binoculars into the right-hand bedroom, then with no candle lit, parted the curtains just enough to see out.

Although being very high up and a long distance away, the view was very good. With the naked eye, I could just see the front of the terraced houses on the far side of the road. Most importantly I could see the end terraced house on the far side of the road next to the wood, with a path leading down to the road. This was the house I had seen the boy run into all those months ago. The small piece of land on the right of the end terrace house was encroaching into the wood and was like a scrap yard, with what looked like old tyres and odd bits of metal scattered about. To get a clearer picture I directed the ordinary binoculars at the front door; the house was at a distance and found the view too wide, so decided a closer image was required. Removing the astronomical binoculars from the case, I tried pointing them at the target and received a very good visual image indeed. There were a few leaves and branches from the hedge in my line of sight, which needed clipping in order for me to see the full picture of the front door and front path. Hopefully one of the men we had come to spy on, lived in the end terrace house.

Leaving the astronomical binoculars on the dressing table, I ventured into the left-hand bedroom. This room was slightly darker, the curtain material in this bedroom was probably thicker. I parted the curtain with care, poked the birdwatching binoculars through and surveyed the scene below. Disappointingly, my view was blocked on the far left by the barn and trees, not allowing me to see the first two properties. I trained the glasses slowly to the right; this enabled me to see four well-spaced semi-detached properties with unusually large rear gardens. Although I couldn't see the front of the semis, I recognised the design to be the same as the houses I had seen from that awkward bend in the road all those months ago. The last two gardens seemed to be well looked after, the middle two were not looked after at all and were larger than the others, also totally overgrown with very high perimeter hedges. The left-hand side one of the middle two was a mess, not unlike the garden of the end terrace house. The word 'mess' was doing it a favour because it was like a tip. A large pile of discarded wood, which included a table, a couple of old chairs and a box full of old tyres, formed a sizeable rubbish heap to the right side of the garden. Further away from the house to the left, was what could only be described as a small tidy bonfire, occupying the back left-hand side of the garden. On the same side, nearer and to the left of the house was a large static caravan, which looked in reasonable shape, possibly in far better condition than the rear of the house. A second glance indicated occupation of the caravan.

This wasn't the time for seriously surveying, so I put the binoculars on a nearby table and sat down on a chair thinking, 'we can safely assume this grubby semi-detached property to be the second house we have come to spy on'.

I could feel the excitement welling up inside me again, this time I let it flow and enjoyed the euphoria. My initial thought was to take notes, but I rejected this thinking surely this would make the situation too intense, it would be much better to store the scenes in front of me in my head, keeping continuous rough memorable pictures. This would hopefully produce more creative ideas and ultimately be more of an advantage.

Standing up, I went back downstairs to the kitchen and joined Daphers.

"I've made tea and a sandwich for a late lunch," she said.

"I didn't think I'd been upstairs for that long," I said, shaking my head in disbelief. "I have really good news, this house is in a better position than we thought. The hedge needs trimming a bit, but apart from that it's perfect."

"Tell me what you have decided to do upstairs," and she produced a huge grin as she said it – maybe she saw my excitable schoolboy attitude creeping out.

I smiled in return, and as calm as I could, said:

"Your binoculars are in the left-hand bedroom, that's your normal watching point. My normal watching point is the right-hand bedroom, I've put the large binoculars on the table in there. It sounds a bit military, but it is a good idea, we don't want us to be focusing on the same man. Hopefully, we will be able to spy on both of them."

She looked at me thoughtfully then, with a cheeky grin, said:

"When I am spying and you're not here, will it be all right if I look from either bedroom occasionally? Then in the evening, we can share information."

I didn't say anything and she took this to mean she ought to continue, so she did.

"I realise the importance of gathering this information and you never know, it may help you to decide exactly what we are going to do. Don't forget I am still in the dark as to what's going to happen." She was now in full flow.

"Although I am aware of the reason we are here, I am still unaware of your exact intention, and I might add, I don't want to know your exact intentions until you know precisely what you are going to do yourself."

She said it all in a way I'd never heard her speak before and ended it in a slightly stern manner. It made me respond:

"I'm sorry I'm keeping you in the dark, love." I drew her towards me and hugged her.

"I have various ideas but nothing concrete. Please do whatever you want to do. As long as you are discreet, and nobody detects we are here, it is fine, anything you find will be invaluable."

I held her by the shoulders and gave her a kiss. "I'm going to explore inside the barn now, will you be OK?"

"Of course I will," she replied.

Taking the keys, I slowly edged open the front door. The cooler air on my face was a pleasant surprise, it felt English and gave me encouragement. The bottom half of the house couldn't be seen from the road below, but I was still not taking any risks, I didn't want to be seen by anyone in the village, it wasn't the time to start waving my arms about.

After closing the door behind me, I crept swiftly to the left, feeling safe, knowing I was hidden from below by the hedge, and completely concealed behind the barn. This was set in such a position, the only part possibly to be seen from the road below was the far section of the roof. I crept my way round to the doors which were entirely hidden by the hedge and were set at a slight angle towards the house. These old fashioned wooden sliding-doors were high, with steel runners fixed to the top and bottom. A smaller entrance door was fitted on the right, built into the main door. The lock released easily with the right key and a jerk on the handle opened it.

# Chapter Thirty-Two

The barn inside was dark. I wanted to close the door behind me and keep things private; what stopped me was the darkness – the barn required further illumination.

Stepping inside with the door slightly ajar I searched for a light switch and saw two on the wall just out of reach. Sidling over gingerly to the right-hand wall I prodded the nearest switch. The space inside the barn glowed a little, rather than burst into glorious luminance. Frightened someone might see the light through the open door, even though it was only a glow and daylight outside, I turned back and closed the door.

Much to my delight, I found the inside of the barn similar to a proper garage, only this one didn't quite make the 'full Monty'. It was more like an amateur car mechanic's garage, with no fixed large machinery to raise cars into the air, only what looked like a sort of pit, in the centre of the concrete floor. The pit was covered over with railway sleepers laid horizontally across, so it wasn't possible for anyone to fall in. I couldn't help thinking 'what a very pleasant surprise?'.

I floated my finger over the second light switch and hesitated, wondering how much more luminescence it would give, finally deciding the dimness was better, as it gave me a sense of confidence. I continued inspecting and scrutinising the whole area in the glow of the dimmer light. A long solid wooden workbench with built-in cupboards hugged the wall on the right-hand side. My eyes travelled to the far right corner of the building and I could see on the back wall a large steel rack with a quantity of very old Jerry cans on the shelves, the type used on American Jeeps in the second world war. These were accompanied by paint tins lined up together in rows. In the left-hand corner of the building was a set of steps, probably older than the paint tins, and next to the steps, were two large cylindrical forty-five-gallon steel drums standing to attention. These drums were specially manufactured to carry large quantities of liquid, usually motor oil and could be difficult to handle because of their size.

Cautiously I made my way over to the bench, bent down and opened one of the doors in the cupboard. Inside was full of plastic bottles, each filled with a liquid. When I reached in and lifted one out, the label revealed 'Oil-Lamp Oil' – presumably these were left over from the days before the barn was wired for electricity. I put it back beside its friends and closed the door.

Continuing my scrutiny, I sauntered over to the paint tins, which were all of different colours, very old and covered in cobwebs. The main feature of my interest from the moment of entry into this barn-cum-garage, was the Jerry cans. Carefully stepping over to where they were, I noted each to be of the very old fashioned type, with firm screw tops. Choosing one, I shook it and could clearly hear a liquid inside. With difficulty, I unscrewed the lid and immediately received the pungent smell of diesel. Replacing the lid and selecting another, I repeated the process; this time the liquid produced a strong smell of petrol. By lifting and feeling the weight of others, I discovered most of them contained a fluid of some description. At that moment an instant and devastatingly cunning plan charged itself into my brain like a bright light; it just blasted its way in. The best plans always came with a sudden burst of ideas. I found a wooden box near the bench, turned it on its end and sat on it. My previous plan, to rid the Earth of these despicable brothers, was to use the silence of crossbows, a difficult task but not an impossible one, or to eliminate them with poisonous mushrooms or shoot them from far away with a two-two rifle. Now, here in front of me was a means of their disposal, in a very different way.

Sitting in perfect silence on my uncomfortable wooden box, I thought more deeply than I had ever done before. The idea developing was far more dangerous and far more grotesque in many ways, but was exactly what these two brothers needed and deserved.

After a very long time thinking, I left my wooden box and sidled over to the forty-five-gallon steel drums in the corner. They were the type used by steel bands to make music, only these two drums were intact and still used for the purpose of carrying oil. Hoping desperately one would be empty because drums like these even half full of liquid were awkward to move, I tried tilting the first one, but by using all my strength only managed to tilt it slightly – which was unfortunate for it looked in really good condition. The other drum had been used and seemed to be alright. Moving it was quite easy and I thought it could be empty. By tipping it on its side and rolling it about, using the light to the best effect, I tried to find any holes in and around the sides. It appeared to be in good fettle and so I decided this one may be very useful indeed. Standing it up and examining the flat bottom end of the drum revealed all to be in good order. I tipped it back, and stood it upright on its end and examined the top. The small plug to let the air out was loosely fitted in place, which was very good indeed; the larger plug for filling the drum was fitted opposite. Although the filling hole was only the size of a small teacup, the plug required a wrench to remove it. I took it out and peered into the hole. The drum inside looked brand new and was in really good condition and empty; perfect for what I wanted to do. I replaced the plug and gave the drum a tap with the wrench; the sound was good and solid.

I replaced the plug thinking, this barn has so much volatile liquid about, it was a bomb waiting to go off. It seemed it was set up for a person interested in very old cars, or more likely because of the amount of diesel oil, very old lorries. I wandered about, peering into corners and examining the railway sleepers covering the pit. Stamping on them and walking on them told me they were in good condition able to support a good weight. The only other thing of further interest was the large drawer in the bench containing many old useful tools.

I had spent far too long in the barn and it was time to return to the house. Making my way to the small door I stopped and thought, 'if it is dark outside somebody might see the glow of the light from down below,' so I figured the light had to be out before the door was opened. Standing by the door, I eyed the light switch over on the wall and saw it was important to get things right and switch the light off before opening the door. The switch was about three steps away so a little practice was required to get things right. This consisted of pretending to switch the light off, then diving for the door handle. Unfortunately, when I switched the light off, I found it was dark, missed the handle and minor groping about was necessary before I managed to open the door.

Darkness had arrived outside, and it was a lot colder. For no reason, I went around the back of the house and entered through the rear door. Standing in the kitchen I called out to Daphers. An answer came from upstairs, but no sound of movement.

I called again and shouted, "I can't see anything with the blackouts up."

After a pause came an audible sound of a match striking, some scuffling, then footsteps down the stairs accompanied by a flickering light.

She arrived slightly out of breath. "I thought I'd keep the light to a minimum, so if I have the curtains open at all, the candles must be out, especially when it's dark."

She gave me a candle. "By the way, do you know what time it is? You've missed coffee and everything. I was beginning to worry about you; can you please be careful?"

She took a step forward and gently put her hands around my shoulders and hugged me. I distinctly got the feeling I'd been missed, but also, ever so slightly, admonished, yet again.

Looking down at my watch-less wrist I suggested, "Let's have dinner now."

"OK," she said with a smile. "I'll rustle something up."

Going through into the lounge with my candle, I put down paper napkins for two places then called through. "It's too cold in here, let's put the oven on and sit at the table in the kitchen, and open a bottle of wine."

Finding tumblers and a bent corkscrew, I unscrewed the wine, tasted it and declared it not bad.

We ate quickly and didn't say very much while we ate. I was complimentary about the excellence of the cooking and the quality of the wine, but that was all; perhaps it was time for reflection. I made coffee, and we sat at the table, warmed by the flames of the oven.

Getting the impression she had information, but guessing the time wasn't right, I waited and wandered over to the window, moved the blackout curtain to one side a wee bit, and looked out into the wood at the darkness, then wandered back and sat down. The warm glow from the oven produced smiles and refilled glasses.

I relayed a little of my information; she listened and showed a lot of polite interest. Garage contents are as interesting to a woman as handbag contents are to a man. I was able to tell from her demeanour, she was full to the brim with news.

# Chapter Thirty-Three

I put on my listening cap and encouraged her to proceed and unravel whatever story she had.

"I have been spying on the semi-detached house with the scruffy back garden," she said. "The house itself is solely occupied by the man; the caravan on the left of the house is occupied by a woman and two boys, one boy striving to reach the age of twenty-one, the other a spotty youth of about eighteen."

By me keeping quiet, she continued.

"The woman rarely leaves the caravan; she sometimes comes to the door, always in her slippers, looks out usually towards the house, then to the bonfires, as if surveying the scene, then goes back inside. The boys have a car and drive it in and out, each time going back into the caravan, I couldn't see any pattern of time, and no clue as to what they were doing."

She took a large sip of wine.

"There doesn't seem to be anybody living in the semi-detached house next door to the one where the man lives. The windows are all closed, and the outside looks as though it has not been lived in for a while. The two boys don't bother with it at all; they treat it as if it's out of bounds."

She stopped and looked at me quizzically.

"It's wrong somehow, the fence between the two houses is intact, and there is no gap for anyone to pass from one garden into the other garden. You'd think they would exploit the other house. Anyway, that's about it."

She paused, saw I was going to remain silent, so elaborated on all the issues she had mentioned previously, filling in minor details. I listened intently, endeavouring to remember all I had heard.

We talked for a while about things in general, finished the bottle of wine, shared the tidying and washing up, then with lighted candles went up the stairs ready to spy on these two predators. We both entered the left-hand bedroom. I positioned one of the electric fires on low heat, away from the window but near enough to keep her warm and watched as she took up the binoculars. I blew out her candle and left the door slightly ajar, to be able to hear her, then with my candle went into my spy bedroom.

After lifting the binoculars from the table, and blowing out the candle, I parted the curtain and watched. It was dark now, no street lighting was visible, only the occasional private lamp. I trained my glasses across the road onto the front door of the end terrace house, wondering and questioning in my mind what I was going to see. Precisely nothing happened, and after a considerable time I became bored stiff; the binoculars I am certain increased in weight, and I put them back on the table and for a time watched in the dark with my eyes only.

My thoughts meandered a bit and I recalled a large set of ladders in the barn, which would be handy up here for the binoculars to sit on, enabling me to watch through them without holding them in place at eye level.

At long last, a light went on in the hall of the end terraced house, and the front door opened. I snatched at the binoculars on the table, only in the darkness missed them, then clumsily knocked them to the floor. I tried my best to see what was happening below and saw the man come out of the house, but he was too far away for me to see any detail. The time it took me to fumble about under the table to recover the binoculars and position them to my eyes, he had gone.

What a blithering idiot! The main reason I was there was to identify the man and I had missed him!

The time was important so I shouted through to Daphers. "What's the time?"

She shouted back. "Quarter to ten. Are you all alright? I heard a noise."

"Yes, I'm fine." Thinking I must remember the time, I went back to watching with my eyes only. After all the excitement of the last few days, missing him like that was indeed annoying.

I sat down on the chair. It was a good time to think and make some progress and develop my plan, which was now quickly gathering momentum, growing considerably, and taking shape. Although it was a bit patchy and blotchy, I knew it was there!

From my seated position I suddenly saw the man come into view, walk across the road, up the path and disappear through the front door into the end terrace house. I shouted to Daphers;

"What time is it?"

She shouted back. "It's quarter to twelve."

His face was turned away from me all of the time, so I couldn't say positively whether he was one of the brothers or not, but he was of the right height and shape.

Assuming he would now go to bed, I shouted through to Daphers," I'm coming through," and proceeded to wend my way in the darkness to the other bedroom.

"The boys went out twice, then came back in their car, nothing else," she said.

She looked completely shattered. We didn't say very much, just had the biggest cuddle possible, undressed, put on nightclothes, jumped into bed, blew out the candle, snuggled up and went to sleep immediately.

We slept late; Daphers took her shower first.

We now had breakfast each morning, so when I arrived in the kitchen, the tea, toast, and jam were ready. We sat at the table, and after recounting my clumsiness with the binoculars, I repeated my diminished information and said:

"Once I have positively identified the man in the end terrace house, I will join you, we can take turns and share the watching together in your spy bedroom."

She returned her teacup to the saucer.

"That's a great idea, I was exhausted last night. More happened than I said; there were some strange goings-on in the garden of that house. The boys came back with a truck, one started chopping firewood. Why didn't he do it during the day? Granted, there is a big light outside on the wall so he could see. It seems they just enjoy making a noise at night."

She stopped for a second and looked at me quizzically.

"They have added to the bonfire in the corner, not the big one, the little one. Another odd thing, they are preparing a space in the garden at the back of the house for some reason, and I haven't got a clue why."

It was time for me to listen. So sitting back on the chair and folding my arms, I waited patiently for more.

Suddenly she blurted out: "Oh, I forgot. The man goes to the little bonfire on the left from time to time, he goes around the far side of it. I'm not sure what he is doing, he fiddles about, moving things and maybe taking things out, I don't know, it is difficult to see. He bends down and does something. We must keep an eye on him."

After we finished breakfast, it was time for me to move.

"Look, love, I need to go into the barn again," and immediately I shot off out of the front door to the barn with the keys, tape measure, paper, and a pencil. Outside the air was fresh, giving an indication autumn was nearly in full swing, and I was pleased to have donned a warm shirt and jumper. After opening the small barn door and closing it, I managed in the dark to hit the light switch at the entrance without a fumble. I took a few measurements, logged them then went to the far wall, collected the steps, ran back into the house up the stairs and positioned them in the right-hand bedroom, went out again and discreetly made adjustments to the hedge with an old pair of clippers.

On arriving back at the house I found Daphers was already in position in the left-hand bedroom. We still maintained the curtains closed at all times – thankfully, we had just enough light to move about without candles; it was crucial to be constantly aware we mustn't be seen, it was so, so important.

I returned to the right-hand bedroom and nestled the binoculars onto the very top of the ladders noting they took their stance very nicely.

I shouted through to Daphers, "Are you all right in there?"

"Yes," was the reply. "Are you? Do you realise we have missed lunch?"

"Yes, I know, but it is really important for me to clock this fellow," and I settled down to watch.

At no time did I think this activity strange; this spying had to be done, it was vital to identify these two men without any mistakes. The sun was out, and with ordinary eyes, I spied on the front door of the end terrace house.

Then, suddenly, without any warning, the front door opened, and out came the man. I was ready this time and bent my shoulders slightly, gripping the top of the steps with my thumbs and looked through the glasses.

The man was hatless. His face brought only a twinge of recognition, for it had been a long time. His hair had shrunk due to it recently being cut with a razor. The grimace on the face, I reflected, was the same and the eyes peering suspiciously all around were the same. He wore a shirt and a scruffy jumper, jeans of the baggy type and boots not shiny. He now had a paunch, not a big one but it was visible which was an addition to the last time I had seen him, all those years ago. I was nearly sure this was the man, but I needed some sort of proof to be absolutely certain in my mind.

He closed the door behind him, squinted his eyes in the sunshine, turned his face to the left then slowly to the right, screwed up his nose, drew his head back and gobbed with tremendous power into next door's garden. It wasn't a spit, it was a full nasal, phlegm gob.

From all I had just witnessed, I knew immediately this was the right man.

The last time I had seen him was after the murders, when a full investigation by the police had taken place and amazingly found nothing. All those years ago, evidence was not collected properly, and nobody in the area where they lived would help the police, mainly because these two men were thugs and had dominated the little village where they lived with fear. At the time, the people were too frightened to come forward with any information.

I had tried exhaustive and extensive means to find out about this man. In the end, by asking questions of lots of people, and from the nods and the whispers I received, I became sure he was one of the murderers, but without any evidence it was useless. One day, a year after the police had abandoned the investigation, I followed this man right to the house where he lived. Just before he entered the front door I confronted him. Very afraid, and rather sheepishly I asked him:

"It was you and your brother who killed them, wasn't it?"

He squinted his eyes. I could see he recognised me, probably from photographs in the newspapers; then with his eyes constantly watching me he sneered and grinned. His mouth turned into a snarl and he showed his teeth. Still staring at me he growled:

"If me or my brother ever see you again, we will do the same to you."

Still staring intently, he followed this by snarling, "And your bloody wife."

He then moved his head back even further and with full force gobbed straight at me. The phlegm flew through the air and hit me on the left side of my jacket, I looked down at the horrible slimy mess in complete disgust, distaste and revulsion. By the time I looked up again, he had gone inside the house.

I stood with my head bowed, completely dumb for a while, but with the definite knowledge the two brothers were the murderers, also I knew that after trying for a year, it was impossible for me to do anything about it.

Gathering myself together, I slowly turned away – what else could I do? The emotion in me was one of overwhelming sadness. On returning to my car my sadness had been joined by anger and a feeling of emptiness. Going straight to the boot, I found an old plastic bag, took my soiled jacket off, folded it inside out, put it in the plastic bag and tied it tightly at the top. My immediate thought being the nearest bin for disposal, where it would be buried forever.

# Chapter Thirty-Four

That had all happened more than twenty-five years ago, and now, returning to the present, I watched this murderous man walk down the path, turn towards his right, walk across the road in front of the semi-detached houses, and out of my sight.

Taking the binoculars and placing them gently on the table, I realised this was a very poignant special moment, and suddenly had the distinct feeling we were going to get more of these special moments. Emotions of all descriptions passed through my mind, but keeping firm resolution and good judgement sprang positively to the fore.

Having not told Daphers beforehand about the first spitting incident, I decided not to tell her of this one, only that I had now positively identified this man as one of the murderers. The thought made me turn my face towards the left-hand bedroom. She had lit a candle, the light from which flickered in the darkness, giving me a scene to savour; this, in turn, encouraged me to sit down on the chair and give myself time for a moment's thought and an attempt to relax.

Eventually, I rose and trundled my way towards the flickering light. She was about to blow the candle out but left it burning when she saw me coming.

"Have you clocked him then? Is he one of the men?"

She said it with a voice of firmness and enquiring declaration.

"Yes absolutely, positively, definitely he is one of the men."

Then with quiet sadness, she said, "Are you joining me in here?"

"Yes, it will be nice to be together at this time." We hugged until we could hug no more.

She blew out the candle, and we took it in turns to watch the back of the semi-detached house, the caravan, the bonfires, the garden and everything else in view. Nothing unusual happened until late afternoon when the spitter and the fat man came out of the back door.

We both took up our binoculars.

This was the first time I had seen this other brother for more than twenty-five years. He was fatter now and strangely shorter, his stomach was bursting from his belted trousers. He wore a collarless shirt and he had more hair than the other brother, but the same snarling features. The pair of them together looked inseparable; it was also nice to confirm where the spitting brother had gone.

Together they went round to the far side of the small bonfire, which we could now see clearly. Sensing there was more to learn about this pile of wood, I took the powerful binoculars to hand and trained them on the bonfire itself. They both bent down and shifted upright slabs of wood away from the base, placing them neatly to one side. It appeared they were attending to something important as if there was something of great value secreted under the bonfire. As they penetrated deeper, more mysterious manoeuvrings occurred until they finally found what they were looking for. They tried to hide their hand movements when removing whatever it was they were removing, before replacing everything on the bonfire exactly as it was before. I visually searched each of them for any sort of packages and saw both now had bulging pockets. Was that part of a plastic bag sticking out of the right-hand pocket of the little fat man? This could only mean one thing, somewhere under that so-called bonfire was their source of income.

"There!" Daphers said. "What do you make of that?"

We watched the men walk back to the house. As they did so, a truck entered the drive, swerved to the left and parked. The two boys jumped out and began unloading the cargo of branches, carefully adding them to the other big bonfire. We watched them finish their unloading, then jump back in the truck, but before they drove off, the fat brother handed them a package from his pocket, they took it and disappeared out of the drive. Both brothers watched them go, purposefully, like a couple of untrusting supervisors, then they both disappeared through the door into the back in the house.

Things remained still for a time, until the return of the truck, with old fencing and fence posts. The vehicle doors opened and out slid the two youths; one went to the back door of the house where he met the fat man who took something from him. Because the brothers were now out of sight, the youths reluctantly and lazily unloaded the cargo off the truck and placed it on top of the big bonfire. On completion of their task, they sort of hung about, seemingly not knowing what to do, terminally waiting it seemed, for someone to give them instruction.

The boys were not slaves, they did things with a percentage of willingness and freedom, but on first observation, it seemed they were totally dominated by the two older men.

Before long, 'the spitter', who was the taller of the brothers, came out of the house and immediately the two boys leapt back into the truck as if they had knowledge of some sort of a plan. The brother climbed in beside them, and they drove noisily out of the drive.

We spied without binoculars for a while because it was easier. Not a great deal happened, and the late afternoon sped on to the evening. Daphers slipped downstairs, cooked omelettes, brought them up to the spying room where we ate sitting on the bed, plate in one hand, fork in the other. The omelettes were welcome and delicious, and the decision to have tea instead of wine was a good one.

During this lull, we took time out to have a cuddle on the bed and discuss what we had seen and how long we ought to stay here in the house, thinking it was very important not to stay too long and even more important not to be discovered. We came to the conclusion it would be a good idea to leave as soon as we had collected enough information, but not before.

The plan of how to deal with these two brothers was developing quickly in my head, although it did require a touch more inspiration to be set in concrete.

We both put our heads on the pillow and within seconds we were asleep, glorious sleep.

# Chapter Thirty-Five

We were woken, in a startled manner, by the noise of a heavy vehicle entering the garden down below, and both sprang immediately out of bed. It was now very dark in the spy room and fumbling and rummaging around was necessary to find the matches to light a candle.

I asked Daphers the time. "Twenty to ten," she said.

"Mmm," I replied thoughtfully, reaching for my binoculars, and was about to part the curtain when a voice said:

"Wait, put out the candle."

Oh for the clever, alert Daphers! A quick blow extinguished it.

By moving the curtain to one side, I could see the electric light fitted to the wall of the semi-detached house shining brightly onto the rear garden. It revealed the motion of a very large, old tipper lorry slowly and noisily being driven into the pre-prepared space between the two bonfires. The sides of the tipper lorry had been extended upwards more than normal, making it look dumpy and also high enough to blank out any view from the caravan behind. The tipper appeared to have a load in the back, consisting mainly of bricks, rubble and soil.

The driver pulled up and stopped in the exact position where the light shone brightly onto the near side of the tipper lorry. Fumes were belching out from the smoky exhaust pipe sticking up from the side of the cab, the constant bobbing up and down of the flap on the top indicating the engine was rhythmically ticking over. By listening intently, I could just hear it grumbling away. Daphers' watch showed quarter to ten; a very familiar time.

I trained the binoculars behind the lorry, focusing on the drive along to the road, trying to see any sign of the youths, but there was nothing. I couldn't quite make out who was driving the tipper as the person was sitting on the far side of the cab, but guessed it would more likely be the spitting brother.

For a moment or two nothing happened, then the door of the cab facing us opened, and to my astonishment, a pair of legs appeared, along with a very short skirt. These were not a pair of youth's legs or a pair of man's legs, but a pair of girl's legs with high heeled shoes attached to the end. The owner of the legs edged forward, and sat half in and half out of the cab looking at the ground, probably trying to figure out how to get down from the position so high up. She was a woman probably in her thirties with shoulder-length hair, some of which was hanging over her face. The dress she wore was askew and from what I could see rather grubby.

The advent of the legs popping out of the cab caused the rear door of the house to open, and out burst the fat brother wearing Wellington boots, a shabby jumper, baggy trousers, and a strange excitable expression on his face. He went straight over to the cab of the lorry, where the legs were dangling. He gesticulated to the owner of them, waving his arms about, indicating to the girl to come down. On getting no response he made an almighty grab at the ankles, which resulted in a lot of fumbling and kicking. The action of the girl pushing him away caused her to slide in a most ungainly and undignified fashion down the side of the cab. She eventually settled her bottom on the footplate, landing on it with a sudden bump and began looking about, wobbling from side to side in a daze. Her facial features indicated a countenance she was decidedly uncomfortable and irritated. It was plain to see she was not pleased with her situation and she looked about the place in an aggravated, stupefied manner. The fat brother, recovering from the scuffle, waltzed round in front of her again and produced something from his pocket and placed it in her hand, she in turn hungrily thrust it to her mouth and swallowed. He then gave her what looked like half a bottle of whisky and she tried her best to totally devour the whole contents of this, only to find it being snatched from her grasp before the task was complete.

She sat there on the footplate dumb, then seemed to think it was necessary to do something, so she slowly placed one foot with awkward indecision onto the ground, then with reluctance allowed the other foot to follow. As her high heels sank into the muddy drive, her persona showed even more discomfort, and it became fairly obvious things were not to her liking for she started waving her arms about.

Beside me, Daphers had her binoculars trained on the scene below.

I said, "What on earth is going on."

A rather naive comment for an experienced sailor like me to utter. I glanced at her, there was just about enough light to allow me to make out the expression on her face. Her lips were flat, accompanied by a trying smile, and her top eyelids raised along with her eyebrows.

It wasn't difficult to figure out the reason for the presence of this lady. I instantly thought surely things were not going to take place in the back garden of this house, I couldn't imagine a more uncomfortable setting for such a scene. My fears were soon dispelled when the wellington-booted brother took hold of the young lady around the shoulders and put his lips to hers in an overly forceful manner. The spitting brother, not to be outdone, dropped down from the other side of the cab, and arrived on the scene by way of the front of the lorry. Encouraged by the activity of his sibling, he threw his arms out and began mauling the chest of this girl from behind.

This was a different world to our world, and I was not at all sure Daphers would enjoy watching it. Both of us had a very good idea where this was going, it was obvious two for the price of one was on the cards.

As I watched through my binoculars, I heard Daphers place hers back on the table and say: "I'm afraid I can't watch this, I think I'll go and make a cup of tea."

She walked to the back of the room, took a candle and matches, opened the door, closed it behind her and slowly disappeared down the stairs.

# Chapter Thirty-Six

More than a flicker of shame for the human race passed through my brain, dwelling especially on the male of the species. This was not going to be nice, but it was essential for me to continue viewing, to further confirm these two brothers were the ones, and to see just how dreadful these two were.

Whilst watching, my mind wondered who the girl was, and what she was, and how she had managed to put herself into such a position. Maybe her purse had already been filled with money. By her actions with the whisky and whatever else she was given, it was plain to see she had received a certain amount of disgruntled enjoyment already.

From the darkness of the bedroom and the brightness of the light shining on to the side of the truck, everything down in the garden was clearly in view, and easy to follow this atrocious behaviour which was starting to get very hectic. It was now an all together threesome, one brother fondling the girl's chest from behind, while the other brother in front was doing whatever he wanted to do. Suddenly it began to rise into a bit of a frenzy, and a lot of clumsy enforced foreplay seemed to be taking place. Then, unexpectedly, in a grasping pincer movement, the spitting brother turned the girl around so she was now facing him, then with ungainly, overzealous fanatic haste, whipped her dress off.

She was now standing between the two men, wearing no bra and naked apart from a pair of pants and high heeled shoes. The aforementioned pair of pants were pulled down in an unwieldy fashion from behind by the brother wearing the pair of Wellingtons. The other brother in front put his hands on the girl's shoulders and forced her into playing her part in his preferred sexual activity, by bending her forward and unzipping his trousers. After a considerable amount of fumbling by the brother, the girl finally managed to get his toggle out, and by the size of things he was feeling the cold. She also must have been feeling the cold, for she participated energetically, maybe wanting things to hurry along a bit.

Round at the rear, a similar sort of incompetence was occurring; the fat man had unbuttoned his trousers and managed to get his underpants down, settling them around the top of his Wellingtons. He now had one hand in between her legs, and the other trying to influence some growth in his toggle. Eventually, after much effort, this was achieved, and his hand was removed from between her legs and replaced by his toggle.

There commenced a lot of bouncing up and down, and in and out from both ends. The two men were having trouble getting their rhythm together, and the girl was being buffeted about in the middle in a somewhat ungainly manner. Both men looked up and found they were facing each other and automatically put their hands on each other's shoulders, which improved their coordination.

The girl's head bobbing up and down at the front did what was necessary for the spitting brother who was the first to slow down and wither away. She maintained her head in the same position waiting for the rear to finish, he retained his rhythm, his pimply bottom wobbling in and out in the bright light.

The spitting brother who had already finished, fastened his trousers and went to the back of the house, flicked a switch, and the light attached to the rear of the house went out.

The question passed through my mind, why he had done that?

It took me a little time to re-adjust to the darkness, the only light available now was the glow through the kitchen window in the house. I pressed the binoculars closer to my eyes, hoping to see more clearly.

The situation had suddenly altered as both men were now gesticulating to each other. I didn't understand what was going on, but the state of affairs had abruptly changed. The fat brother at the rear of the girl was still humping away, but it appeared he was marking time and I began to think, 'this isn't right, he was going on and on continuing with this too long'. To help strive for what seemed to be his fulfilment, he moved his hands from the girl's shoulders to her hair, then he pulled her head back level with his, which enabled him to place his hands around her neck. Suddenly the horror of it all dawned on me, this monster could not reach the height of his satisfaction without doing the worst thing possible.

He was going to strangle her, he was going to kill her.

Good God, what the hell was I going to do now? Oh, the poor girl!

Turning my eyes away from the glasses, I shouted down for Daphers to come upstairs, then returned the binoculars to the revulsion below.

The little fat monster's movements were slowing down, and it looked as though he was sagging, although he still had his hands around the girl's throat. When he was spent, he let go of her, and she flopped and crumpled to the ground heavily, in a way only dead people do.

This time I cried out even louder, disdain and anguish in my voice.

"What the hell has he done?" I whispered to myself.

A flickering light appeared as Daphers opened the bedroom door; she entered and blew out her candle.

Lowering down my binoculars, and with my face screwed up in torment I blurted out.

"Bloody hell, Daphers, he's killed her, bloody hell, he's killed her."

She put the candle on the table, and in disbelief gasped:

"God, surely not."

Suddenly, I started to shake and cry, I put my head in my hands, unable to do anything and pressing my fingers into my eyes, re-seeing the act in my mind in disbelief, finding it impossible to come to terms with what I had just witnessed.

Daphers took hold of my head and pulled it towards her, hugging me as close as she could, and began crying herself.

We stayed like that for a long time.

The revving of a lorry disturbed us, and I angrily returned the binoculars to my eyes, focussing into the semi-darkness. I could see the exhaust fumes belching out from the pipe above the cab as it got ready to move.

Something white caught my eye in the back of the tipper.

"Oh no, look in the back of the tipper," I said.

Daphers put her binoculars to her eyes.

From where we were, up high, we were able to see into the back of the lorry. The girl's body was on top of the rubble of bricks and soil, lying there, broken and dishevelled, legs and arms at strange uncomfortable angles. They had tried to cover her up with planks of wood, but I could see she was there.

Daphers shifted her binoculars to see, mournfully saying:

"That's not her in the back of the tipper, is it?"

I nodded, and with disgust and revulsion managed "yes".

"Oh dear, oh dear, this is not right, this is not right, this is awful, that poor girl, it's not right, it's not right."

She began to cry again and dropped the binoculars on the floor putting her head in her hands. I took hold of her and tried to console her as best I could.

We stayed like that for a long time.

# Chapter Thirty-Seven

The noise of the lorry's engine accelerating forced me to peer around the curtain. I watched the lorry slowly move and was just able to see parts of the white body in the back under the planks of wood as it vanished down the drive.

"We must call the police, where's the phone?" I said.

"We can't get a signal, don't you remember?" And she walked over and sat on the bed.

"If you really want to try, it's in my handbag."

Finding the matches I lit a candle and sat down beside her. We were both shaking as we sat there, doing nothing, saying nothing.

Eventually, I spoke.

"We could get in the car, go into the village, get a signal, phone the police and tell them what's happened."

There was definitely some sort of panic in my voice, which was not like me. I tried to calm myself and think about what we could do.

In the candlelight, Daphers found her handbag and after rummaging about discovered the phone, fiddled with it, then said:

"No, I can't get a signal."

I sat down on the chair, my mind in complete disarray and my movements on automatic pilot. My arms folded themselves and rested on my knees and my forehead slowly lowered itself. Daphers came over, put her hand on my head, and held out the phone with the other.

She stood and we had a quiet moment.

Eventually, she broke the silence. "Are you all right?"

Still wiping tears away, she paused, then softly whispered.

"What happened down there?"

I was unable to say anything, needing more time to think it through.

Then even more softly she whispered, "Are you going to try and use the phone?"

My thoughts were eventually disturbed by her kissing the top of my head. I raised myself, turned, and we hugged again and kissed. What would I do without this beautiful woman?

She needed and required some answers.

"Yes, my love, I'm all right, I'll be even better after a cup of tea and a couple of glasses of wine."

The phone was in my hand. I looked weakly at it and declared:

"Ringing the police is a difficult one, by the time we get ourselves together, drive into the village, find a signal, phone the police, it will be long while after the event, and because of the seriousness of the crime, we'll both have to go to the police station, wherever it is. We'll be there for days, it will continue forever, if not longer. The brothers will see us at some point and they will know who we are. I know it sounds heartless, but it's probably best for us to stay here and not go."

In my mind, I wanted to say, 'If we tell the police, the brothers will say we are making it up out of spite, and as before, with good lawyers will probably get off'.

I also wanted to say, 'Let's just kill them,' but I didn't.

I held her at arm's length, looked into her eyes and asked:

"What do you think?"

She gazed at me in a calming, reassuring way and gave me the candle. "I think it would be a good idea if we went downstairs to make that cup of tea."

We did exactly as she suggested and sat at the table in the kitchen, trying our best to return to normal. Daphers patiently waited for me to steady my nerves, wanting me to explain exactly what had happened to that poor girl down there. After having witnessed a certain amount of death at sea, I found this kind of death different; this was brutal, these two men were evil, but I already knew that. They had avoided conviction in the past, if there was ever any evidence against these men, people were too frightened to speak out.

She waited patiently, there was no point in being too explicit, so I just told her terrible things had happened and the girl was dead. The brother had strangled her and thrown her on top of the rubble in the back of the tipper. By now it would have been tipped, and she would be buried under all the bricks, stones and gravel, somewhere unknown to anyone but the driver. We couldn't help her now.

She showed a lot of expression in her face and said:

"We have got to do something, haven't we?"

I hugged her again and with grave determination in my voice, said:

"We will, I promise you, my love, we will, and sooner than you think."

We sat for a while and said nothing. It was far too cold in the kitchen, so we went into the lounge, collected two bottles of wine, two glasses and returned to the electric fires in the bedroom.

On entering, I parted the curtains and glanced at the scene below. It was in darkness except for a glow from one of the caravan windows. I opened the wine, poured out two full glasses and placed one on each bedside table. We prepared for bed and after climbing in, each took the glass of wine and emptied it. Filling them up again, I watched Daphers take a hefty drink from her glass, then finally put it back on the bedside table.

She wanted to know more about what had happened.

Keeping it as brief as possible, I spoke slowly and intermittently, really struggling at the beginning, finding it sometimes best to lie back on the bed with my head on the pillow, my eyes fixed on the ceiling.

"Before you went to make the tea, you must have had some idea of what they were going to do. Together, they took the girl, one at the front and one at the back; at first she didn't object or fight. The brother at the back had an awful lot of trouble bringing himself to a crescendo, but the girl with some reluctance played her part. In the end, tragically to bring himself to a crescendo the brother at the back had to eventually strangle the girl."

I waited a little longer, then said, "I wonder if they have done this before?"

The moment it came out through my lips, I regretted it.

Daphers suddenly retorted, "Oh no! Surely not."

As she said it, she sat up and turned and faced me.

Quickly recovering myself, I responded.

"I think you are probably right; maybe he needs some bloody horrible cruel act, now he is older. I'm pleased you didn't see it because it wasn't for your eyes."

Then I looked at her again in the gloom hoping she wouldn't ask any more questions, and that my words had pacified her; thankfully they seemed to.

After opening another bottle of wine, we automatically kissed and drained our glasses again and again, then, with the electric fire and the candle out, we cuddled and went to sleep.

# Chapter Thirty-Eight

Surprisingly, we both slept through the night without waking, maybe due to exhaustion and a bottle of wine each. I awoke before Daphers, and lay back on the pillow with my eyes wide open, seriously studying the previous evening in my mind. I knew these two brothers were very, very evil, but what they had done last night was taking evil to another dimension. I was now more determined than ever to rid the world of these two. This morning I needed time to survey and inspect the contents of the barn thoroughly for my plan to be finalised.

The thoughts must have made me fidget, for Daphers stirred and opened her eyes. We both then wriggled to a sitting position and kissed.

I started the conversation deliberately slowly and calmly.

"I know it's difficult, but let's see if we can put what happened last night behind us; maybe we should have called the police, but we didn't; we have our reasons. We now need to stay calm and work out what we are going to do next. I have the beginnings and the middle of a very good plan."

She looked at me. "Hopefully I am included in this plan; I've told you already, I'm totally with you every step of the way."

Under the circumstances hearing her say that was a huge step for me, all in the right direction.

My reply was easy. "I'm very glad you are, I certainly can't carry it out without you."

She looked sadly pleased.

"I need to go into the barn again, to have a good look round, also measure those scaffolding planks outside the house. This afternoon we need to walk along the road past both houses; I need to see the front of this semi."

She looked thoughtful and whispered, "That's going to be dangerous, what if they see us?"

"They mustn't see either of us. We must both be extra careful."

There was a pause in the conversation.

"When are we going back to France? I can be ready at a moment's notice if necessary."

"I've been thinking about that too, I reckon it has got to be early tomorrow morning."

"Right," she said, "I'll make the tea. You use the bathroom first, then you can do the business in the barn, OK?"

There was no need for me to reply; I was up and away and in the shower. After dressing, I had a sly look from the bedroom window at the garden below. It was as if nothing had happened, all was as still and silent as the grave. The neighbours over the years had learned not to interfere or even try to look over the hedge. Noise at night from the semi was normal.

I sauntered over and sat on the chair, and placed my head in my hands. The question again arose in my mind. 'Had we done the correct thing by not ringing the police?' What I had seen and witnessed was horrendous and was totally beyond belief, and so, so evil. Dulled thoughts scrambled across my brain. This was a difficult and very serious moment. It ended with me telling myself to leave it, and remain positive from now on. So, standing up quickly, I marched down the stairs to see Daphers making preparations to leave. She looked up when I arrived.

"Have some tea and toast before you go in the barn. I presume the idea is to come back here to this house at some stage in the future – what do you say we leave all the heavy things behind?

Everything else I'll pack in a bag ready to put in the car."

With cup in hand, I replied, "Brilliant. Don't forget we have at least one more night here, although getting ready sounds a good idea to me."

After breakfast, I went out by the front way, crept across the gravel drive and unlocked the barn door. It was dark inside, so as usual, I danced between the door and light switch once again, this time managing to get it right. I stood for a moment just gazing, trying to remember everything in front of me for the future, and mentally noting exactly what was there and how much. I stepped out the length and width of the total space available inside, registering one step equal to one metre or three feet, and I spent a lot of time estimating the available height inside the barn, which was very important.

When sure enough information had been gathered, I turned the light off, opened and closed and locked the door, ran across the path to the scaffolding planks in the long grass and checked their dimensions. They were of considerable length and capable of carrying a substantial amount of weight, which was pleasing. As always time seemed to pass me by whenever planning in the barn was involved.

We finished our soup, donned hats, coats and scarves to partially cover our faces, made sure the car, back door and front door were all locked and set off walking along the short driveway to the main road. We continued walking following the road, winding around until we found houses on either side, then we turned left and left again which brought us back on ourselves, and on to the entrance of the road of the two murderers.

Before going any further, I took Daphers to one side and told her it was necessary for me to watch her walking along the footpath to take some mental measurements of the front of the semi-detached house. The only way to do this, was for her to walk along the right-hand side of the road directly in front of the semi-detached house, with me following along on the left-hand side.

"Walk as smartly as you can past the front of the semi, the one with the big bay window–" indicating it by an excessive movement of my eyes and eyebrows.

"Yes," she whispered.

"When you are passing, keep looking straight ahead; don't under any circumstances look at the house, just look straight ahead all the time." A cross between nervousness and excitement was evident in my voice.

"Yes," she whispered and started off a bit uneasy at first, then slowly increased her stride along the pavement on the other side of the road. I followed on the left-hand side, with slumped shoulders and head bowed. Her increased pace made me lag behind, which possibly helped, because it gave me a better view and allowed me to use my eyes only to watch her, without turning my head.

As she approached the semi-detached house, I took a mental picture of the height from the ground to the bottom of the very large bay window. On previously seeing these houses from the car months ago, this feature had stood out, I also noticed the fence in front of the tiny front garden was now missing. I clocked the measurements of the height of the wall from the ground to the bay windowsill to be waist high on Daphers. I also noted the distance from the pavement edge to the brickwork under the window, to be a good twelve feet. We maintained our casual air and using the same walking pace carried on, hoping no one would see us – if they did, we hoped they would think we were ramblers or birdwatchers.

As I watched her striding along on the other side of the road, then cross over and enter the wood, my walking pace along the tarmac pavement on this side inadvertently slowed as I neared and drew very close to the spitting brother's front door. I became more and more aware of who the owner was, and an uncontrollable angry panic welled up inside me and sweat suddenly appeared over all my body from nowhere. I didn't know whether

I was going to break down or go into the house and bludgeon him to death. A great deal of effort and much of my strength was seriously employed helping me pass the garden gate; with enormous difficulty I managed to do it.

Unconsciously, my hand strayed to my jacket and wiped off an invisible mucus mark in remembrance of that horrible vile spit at the house in the other village. By using deep breathing and some resourcefulness, my thoughts reverted to reality, and I returned to a normal walking pace. The changes in all these emotions left me completely exhausted.

Fortunately, I joined Daphers in the wood, which helped me and we continued along the path, climbing and traversing the slopes.

Glancing up at this stage, I tried to see our little cottage but couldn't because of the denseness of the trees. After a short walk, we went left and came to the road, turned right and climbed up the hill towards the house, turned right and strolled along the drive to the haven of the front door.

Once inside we had a relieved hug, but not many words. I walked through to the kitchen, opened a cupboard, lifted out a bottle of wine, and we sat at the table in our coats and nursed a full glass each. Daphers, with a quizzical look, enquired:

"Did you see all you wanted to see? I had a discreet look at both of the houses if you ever want any help?"

"Thanks, love, everything, in the end, was good. There were a few emotional moments on that walk for me, but it all feels a lot better now."

I took another gulp of wine, then repeated, "It really does feel a lot better now." She clutched my hand across the table.

"Tomorrow morning we need to get up about seven. It will be a good idea to be down the road before eight. Can you set the alarm on the mobile phone?"

"Yes, that's OK." She smiled. "Do you think anybody saw us on our walk?"

"No. If they did, I don't think they would have taken much notice of two old people."

She looked across at me and smiled a smile so huge it engulfed her face.

"You made a promise to this one old person, a promise to do something."

"Yes, I know, and it is a promise I shall keep."

The remaining time in the day was deliberately planned to relax us and consisted of a nice dinner with plenty of wine, carrying out gentle ablutions and donning night attire.

The last feature of the evening was for us to spy on both houses.

For me, this entailed taking a candle upstairs, setting myself in position, blowing it out and watching the front door of the terraced house across the road, then waiting.

At about quarter to ten, the light went on inside the porch, and sure enough, out he came right on queue. He stood for a moment, gobbed into next door's garden, then walked down the path and onto the road. He only had one place to go, and that was his brother's house.

The time was important. I shouted, "What time is it?"

"Quarter to ten," came the reply.

A useful habit for us, and one I hoped he would never stray from.

On strolling into the other bedroom, I found Daphers watching the back garden of the semi without her binoculars. She looked up.

"The light has gone on and off in the kitchen, and there's a glow from the caravan, but nothing else."

Eventually, just before midnight, the brother returned to his house and we settled down. That night, sleeping was not a problem.

# Chapter Thirty-Nine

The following morning the alarm woke us. A morning kiss started the day well, followed by the usual showers and stuff. We made the bed properly, packed the rucksacks, had a last inspection round the rooms and went downstairs.

It was decided not to take any wine or whisky or any non-perishables with us back to France, as they would be too heavy for the rucksack, so we left them.

After breakfasting, washing and tidying, we returned to the table, wrote a precise uncomplicated note for Mrs Ramsbottom, informing her we had turned the gas bottle off, turned the electricity off at the mains, closed all the windows, locked the barn, and the house. It also informed her we wanted to return at some point under the same terms, and would be only too pleased to pay a further three hundred pounds and would telephone before we came.

The car was secreted in such a good place alongside the barn, we had no problems in transferring our personal effects from the house to the boot of the car. My wife settled herself in the passenger seat, but before getting in myself, I glanced back at the spy house with all the curtains drawn; all seemed to be in order. The car needed to be turned around, so, as a precaution, I went round to the end of the barn, and peered down at the garden below. A strange smile-cum-snarl appeared on my face in the knowledge that next time we came, it would mean the end of these two evil men.

After a deep breath, I walked back to the car, slid into the front seat, and without too many revs, turned the car around and drove along the drive and out onto the road.

I found it surprisingly good to get away for a while after what had happened. As we headed away from the village a glance at Daphers told me she was pleased too, for a gentle smile had appeared on her face. The clock in the car read ten to eight. We had been in England enough time for me to gather information to carry out my plan, plus I had acquired a steely determination from the horrors of the other night.

As we drove along, my wife must have been thinking about the note to Mrs Ramsbottom, for she asked, "Do you seriously think we will be back in a week?"

"We will make it before that if things go right. Our first job now is to find a cobbler's to get these keys copied."

She pulled a face. "That's a bit deceitful, isn't it?"

"Yes, I know, but they may be useful. Don't worry, I have no intention of doing anything illegal." We both laughed heartily at the ridiculousness of the comment, knowing what our intentions were.

The nearest town produced a key-maker and we drove on to Mrs Rambottom's and parked the car ahead of the house. I placed the original keys in the envelope with the note. Daphers scooted out of the car, posted the envelope through the letterbox and was back in the passenger seat in no time. Doing this meant the old lady would only see us one more time.

Our next stop was the car hire company, where with the necessary formalities we discharged our hire car. The company supplied a driver who shipped us to the ferry terminal. With rucksacks strapped in place, we strolled across to the berth and boarded the ferry.

Within a couple of hours, we were back in France, docking at Calais, and alighting from the boat down the gangway to our parking place. The pick-up truck was there to greet us, with all the boxes and suitcases unmoved in the back. Our immediate priority was to remember to drive on the right – at the first roundabout, we achieved it.

# Chapter Forty

In the first few miles, it was important to concentrate in order to get the driving absolutely correct. On the journey, we had plenty to discuss, mostly about what we had left behind in the spy house, and whether it would be alright left there.

One of the other issues of concern was the amount of personal effects and equipment in the back of the pick-up truck, and whether it was enough for us to live comfortably in our new house. We both agreed we had made the right decision to complete the signing and selling of our French house before we left for England, and felt selling most of the furniture and heavy items was a good thing because storage of such equipment would be a real problem. Finally, the conclusion was, we had done it, and therefore, it was too late to change it.

The motorway roads created easy driving and gave me the ideal opportunity to think and try to finalise the idea swirling around in my mind. This was good and eventually, my brain contrived a plan to rid the world of these foul people.

Halfway to Eeee, in the evening at dinner in a quiet corner of the restaurant, I decided it was time to bring my plan to the fore, so I took hold of my wife's hand and quietly said:

"Over the last week, I have been working hard, and have finally devised a plan that will rid the world of the two brothers. Oh, and I am absolutely certain the two brothers we have been spying on are the two men who killed our beautiful twins all those years ago."

At this point, I faltered. Saying what I said made my shoulders and my head sag forward. Only by slowly taking a deep breath and bringing Daphers' hand to my lips and kissing her fingers brought life back to me.

"Unfortunately what I want to do is just too much for two of us; we need some help; we need a third person."

I paused for a moment and hesitated then repeated, "To carry out my plan by ourselves would be very difficult indeed, we need someone else to help us."

She looked across the table at me, then with a solemn and curious expression on her face she quietly asked:

"Your plan, and what you aim for us to do; it is going to get very serious, isn't it?"

"Yes, it is," I said. "We are going to kill the two brothers, you, me and another. We are going to murder both of them. You and I are going to end up both being murderers."

This was a defining moment: It was important to tell Daphers this from the beginning, she looked at me and went very, very quiet. I thought it best to leave her with her thoughts.

We didn't speak very much through the rest of dinner, or breakfast the following morning, even when we took our seats in the pick-up and left the hotel, I knew not to say anything. I only glanced at her from time to time, then back at the road. Most of the time she was staring directly at the windscreen, not flinching. I began to think, maybe my words had been too harsh, or too direct? Now that she knew what we were going to do, was she going to say she couldn't do it? Possibly situations like this were going to crop up again and again in the next few days. I waited in agony; all my planning was hanging in the balance.

If she stumbled and wavered and said she couldn't do it, we would just go down to Eeee, stay for a little while, then move on further down to Southern Spain somewhere. I would never try and persuade her to do otherwise. If she was going to do this thing with me, she would have to agree to do it wholeheartedly. My thoughts started to stray again; maybe I was asking too much, maybe after all this time I was wrong, maybe the two brothers should be allowed to carry on and kill undisturbed. They had managed to do exactly that so far.

I continued driving with the car engine and the road noise as company. The straight road meant driving was possible without making any sudden movement, which helped me to stay composed, calm and steady while Daphers decided on such a seriously decisive issue. During this quiet period, it was a good time for me to think more deeply about the situation. I concluded I would be unable to stop myself from killing these two.

I drove and waited and drove and waited. She sat beside me in silence then suddenly moved in her seat, and I sensed she had made a decision. It must have been the excitement, for my foot increased pressure on the accelerator, and we speeded up.

"With this plan you have, are we going to kill the two brothers outright, and you are absolutely certain they are who they are?"

I replied, "Yes, we are going to kill them outright, and yes I am absolutely certain they are who they are."

"Then I'm with you all the way. It is time somebody stopped these two – if we don't do it, nobody will. All I ask is, when we start preparing, we continue and we don't stop until the plan is completely carried out and the whole thing is finished, and I mean completely finished. Will you promise?"

I understood what she meant and glanced at her, really wanting to stop the car, take her in my arms and give her a big hug. The traffic and the motorway stopped me.

Beaming a smile, not a happiness smile, a satisfactory smile, I gave a definite reply:

"I promise, I promise."

From this, rose an atmosphere of euphoria inside the car, it was retained until we finally left the motorway and drove at a slower pace through other villages, and on to the village of Eeee.

On this little passage, it was she who broached the subject and enquired: "You mentioned another person, someone else to help us – have you someone in mind?"

Ever since we left the spy house and maybe even before, my thoughts had drifted from time to time, as to who could help us with this fatal decisive criminal act, and the person who came to mind each time was Auguste. He had enough character, courage, and skill to help us with this plan and he also knew how to keep a dark secret; whether he would be willing to do this thing, was a different matter.

For the first time in our lives, we were going to deliberately and seriously break the law in a big way by killing these two, and we were going to do it knowingly. It ever so slightly took my breath away and the thought changed everything from being a possibility, into a positive must. From this moment on, until the job was done, life, or part of life, would have to be very serious, and different, also we all had to be cleverer than clever, and determined.

During the rest of the drive, my thoughts strayed to 1972, nearly thirty years previous, when I was Captain of a large cargo ship, a beautiful vessel with gracious lines. We were some days from Hong Kong when we received a radio message telling us we were heading directly into a hurricane called Rose. Hurricanes at sea are very dangerous adversaries and can be devastatingly cruel and deadly. Seeking a port to hide away until the worst is over is an option, but not always the answer. If the hurricane follows the ship and finds it tied up at a berth, there is a strong possibility the force of water and wind will batter it against the dockside, severely damaging it, or even possibly sinking it. The situation we were in was very serious indeed. After discussions with other senior officers, I decided our best hope of survival was to take our chance at sea, and steer the ship directly into the force of the wind and waves. Preparations were made and all cargo hatches were battened down and made more secure than ever before, and all-weather doors were shut tight. This made it watertight, but still, under no circumstances must we allow the ship to face the waves side on, for the sea would eventually sink it.

As the light of day broke, the hurricane hit us full force. The helmsman steered the mighty ship to plunge headfirst directly into the rising barrage of saltwater. Time and time again I watched the forward section of the vessel completely disappear beneath the waves. There was a split second every time this happened when my brain queried whether the ship would rise again out of the all-engulfing sea. Holding on to something solid on the bridge I watched as the whole of the forward section of the ship rose out of the water like a great beautiful monster. The ship survived and all the people on it survived. We were battered and tired when the hurricane passed, everyone on board was mindful of the experience we had encountered and the fact we had all endured it and lived through it.

We carried out our plan to the full, and it worked. Now at this present time, we have a plan. It is a very risky and very dangerous plan, but if we prepare it properly and carry it out correctly, we have every chance we will succeed in killing these brothers outright. It would require all involved to play their part to the full; any mistakes will result in failure.

Entering a tunnel on the motorway disturbed my train of thought, and I heard Daphers say:

"Well, are you going to tell me who is going to help us?"

I took my eyes off the road for a second and met her gaze. "Yes, I have someone in mind, but I've got to ask him first."

She smiled and shook her head as if to say, 'I already have some idea'.

We continued along the open French motorways until Daphers spotted the possibility of a good signal on her mobile. After several attempts, she must have had success, for I heard her say 'hello' to Nicole and inform her of our approximate time of arrival and then accept the offer of an aperitif before we moved into the new abode. I was not absolutely sure where this holiday home was, only that it wasn't far from Auguste, which was more than acceptable to me.

# Chapter Forty-One

We entered Eeee at about the time Daphers had indicated, passed through the gates, and parked the pick-up in the drive of Louis and Nicole.

The front door opened as we approached, and Louis stepped forward and greeted us both.

"Nicole is attending to supper, come in."

After a minor search in the back of the pick-up, we found bottles of wine, and gave them to Louis as we entered. The supper was typical French fare, the wine was good, and the conversation never stopped. They asked politely about our holiday to England; we rambled on explaining it was to see friends, casually mentioning we would be popping back across the pond again shortly.

They told us all about their cottage, which was going to be our new home, elaborately explaining many times over the plan of the rooms, cupboards and things in the kitchen. Why they didn't take us and show us was a mystery.

Eventually, the evening drew to a close. After luxuriant goodbyes, keys were placed in our hands along with directions.

The cottage was not far, only a short drive along a twisty single file road. Soon the welcome porch light came into view along with our French car. I parked the pick-up truck next to it. We both stood for a moment in front of the cottage not saying a word; eventually, Daphers linked my arm.

"Well, this is another beginning."

"Yes," I said, and secretly wondered if the end of the beginning was going to be as pleasant as the beginning.

Everything seemed to be to our liking, the house was small, but comfortable and fashioned with typical French furniture. Fortunately, there were plenty of wardrobes for personal stuff. After showers, bed was a welcome companion.

We slept late, had a cup of tea for breakfast, meandered around the house trying to settle in, finally ending up with a wandering jaunt in the garden.

Pleasantly situated at the rear of the house was an open gazebo with an inviting table.

"Lunch outside maybe, today?"

She took my hand and patted the back of it with her other.

"I think we will both require a warm, woolly jumper if we do."

Still holding my hand, she smiled.

"I think this little cottage will do very nicely. Maybe I'll take a walk through the village, and pop in to see the mum of Jean and Genevieve, and ask her if they are coming here to visit in the near future. I presume you want to go and talk to Auguste?"

She led me further along the garden.

"If you look through those branches there, you can just make out a building." She pointed to it. "I do believe that is the rear of the garage of Auguste."

She had already figured out who the third person was going to be. We returned to the house and she prepared herself to go to see the mum of Jean and Genevieve. We kissed and I watched her until she was out of sight

Afterwards, I sat in the lounge in a comfortable chair, going over in my mind not only what to say to Auguste, but more importantly, how to say it. I couldn't just go up to him and say, 'look I want you to help us kill two people'. If I did, I might find him turning down my plan, before I could fully explain what it was all about. Most crucially,

I wanted to justify to him how important it was for us to complete this killing task and exactly why we were doing it. The difficulty was not only introducing the subject but how to approach it without causing alarm.

It was not going to be easy. I thought maybe in this situation it might be best for me to let him do most of the talking, and for me to act as calm as possible, allowing him to lead the conversation, then see if I could edge it round to where I wanted it to be. Not having seen Auguste for a little while, and always finding him full of life, I hoped it might be easier than the difficult thoughts I was having.

It was only a short walk round to his house and I sauntered in through the open garage doors into a very neat, tidy and spacious workshop. It was a conventional small garage and reminded me of the barn in England.

As there was no sign of Auguste, but assuming he was somewhere near, I went through a back door, peered around the corner and saw him in the garden with a spade in hand. As I moved towards him, he must have sensed my presence for he turned, saw me, speared the spade into the ground, and with a beaming smile came towards me, thrusting out his hand. I received an abundant impression he was pleased to see me.

He spoke to me at a quick pace with a strong accent. A wave of my hand indicated for him to slow down, he did so and invited me into his house. We sat in his tiny but cosy kitchen in the company of an old sink and an even older fridge. Through an open door, I could see another room, with an armchair and some very old ancient higgledy-piggledy, scattered French furniture.

I accepted the offer of coffee, but turned down the splash of whisky, telling him coffee by itself would be fine. We talked in general about my visit to England, then about how things were here in Eeee. His reply was genial, although it lacked a certain conviction, and it was easy for me to hear in his voice and see in his manner some sort of anxiety. My curiosity was aroused as to why this was, and why he was like this – his enthusiastic greeting when we met had assured me, my presence was not the reason.

We continued with the customary chit chat until suddenly it ran out, and we had a strange silence. In the end, I forced myself to say something, so I softly ventured an enquiry.

"Are you sure you are alright, Auguste?"

He scratched his head, screwed up his face and said: "It's very difficult."

I chose not to say anything, deliberately encouraging him to carry on; eventually, he rather reluctantly continued.

"Maybe you are the one person I can tell, Matthew."

He took a sip of coffee, leaned back on his chair and slowly began:

"I've rented this house and the garage for a long time now, and have always made sufficient money to pay the rent and live to a reasonable standard."

After saying it he struggled, so I said, "Go on."

He gave a big sigh.

"I have received a letter in the post, from the owners of the property, telling me they intend to sell the house and the garage. They will be putting a 'for sale' sign up shortly, and they say, when they sell it I won't be able to rent it anymore."

After he said it, he looked very sad.

"Why don't you buy it?" I queried. It was a silly statement really, because if he had had enough money, presumably he would have bought it.

He cogitated and I could see him thinking whether to tell me or not. He was a village man, not a city man and proud where money was concerned, like a lot of old French.

"I haven't got enough money. The house is small, and the garage is just a building, so they don't want a lot, but I just don't have enough." He looked at me despondently.

"Have you tried the bank?" I suggested.

"I can get a little from the bank but they will only allow me to have so much because of my age. I was quite surprised they would let me have anything at all."

He became agitated and began to wave his arms about in a hopeless fashion.

"I have sold all the cars I have spare, which didn't come to much, and I am still a long way short. My only hope is nobody wants to buy it."

Then he quickly embarrassingly added, "I don't want the whole village to see the for sale sign going up."

That was the crux of the matter, he didn't want the village to know his business.

Previously, when walking through the garage, I noticed his yard was empty of any cars for repair.

"I can see from the garage you are not very busy."

He wrinkled his brow and scratched his head again. "I think my lack of enthusiasm in the business is showing through."

# Chapter Forty-Two

Now was the perfect opportunity for me to broach the subject of my dilemma.

"Would it be possible for you to do some work for me, on the pick-up truck?"

"Yes," was his instant reply, then he said, "Wait a minute, your truck is fairly new, I don't want to do things for you that are not necessary, Matthew, just to help me along."

From this reply, it was important for me to take him completely into my confidence, or else it might get somewhat complicated. Deciding that going in at the deep end would be best, I took the bull by the horns and took a chance.

"What I want you to do on the pick-up will need you to be as discreet and secretive as possible, like you were during the war."

His ears pricked up, and his eyes stared at me with renewed exuberance, a broad grin arrived on his round face, and he sat back in his chair and waited. It was so very, very important to get right what I was going to say, and because of what it was, it would need all my courage, strength and endurance to say it.

"The reason why I want you to work on the pick-up is long and complicated, and must be told from the beginning."

I stopped speaking and settled myself. He sat back and prepared himself to listen.

"After Daphers and I were married, we were blessed with twins, two of the most beautiful babies in the world. One was a boy, William, and the other a girl, Rebecca. They were wonderful children, both full of life, and because they were twins they tended to do things together."

Auguste sat and didn't speak, he just listened, his visual expression changing to curious concentration.

"As a family, we all grew up very happily, we were as one. My work in the Merchant Navy took me overseas, Daphers stayed at home and looked after the twins; our lives were wonderful. When I was on leave we spent all the time together as a family, going on holidays, or encouraging the children with their hobbies, or in their education; life could not have been better. We didn't have any more children, the twins were enough and they filled our lives with happiness. They went to the same school, both went on to university, finally after getting their degrees in the early part of 1970 they came home and lived with us. One evening soon after they qualified, they decided to go in the car to a pub quite a long way away, to meet some friends."

I shut my eyes at this point, finding it so difficult to go on. The tragic, cruel travesty of what had happened was always in some dark corner of my brain. It was very important for me to go on, so with all the willpower I could muster, I slowly continued.

Auguste listened intently; he now had a solemn face and sat stock-still. The explanation was now getting more and more difficult for me to share because it all came back to me, I had to force myself to speak.

"The twins had enjoyed themselves in the pub as far as we can gather, then for some reason, they decided to take the scenic route on the way home down one of the more isolated roads. On the journey something caused them to stop, nobody knows why, or what for."

Feeling a lump in my throat, I found it difficult to continue but knew I must.

"When they didn't arrive home, Daphers and I became worried and phoned the police.

Eventually, in the early morning, we received a visit from the police. There had been a fire, they said the twins' car had been found burned out, with both of them still sitting inside."

I began shedding tears uncontrollably, I was unable to continue speaking. Auguste sat and waited for me to recover. Eventually, I wiped my eyes.

"Daphne and I were completely and utterly destroyed, unable to understand how anything like this could happen to our beautiful twins."

At this point I broke down again as before and cried in the memory; eventually, it developed into a sob, a continuous sob. August placed his hand on my shoulder, it helped and I looked up.

"We went to see the burned-out car. Everyone told us not to go, including the police, but we felt we must go to see the last place our twins had been alive. They were not inside the car when we got there. We stayed for a long time until the police truck came and took the car away."

Auguste shook his head slowly from side to side, his face a mask of sadness. He remained silent.

"Then came the hardest thing of all; we had to identify the bodies. I tried my best to stop Daphers from going, but it was impossible, she absolutely insisted, reaching the stage where she became very angry, which for her was very rare indeed. In the end, I relented."

I stopped speaking and restored myself to a level where, with controlled deep breaths, I found I could very nearly speak normally.

"We went to where the bodies were laid out, both of them were as black as charcoal. We cried and hugged each other tightly for ages, trying to hold ourselves together. It was the most difficult thing I ever had to do in my life. Instinct only enabled us to recognise the twins. The police told us they had been unconscious before the fire had started, which somehow seemed to help us, I don't know exactly how, but it did. They also told us someone had set fire to the car deliberately."

Auguste spoke for the first time for a long time.

"Who would do such a thing? Did the police find the people who did it?"

"The police were sure it was two brothers, who were notorious in the region for causing dreadful trouble and carrying out appalling acts of violence."

"Did they both go to prison?" he asked solemnly.

"No," I said. "The police didn't have enough evidence, neither of them went to prison. It was never proved they did it."

Auguste gripped me by the arm.

"My God, my friend, was it them? Did they do it?"

"Yes, they did it, the trouble is nobody at the time could prove it was them, and now, well, it was a long time ago."

We sat in silence, and I wiped my eyes. Auguste turned his head to one side peering out of the window, then down at the ground. I could see him thinking, then he quietly spoke:

"I cannot see why you want me to work on the pick-up truck, what has it got to do with this horrible time for you?"

Then again he repeated, "What do you want me to do with the pick-up truck?"

I waited for a few seconds knowing the moment had arrived for me to tell him what we ultimately wanted to do.

"We want you to do more than help with the pick-up, we want you to help Daphers and I kill both these two murdering brothers! We have a plan."

He was completely stunned by what I had said, obviously not expecting me to say that. His face took on an expression of absolute horror and disbelief. He did one of those scratches to his forehead, then put his hands on his knees. We had a silence; nothing moved, we didn't seem to breathe, we just stared at each other. All the nerves in my body were awakened, I felt them in my head, and my fingers and feet. Having no idea what his reply was going to be, I sat and hoped he would say the right thing; it would be nearly impossible to kill these two brothers without his help.

Waiting in this silence was very hard indeed. Eventually, he turned his head and looked out of the window again, then back at me and whispered.

"I remember the war and Jacques and the Germans." By the expression on his face, I could see had returned to the past, his eyes glazed and he breathed a smile.

"I will help you do this," he said.

He put his hand out for me to shake. I took it with gratitude and hugged him like a brother.

He continued in a serious voice, "I've never felt like this for years, you know, I told you about the incident during the war, watching that steam train and the German guns lying on their side."

He didn't move, only focussed his eyes on mine. "I think I need to know a lot more about your plan."

"I agree," I said. "We need to carry out the first part of our plan very shortly. Can I bring the pick-up into the garage tomorrow, for you and me to work on? All three of us want to be leaving for England on Thursday morning if we can."

He spoke again in a slightly raised voice. "You mean Daphne is in on what you want to do, she is going to help kill these two brothers with us?"

"Yes," I said. "We can't do it without her, and she wants to help to do it."

He shook his head from side to side, smiling a smile of disbelief, then said, "Tell me about your plan."

"With help from you and Daphers, I'm going to set fire to the two brothers. I'm going to do to them, what they did to the twins." I didn't say it in a vengeful way, just in a matter of fact way.

He looked at me a bit bewildered. "I presume you want me to go to England with you?"

"Yes! Oh, I have a big question for you, have you got an identity card?"

"Yes, I go to Spain for various cheap stuff, mainly diesel; I have a contact there, so my identity card is always up to date." After saying it he raised his eyebrows and winked. I didn't know exactly what that meant – Frenchmen like Auguste were always up to something, another Frenchman would have known exactly what that was about – but I chose not to go any further along that route, and didn't ask, but managed a smile.

"I have a sketch of the structure for us to make," I fibbed, "I'll bring it with me in the morning."

"I'll be here ready any time after eight," he said with renewed vigour for life.

Before leaving I asked to see the letter he had received from the owners of the property, jotting down the name, phone number and the asking price, which looked fair to me considering the size and quality of the property. It gave me an idea.

# Chapter Forty-Three

Walking slowly back to the house rendered me enough time to think about Auguste's dilemma, and it set me wondering whether Daphers and I could help.

She was waiting with the table set in the garden.

"You've been a long time?"

It wasn't a rebuke it was more of a question, for it was accompanied by an enquiring half-smile. "I must start wearing my watch regularly. What time is it?"

"After three."

The conversation paused, finally she added: "Are you going to tell me whether he is going to help us or not?"

My Daphers didn't miss much, what a combination of beauty and brains.

I couldn't stop myself from having a chuckle.

"Yes, we have help, enthusiastic reliable help, but unfortunately he didn't give me any lunch."

"I'll have ours ready in a minute. Can you open the wine?"

The heat from the sun slowly diminished, Daphers talked about her visit to the mum of Jean and Genevieve and other village gossip. It began to get cold so we cleared the table and retired to the lounge.

Over coffee, I broached the subject of Auguste's dilemma and the sale of his property.

"He is going to be left without a home, or a garage, and I'm sure his pension is not enough for him to live comfortably if he had to rent somewhere else. He's in a bit of a pickle."

There was a hush between us then she said:

"Can't we help in some way?"

I showed her the information gleaned from the letter.

"Look, I am certain we can, and I am hoping you will agree. Now we have sold our house we can easily afford to buy his house including the garage."

She smiled. "You mean, we buy it all and give it to Auguste?"

"Yes, I've seen how much they want for the property, and it is not a great deal. Would you agree to us buying it?"

She smiled again. "I think it's a lovely idea."

"We can't just give it to him; we'll leave it to him. In the meantime, we will ask him to take care of the property and both cars, in return he can stay in the property rent-free. With a bit of luck, he will end up having more money than before."

She folded her arms. "Why don't you phone now, and see if you can sort something out?"

I took the phone and dialled the number. It was answered by a man with an elderly voice. He could tell I was English from the beginning and sounded surprised and a little unsure. Eventually, after a fairly lengthy chat, we arrived at the crux of the matter and discussed the price to purchase the house, the land, and the garage. After buying and selling other houses in France, I was aware of one or two money saving moves; one of them being to bypass the estate agent, which could save an awful lot of money on both sides. The discussion continued until the asking price for the house and garage were reduced to an agreeable sum, which didn't involve estate agents. It was also more economical to use the same solicitor, and I asked him to arrange a letter to be sent to our address here in Eeee, confirming all the details. He agreed to this with enthusiasm and elaborate politeness.

I put the phone down and turned to Daphers.

"He seemed to be content to sell the house quickly, with minimum fuss. Hopefully, it will go ahead without any problem," and I smiled a wincing smile.

"Well, I'm really pleased we've done that. Will you tell him in the morning when you see him?"

"I shall pick my moment carefully," I said.

We finished our coffee with more thought than conversation until Daphers went to bed. While she slept, I sketched on paper the plans for the alterations necessary to the pick-up-truck, continuing my task late into the night.

I couldn't wait to get started the following morning and drove to where Auguste was waiting with garage doors open. He indicated for me to park the pick-up right in the centre. A bench at one side was clear of his tools for me to spread out one of my drawings. The first was of the pick-up, with the full timber structure and apparatus assembled into and onto the back section. It did look a startlingly daunting sight.

We both stood and studied it for a few minutes, well, more than a few minutes. The drawing must have clicked with him, for he immediately saw what it was all about, and exclaimed:

"My God, what's that?" Pointing to the large round object perched right over the top above the cab.

"It's a forty-five-gallon drum, you know the ones for storing oil," and I pointed to one he had in the garage.

He looked at the drum in the corner then back at the drawing.

I continued.

"You see on the drawing these scaffolding planks sloping from above the top of the cab down to the other scaffolding planks sticking out the back end of the truck. Well, we are going to half fill a forty-five-gallon drum with the most volatile and inflammable liquid we can find and strap it in place at the top of the sloping timbers above the cab. When we have everything perfectly in place we are going to drive the truck down the road to the brothers' house, reverse it, and at the right time roll the drum with the liquid inside down the planks of wood and off the end of the truck, and through the bay window of the house when the two murderers are inside, and kill them both outright."

There was no doubt, what I said shook him. He looked at me, then at the drawing, but didn't say anything, so I repeated:

"The drum and its contents will be like a bomb, they will be delivered at speed off the back of the truck, and rolled through the bay window of their house when both brothers are inside."

Auguste scratched his head in his usual manner but still didn't say anything.

"The reason we recently went to England was to find these two brothers. We not only found them, we made absolutely sure they were the ones who killed our precious twins. We also found where they lived, and spied on them for three days from an isolated house in the woods. By doing this, we discovered without any doubt they were the two who had carried out the murders."

I only had a moment's hesitation then continued.

"This next time we go to England we will stay in this isolated house, and carry out our plan. There is also a garage like this one along the far side of the garden and there are two large round forty-five-gallon steel drums in one corner, one of which is empty. Also scattered about the garage are cans and bottles containing various forms of very volatile liquid. All this is there waiting to be used."

Auguste looked at me in disbelief, then again at the drawing on the bench.

Unrelenting, I continued: "I have found a lot of long scaffolding planks on the grass outside the house, which we are going to fit to form the slope for the drum to run down. We can position some of them to stick out the back of the truck and use them as a battering ram, to blast our way through the double glazed window and propel the drum through the hole we make."

I replaced the drawing on the bench with another and gave further explanation.

"This one is a detailed drawing of what we are going to make and fit into the back of the pick-up."

This one was less complicated than the first; he didn't say anything just became more interested.

"Everything we take to England we must bring back; we must not, under any circumstances, leave anything behind. We must try our best not to give anybody any evidence of our presence there."

He shook his head from side to side, smiled a broad smile then did the same again. No further words were spoken as he absorbed the details of the drawing in front of him.

"Once we start getting things in place, you will see how it all fits together. We need other timber to build a base in the back and timbers for a goal post affair and two straps to secure the drum onto the top, also packets of large screws, and a screw-gun."

"I have lots of straps," he said, "and I know where to go to get everything on this list. How about we make a start."

It was a good idea, we drove about twenty kilometres to a very large store selling everything. We bought the items we needed without any complication and arrived back at the garage within a couple of hours.

It was necessary to build a timber platform in the cargo bay in the back of the pick-up to support the scaffolding planks and made it just a little higher than the sides of the truck. We constructed it like a stage with a storage space underneath, sawing it to the correct length to allow us to replace the tailgate. One set of scaffolding planks at the spy house would eventually be placed on top of the platform.

"We'll need to wedge it in place solidly so it can't move. Can you make some wooden wedges?" I asked.

He set about this and hammered them in place. When we had finished this section, it appeared a substantial structure and very much looked the part.

I then said, "Next, we want to construct the goal-post affair to stand up behind the cab. This will support the steel drum and the sloping scaffolding planks running from the top of the cab to the back of the truck."

We made the goal-post affair and screwed it in place. Later we would take it apart and stow it under the platform – already made would make it a lot easier and quicker to assemble when we arrive in England.

We stood back and agreed it was time for some lunch.

# Chapter Forty-Four

It was while we were sitting in his little kitchen having bread and soup, I approached him about the business of the sale of the property.

"I have a proposal for you," I said.

He looked at me enquiringly.

"Daphers and I have rung the owners of this house and garage, and they have agreed to let us buy it."

This stunned him somewhat. He stood up and appeared quite frantic as if he didn't understand.

"You mean you are going to buy the garage, and the house as well?"

He blurted this out with his eyes wide open, throwing his arms in the air like a typical Frenchman, walking backwards and forwards across the room in a very irate manner.

"Yes, everything," I said, and calmly put my arms out, encouraging him to sit down.

I looked at him and knew without a doubt I had approached the whole thing the wrong way. I kept my arms out slowly and deliberately, trying my best to settle him down.

"Listen to me a minute. We don't want the property, we would like you to continue to live here all the time, and work the garage. We don't want to live here."

He pondered this for a moment. It seemed to pacify him a bit, and he sat down. I sat opposite him, sure I'd gone about this the wrong way – maybe a more gentle approach would have been better.

I repeated: "We want you to continue living here as before, exactly the same."

I stopped and let him take it in. It seemed to work for his eyes went back to normal.

"We would like you to look after both cars for us, and to look after the house and the garden exactly as you did before. What do you say?"

The expression on his face went from misunderstanding to nearly understanding and finally to jubilation. He put his hand out for me to shake, but it was a shake of slight disbelief.

Tentatively he asked, "Are you going to live here as well?"

I shook my head unable to conceal a broad grin, it nearly developed into a laugh.

"No, no, Daphers and I are going to live in Spain. You can live here forever and do with it what you want. We ask you only to pay for the electricity, water and house taxes, that's all."

With exuberance he exclaimed, "I've always paid them."

Then innocently he enquired, "What about rent? Can I pay the same as I used to pay?"

"No, we don't want any rent, thank you."

His face was a picture. "C'est pas possible," (that is not possible) "I must pay something."

"We will talk about it later." An unpreventable smile appeared on my face.

He was shocked and went very quiet. He shook his head a few times from side to side, peered about the room, drank the remainder of his glass of wine, poured another and drank that. I watched and waited.

At last, he stood up, beamed and said, "Let's get on."

He strode back into the garage with renewed enthusiasm. We studied the second drawing, which depicted the whole timber construction on the back of the pick-up. He pointed to the scaffolding planks sloping from the top of the goal-post down to the back of the pick-up.

"I have some similar planks to those at the side of the garagel we could try them in position if you want?"

I thought this a great idea, and we brought them into the garage. They were indeed similar, to the ones in England, and would give us an idea of how things would look and work. First, we laid some along the platform base we had already fitted, protruding them out of the back of the pick-up, over and past the tail-gate. Then we positioned the other planks sloping them from the top timber beam of the goal post above the cab to the end of the pick-up. On completion, we stepped back and surveyed our handiwork, it seemed a lot bigger in reality than on the drawing.

Auguste was a little in awe of the size and he spoke my thoughts. "It's big, isn't it? And we haven't put the drum in place yet."

"Yes," I said in agreement. "It is big," and I took another step back. The structure now on the back was like a child's slide, only bigger with a very steep slope.

"We'll try the drum in position tomorrow."

He turned his head towards me.

"We will never get the cover over the back of the truck if we take the drum as well."

"No, no." I said. "Don't forget there is a drum in the barn at the house in England, we will use that."

"Oh good," he replied, becoming more knowledgeable of the situation.

"When we take all the goal-post timbers apart, hopefully, they will all fit in the space under the platform we built in the back of the pick-up." I said this with a certain amount of trepidation. "I'll leave the drawings with you. We need a rubber bung or wooden bung to fit securely in the filling hole in the side of the drum, some strong rope and do you see these straps holding the drum in place at the top above the cab? We need two for tomorrow to do a trial run, also we need something for Daphers to sit on, inside the back, under those temporary diagonal scaffolding planks; possibly a wooden box."

Auguste looked directly at me, completely startled with an expression on his face of total disbelief.

He went over and pointed directly into the triangular space under the sloping planks. He then stared at me and grimaced in mental objection.

"She's not going to sit under there, with a forty-five-gallon drum full of volatile explosive liquid over her head?"

For me, this was a moment of complete despair. I'd thought about this for a long time, but I couldn't think of any other way of doing what we wanted to do. I stroked my chin with my right hand, screwed up my face and softly uttered:

"There is no other way. I've sat for ages and ages and thought about it long and hard and even been in torture thinking about it, but I can't come up with any other solution."

Still, with a startled look on his face, Auguste repeated:

"All that highly dangerous volatile liquid is going to be sitting in the forty-five-gallon drum directly above her head. Are you sure she will be alright?"

I bowed my head and my hand let go of my chin.

"I can't think of any other way of killing these two brothers."

He shook his head slowly from side to side and scratched it. We stood looking at each other, I sensed he wanted to say more, and eventually, he muttered:

"I hope you know what you are doing."

It was one of those moments when doubt could have crept through a crack in my determination. I looked back at the structure, then turned to him.

"We shall see what Daphers says tomorrow."

He stared at me in amazement.

"Are you telling me she knows nothing about this. Are you saying she doesn't know she is going to sit inside that tiny space with all that lethal liquid above her head?"

I puffed out my cheeks.

"Yes, I'm afraid she is going to sit under all that lethal liquid, and she doesn't know anything about it."

He scratched his head with both hands, held out his hand for me to shake, then with resolution said:

"I'll have the straps, the box and everything else ready in the morning at eight o'clock."

# Chapter Forty-Five

I solemnly and slowly walked, or rather dawdled home, with a lot of serious thoughts in my head. Was I asking too much of Daphers? Was it far too dangerous for her? What if things went wrong, I wasn't fearful at all for myself, but if anything happened to Daphers I would never be able to forgive or live with myself.

When I arrived she greeted me, and I relayed the day's progress to her. She must have spotted something in my manner for in a concerned voice she said:

"Are you all right?"

I quickly replied, "Yes."

I saw her staring at me, so rather quickly went into a detailed account of how the day with

Auguste had gone, relaying what we had done to the pick-up.

When I finished she enquired, "When will you need me? I really would like to get involved."

"Don't worry," I said. "You'll get involved alright. Can you come to the garage at about two o'clock tomorrow?"

"Yes, she said, "I think I can make that."

After collecting papers in the office I asked her if she could arrange two rooms in a hotel, in the usual place halfway up France for Thursday night, then said:

"If you do that, I will organise the ferry to go to England on Friday and come back on Sunday."

She looked at me. "I thought we were going in a week's time, suddenly it's a few days. What happened?"

"Everything went surprisingly quickly and slipped into place. Oh, and Auguste eventually liked the idea about his house."

"Why eventually?"

"He misunderstood in the beginning, but in the end, he was delighted."

"Mm, that's good. What sort of hotel do you want, just run of the mill nondescript?"

"Yes please," I responded. "From now until Sunday, which is when we arrive back here, everything has got to be run-of-the-mill; we don't want anything to happen out of the ordinary."

She intervened. "What about clothes? Do you want a minimum number? If so, we had better wear a wind jacket of some description. By the way, what about food?"

"Yes, a minimum change of clothes, take only one bag between us, the same as before. On Thursday we will have an early lunch before we leave, eat in the hotel Thursday night and on Friday morning have lunch on the ferry. Hopefully, we will have a celebratory breakfast or lunch on the ferry on Sunday morning coming home."

She deliberated for quite a while. "I think I've got that. Don't forget, we left tea and coffee there. I'll put an extra few things in a cool bag and put it in the back seat of the pick-up."

I added: "We don't want to stop anywhere in England for petrol or any kind of shopping. Hopefully, we will only make two stops, one to call Mrs Ramsbottom on a payphone, and the other to call at her house, pay her and collect the keys. When you go, it is very important you tell her when we leave we will put the keys back through the letterbox and switch everything off. I want her and everybody else to keep away from the place for as long as possible after we depart, to reduce our chances of being caught. The minimum number of people who know of our presence, the better."

She wrinkled her brow, and probably for the second time, realised how serious this was going to get.

"You have planned this to the final detail."

A smile released itself. "There is every chance it will be all right; the only problem we will get, is if the unforeseen happens, but let's hope it doesn't."

I refused to say, if we left evidence, or if we were found out, we would spend the rest of our days in prison.

Whilst we were having supper and before we went to bed I reminded her to come to the garage at 2 o'clock, and she replied she was looking forward to it.

The following morning over a cup of tea I asked Daphers to invite Louis and Nicole for supper in the evening, so we could at least tell someone we were going back to England.

I took my time sauntering round to the garage. Auguste was waiting in the small kitchen with a cup of coffee and a beaming smile on his face. He shook my hand warmly.

"Are we nearing our trip to England?" he enquired.

"Yes!" I said. "We go tomorrow. Can you take a change of clothes, we will stay in a French hotel on Thursday night, take the ferry on Friday and come back on Sunday. Is that OK?"

"Yes," he replied and stood up. "Well, if that's the case, we had better get on. I've got the straps and the rope ready, and I've cleaned an old empty forty-five-gallon oil drum to try it in position. I know we are not going to use this one, but it might help in setting things up. I've fitted the steel plug in the small hole at the end of the drum and I have found a rubber plug to fit in the other larger hole. We can take them with us to England."

We moved into the garage. The structure on the back of the pick-up had not reduced in size; if anything, it was looking bigger. He brought the two strong woven adjustable straps to the bench. They were the type used for securing heavy loads on lorries.

I gave instructions. "We need to roll the drum up the diagonal planks, right to the top, then throw each strap over the drum, then fasten it to a wooden beam underneath where the quick release mechanism will be fitted in position."

He scratched his head. "We haven't got a wooden beam or a quick-release mechanism in there."

"Yes, I know. We can only do that when we find the right position for it. Let's try it now, if we get everything ready, we may be able to fix things in the approximate position. If you help me, I'll push the drum up the diagonals, then you can scramble up onto the top of the cab and screw one end of each strap in place."

We found it wasn't easy, and required the small steps to be positioned at the back end of the truck for me to clamber onto the wooden platform structure we fitted yesterday. Manoeuvring the drum was difficult, but together we managed to roll it all the way up the slope finally settling it at the top of the diagonal planks close to the top of the cab.

Auguste, with the aid of the steps, climbed on to the top of the cab, and screwed each strap in the right position, then threw them over the drum. We needed to know where to fix the quick-release mechanism for Daphers to operate. He then quizzically looked at me again, I winced and knew what he was thinking; it was another of those moments. Without any more glances, he descended down the ladder from the top of the cab, shuffled himself through the triangular hole under the diagonal timbers, and sat down with his back to the cab.

"Right," he said. "Can you push the straps down to me, so I can get hold of them." There was a pause. "Right I have them, do you want the two together?"

"Yes, when we make it, we'll push the quick-release bar through the eye of both straps, so when

Daphers is there under the drum, she only has one bar to pull out."

"Ah," he said. "I see what happens now. When she pulls the bar out of the eyes of the straps, it will release the drum and allow it to roll down the diagonal planks with some force, and off the end of the truck."

I got a small boost of confidence from that remark, one which I badly needed.

"Yes. It is fairly heavy now, but when we have highly inflammable liquid inside, it will be a lot heavier, and when it is released it will gather speed very quickly and depart off the end of the truck with a lot of force, smashing its way through the lounge window of their house."

He mumbled something which I didn't understand, probably realising, for the first time, what we were going to do.

He shouted, "I've taken measurements from these temporary diagonal scaffolding planks, and marked where the beam has to be positioned, also the length of the beam and where the hole for the quick release bar should be."

"That's great. If we make the quick release assembly here in France it will save a lot of time in England. We are about finished now, this drum is getting heavy; can you crawl out from under there and put the steps at the back of the truck, so I can come down?"

I heard him shuffling about and finally saw him appear at the side of the truck and descend the steps.

He did as asked, and slowly I allowed the drum to roll back down the incline. It certainly was steep, I had a struggle keeping it in check because it wanted to run away, which was pleasing. In the end, I descended the steps, and we lifted the drum off the truck on to the floor.

I remarked, "Daphers is coming at two o'clock, we need to make the wooden assembly for the quick-release mechanism and the rod."

"OK," he said, "I have the measurements."

He cut a measured piece of timber, drilled a hole through it in the correct place, then fashioned a round 'L' shaped steel bar to fit the hole. He crawled through the diagonal hole again and temporarily screwed the assembly in place. I couldn't stop myself from looking at it, and speaking out loud.

"When Daphers pulls the bar out of the hole, the straps will be released, which in turn will release the drum, allowing it, and its contents, to crash down the incline and off the end of the truck with such almighty force, it will blast whatever is in front of it out of the way."

Auguste crawled out of the hole and stepped back onto the floor and blinked his eyes, scratched his head, possibly in disbelief, then nonchalantly said, "I think it is now time for some soup."

# Chapter Forty-Six

Lunch was carried out in a hurry. When we finished Daphers met us, bristling with enthusiasm and raring to go, wearing an old jumper and an old pair of trousers. As we three walked into the garage, she stopped abruptly as soon as she saw the truck with all the timbers sloping down the back of the cargo bay.

"Wow, it's very big isn't it?"

That's all she said, then wandered around the other side, stared at it, then walked back to where we were.

I whispered to her in English: "It's going to get bigger, but first, my love, can you go round to the back of the truck and stand for me to see if things are all at the right height."

She went to the back of the truck and stood.

I assessed it. "Yes, it's all at the right height; and before you ask, do you remember when we went along the street that day, and you walked on the other side of the road past the front of the semi-detached house?"

She nodded.

"Well it was to measure the height of the bottom of the windowsill at the front of the house. It just so happened it was slightly above your waist."

"Oh," she said and raised herself into a little pose.

"It is vitally important to hit just above the bottom windowsill with the very strong scaffolding planks sticking out of the back of the pick-up, so the whole of the glass will crash into the lounge, and the drum and its contents will follow it."

"What drum?" she exclaimed.

It was time to give another explanation.

"A forty-five-gallon drum sits up there above the cab, on top of those timbers, where it is held in place by straps."

She looked up with a curious and somewhat bewildered expression on her face.

I continued. "The drum will be filled with highly inflammable liquid, and you are going to sit in the back of the pick-up underneath the sloping scaffolding planks with the drum at the top."

I then pointed to the triangular hole made by the sloping timbers.

"You are going to sit inside there through that triangular hole. When we ram the front of the house with the scaffolding planks sticking out of the back of the truck, it will smash the double glazed window to pieces, that's when you will pull on the handle, just at the right time, and release the drum, and it will smash its way into their lounge."

I waved my arms about indicating the drum rolling down the slope and off the end of the truck.

The moment I finished my demonstration I knew I had said the whole explanation all wrong.

There was a deathly silence about the place. Auguste didn't understand what I was saying but followed the progress and rubbed his forehead as usual. Daphers stood and looked to where the timbers jutted out and protruded up above the cab.

It was one of those very awkward silent moments. I tried my best to alleviate the situation by further saying:

"When the drum goes through the window the inflammable liquid will spill out and the whole thing will explode. By the time that happens, I will have put the truck into first gear and driven off like hell, out of the way down the road."

She stared at me.

"What about the little hole and the bigger hole at the end of the drum? I've seen the drums in garages, the liquid will come out all over me."

I explained further: "We will screw a plug tightly in the little hole so nothing will come out, and we have a rubber bung to fit in the big hole, to stop anything coming out before the time is right."

"Well, how is the highly inflammable liquid going to come out when the drum hits the lounge?"

Again more explanation: "We will attach the bung to a strong rope, and when the drum enters the lounge at full speed the rope will go taut and the bung will fly out and then, and only then, will the inflammable liquid escape out of the drum."

Daphers stared at the truck in front of her. It continued to be one of those moments, only this one was worse than all the others put together. She went round to the other side of the truck and stared at the other side. Auguste and I stood and waited in silence. I indicated to him with a shrug of my shoulder, that I didn't know what decision she was going to be make. She then returned to where we were standing, and looked at the top of the sloping timbers going down the back of the pick-up truck then at us, and poignantly said:

"The drum will be high up at the top, right up there above the cab."

I nodded.

"And I will be sitting directly underneath it, through that hole there," and she pointed to the triangular hole.

I nodded again.

She then said, "Where's the forty-five-gallon drum?"

"It's in the barn in England, but we have one here exactly the same."

"Let me see it," she said, and we all walked over to where the drum was standing. "It's big, isn't it? You will put dangerously inflammable liquid in it, and you will plug these holes as you say?"

"Yes, tight as we can," I said.

Auguste and I did nothing, we just stood and waited. Although she spoke in English, from Auguste's facial features I saw he got the general gist of what she was saying.

After what seemed like an eternity, she said:

"Is there no other way?"

"No, love, there is no other sure way of killing these two together, many rival gangs I understand have tried and failed. This is a sure-fire way."

In this very serious moment, I didn't mean to make a pun, it just came out, but it alleviated the situation. I tried my best to resist a smile and just managed it.

Daphers looked at Auguste then at me.

"Right, Matthew, if there is no other way, I am with you one-hundred-percent. What do you want me to do?"

# Chapter Forty-Seven

She had spoken in English so I looked at Auguste, and gave him a half-smile and raised my brow indicating that she had agreed to go along with the plan. Relief flooded through us both, for without Daphers the whole thing would have folded completely. I breathed a sigh and puffed my cheeks out. She saw this and smiled.

I took hold of her hand. "Let's have a dress rehearsal."

"OK. Do you want me to go in there?" pointing to the triangular hole.

"Yes, use those steps and crawl in underneath the timbers and sit down facing the back of the truck."

With enthusiasm, she did as I asked. She was smaller than Auguste and found scrambling over the side of the truck and into the space easier.

Then came the call. "I want a box or something to sit on."

Auguste piped up. "I've got a wooden empty toolbox, it might be the right size."

He scurried off, found it, brought it and pushed it through the hole; Daphers manoeuvred it into position and sat on it.

Then, hearing her say, "that's better," I poked my head through the hole. "Can you see the round steel rod handle in front of you?" She looked up and got hold of it.

"Right," I said, "pull it out of the hole."

She did it exclaiming, "It's a bit stiff."

Still, with my head poked through the hole, I explained:

"Don't worry, we will make it easier when we fit it properly in England, we will put grease in the hole."

"What now?" she said wanting to get on with it.

"We are going to climb onto the back of the truck and push the empty drum up the slope."

She nodded.

With Daphers in position, Auguste and I went round the back of the truck and wheeled the empty forty-five-gallon drum along the floor, lifted it onto the timbers in the back of the truck, then clambered on after it. We rolled the drum up the sloping timbers right to the top of the cab and placed the straps over the drum, then passed them underneath to Daphers below.

I leaned over and spoke to her. "Can you push the rod back through the hole and put it through the eyes of the straps?"

She grasped the straps one at a time, and with a certain amount of dexterity held them together, then pushed the rod through the hole and further on through the eyes of the straps.

"I've done what you told me," she enthused.

"Brilliant," I said, unable to think of a better word. "Can you just sit there?"

"Yes," came the reply.

I turned to Auguste. "Can you adjust the straps so they are tight around the drum? I'll hold on to it."

"Right I've done that," he said.

From my position holding the drum, I bent around the side of the timbers to talk to Daphers. "Can you pull the rod out?"

She was already gripping it. She tried to pull it out of its hole, "No," she said.

"Give it a good yank."

As I finished the words, she gave it a good pull, and the drum released itself and nearly knocked me off the back of the truck. Fortunately, I managed to steady it just in time.

"It works," she shouted.

Auguste and I beamed a big smile at each other. I inhaled and breathed out a sigh of relief. Yes, it worked.

I waltzed the drum further down the slope. Auguste descended the ladder from the cab and helped me lift it onto the floor.

I went round to the triangular hole, carrying the steps, and peered in. Daphers was sitting there inside. "It worked," she said again.

"Yes," I said. "Do you want to come out?"

She shuffled along the wooden timbers front first and came down the steps facing forward. I helped her by taking both her hands and she ended up in my arms.

Auguste remained at a discreet distance, we saw him, and by opening our arms, invited him in. For a long time, we held a silent trio hug. It lasted for ages, then eventually, we broke free. All three of us stood and looked at the contraption in front of us.

When Daphers had been sitting underneath the drum, she had obviously been thinking again of all the inflammable liquid directly above her head, for she said:

"Can you tell me again about the bung?"

I gestured to Auguste to explain how the bung works and he instantly came forward.

"Yes, yes, I have a rubber stopper that fits exactly in the larger of the two holes at the end of the drum and while it is tight in the hole, none of the liquid will come out. I will tie a very strong rope to the eye screwed in the stopper, the other end of the rope I will fasten to the end of the truck. When you pull out the rod to release the drum, it will roll down the slope, and when it blasts its way into the room the rope will tighten and the stopper will fly out."

He then went and positioned himself by the side of the truck, and with his arms waving about he gesticulated elaborately indicating the passage of the drum down the slope and the position of the rope.

He then looked at Daphers and saw a query in her expression so he explained further.

"When the drum gets to here," and he pointed to a space some three or four feet after the end of the truck.

"This is where the end of the scaffolding planks will be when we fit them, and by then they will have blasted the double-glazed window to pieces and be inside the house. At this point, the rope will go taut and the bung will fly out, and all the stuff inside the drum will go into the room."

Everything went silent, so he added: "Boom, it will blow the bastards up."

To hear him swear in English was odd, it brought a huge grin to everyone's face including Daphers, who had a little chuckle. She then held her hands up in a gesture of curiosity.

"What will start the fire? What will start the explosion?"

I had pondered this question for some time.

"There are three things that will start the fire. We know there is electricity in the lounge, we have seen lights and flashing from the television; that would possibly be enough. We have seen smoke coming from the chimney, so they must light a fire at night, that would be more than enough."

I paused.

After a while, Auguste enquired, "You said there were three things?"

"Ah yes, the third thing; one of us has to light and throw a Molotov Cocktail into the lounge as well."

There was another pause.

"Well it's not me, because I'm under there," said Daphers, nodding towards the triangular hole.

"And I'm driving," I said.

I met the eyes of Auguste and noticed they were not afraid; as a matter of fact, a tiny smile appeared on his face, a smile that told me everything.

I agreed wholeheartedly with the smile. "That's about it for the day then."

"Yes, you go," said Auguste. "I'll take it all apart and pack everything into the back. We don't require the drum or the scaffolding planks, they are all in England?"

I nodded my head. "They are in England."

Our departure featured more of a hug than a handshake, and an agreement to return the following day at around twelve.

# Chapter Forty-eight

Daphers and I strolled home to our new residence, very slowly, arm in arm. It was the strangest of feelings, we were going to do this thing. Three ordinary people who obeyed and respected the law and all it stood for, were going to kill two men and at the moment were very pleased to do so. There was no turning back.

We had dinner with Louis and Nicole in the evening. Daphers made a story about going back to England to see old friends. She also told them, as Auguste had never been to England before, he was going with us to see what England was like. The meal was beautiful with plenty of wine, which nicely sealed the evening, and later encouraged us to sleep.

The following morning, after an early lunch, we walked with bag in hand round to join Auguste in the garage. The pick-up was prepared with all the equipment tucked away in the back hidden under the cover, which was exactly what I had hoped for.

After the normal greeting, I asked, "Is everything in?"

"Yes," came the reply, "everything's in and I've put my travel bag on the back seat." Ours joined his on the back seat and I dropped into the driver's seat, Daphers sat in the passenger seat. I drove forward to allow Auguste to close and lock his garage.

The roads on Thursdays were never particularly busy in France, and we made excellent progress to the hotel. The following morning, we boarded the ferry, ate, bought more food and by way of the ferry ramp entered the roads in Dover. At the first supermarket, Daphers phoned Mrs Ramsbottom about keys, money, and how long we wanted to stay, informing her when we left we would switch everything off, lock up, then finally put the keys through the letterbox.

On her arrival back from the shop, I noticed she had a full carrier bag.

She saw me eyeing it. "Mainly food," she said. "Oh and by the way, I've been thinking, why couldn't I just use the mobile?"

"I don't know, it didn't seem right somehow," was my paltry reply.

Auguste, in the back seat, hadn't spoken for a while, and it suddenly dawned on me, Daphers and I were now speaking English. I translated: we were now going to collect the keys for the spy house and to pay Mrs Ramsbottom for renting it.

I saw his nod of acknowledgement in the truck rear-view mirror.

# Chapter Forty-nine

We left the supermarket car park and headed for the house of Mrs Ramsbottom and I slowed down, wanting to find a place to park which was as discreet as possible. It was not easy with this pick-up truck. Fortunately, on our approach, we found what looked like an empty house on the corner a little distance away. I drove along at a snail's pace and parked by the kerb.

It was decided from discussions earlier, Daphers was the best person to go and see the old lady, do the business then return to the car as quickly as possible. As she grasped the door handle I couldn't stop myself from making some last-minute suggestions.

"Can we go through things again, please? It is important."

This was met with not the greatest response, but without a word, she sat and listened to me.

"Give her the money first, then get the keys. Tell her what we will do when we leave so there is no need for us to return."

"Yes, I won't forget anything, and I've got extra cash if needed." She then got out of the car and set off along the road.

Auguste and I watched her go, having no idea why because it was a simple journey, in an ordinary street. Mrs Ramsbottom's house was a lot further than we thought, but finally, without glancing back, Daphers turned left into the small garden, halted for a time at the door, then entered.

In the beginning, we both sat patiently waiting in the car, but as time passed we started to fidget, as men do. By the time the door of the house opened again, we were at the nervous stage, fidgeting a lot and saying, 'what is she doing in there?'.

Daphers eventually came out, casually walked along the pavement, opened the car door and sat down on the passenger seat.

"Everything all right?" I said, as nonchalantly as possible.

"Yes," she said.

Putting the car in gear I drove off quietly and slowly down the street. Both Auguste and I were sitting there, wanting to ask a lot of questions about what had happened, but we both resisted.

Leaving the gaggle of houses behind, Daphers opened up.

"She liked the money very much and asked if we would be going again. Nobody had been up there since our last visit, and putting the keys through the letterbox would be fine."

"Marvellous, you were a long time, we wondered if something was wrong?"

"No, I don't think she gets out a lot, and she doesn't see other women, she wanted to gossip, told me all about her ailments. You know, women's things."

I glanced in the mirror at Auguste, he hadn't understood a word. I thought of explaining but came to the conclusion it wasn't necessary. This jolted my memory and I wondered whether it was essential for me to tell him about the death in the spy house of Mrs Ramsbottom's sister, and the fact she had died of leprosy. Here was a man who was going to carry out the murder with us, and I was resisting telling him the facts.

I couldn't help thinking of the moral judgment by me, of not giving him the full information about the person who originally lived in the house. The complexity of the translation and explanation would take a lot of time and could be misunderstood. The possibility of any of us catching leprosy was remote, and telling him could maybe plant a complicated seed of doubt in his mind. At this late stage in these dangerous but essential proceedings, it was something we could well do without.

After a lot of thought, I decided not to say anything.

We motored along in silence, maybe all in the thought of what was to come. As we approached the village, I took the familiar left-hand turn and drove up and along the gravel path, parked by the side of the barn, and switched the engine off quickly to reduce the noise level. There was a small amount of light left in the day, hopefully enough to drive the truck into the barn and position it in the right spot.

Turning around I spoke to Auguste who was already looking around through the windows.

"We have parked next to the barn; the spy house is behind us."

He nodded and turned round to look at the house.

"First we take the bags into the house, then we shunt the car into the garage," adding, "as quiet as possible."

Daphers was quickly out of the car, taking her handbag and opening the front door with the keys.

I stood momentarily outside, noticing all the curtains in the windows of the house still closed, then turned and watched the leaves on the trees rustling in the strong wind. It would be challenging to detect any noise up here, from down below, which was very good for us indeed.

Auguste and I took the rest of the bags inside through the front door. The food and drink we left in the kitchen, the other bags we took upstairs. I showed Auguste into the right-hand bedroom, he dumped his bag in there and immediately returned downstairs.

After putting the bag of Daphers and myself in the left-hand bedroom, I took time out to stand and survey the room in the darkness. There was only a faint shaft of light in the far corner, squeezing its way through a nick in the thick curtain. At that moment, a strange tingling feeling came over me, and the whole room felt dreadfully, dreadfully menacing and alarming. The house was the same as we had left it, nothing had been touched, but this room was unerringly sinister. It was a difficult, awful moment, one of those sensing beyond belief moments, as if someone had been here in the house, as if someone had been inside this room, not touching anything, just strolling about. Was it possible, someone in the houses below had seen us, climbed up here, managed to get in, and walk about inside the house after we left? Knowing those people, surely they would have stolen things, or disturbed things or smashed things. No, it was something else. I considered what had happened in this house all those years ago, the woman who had died, the loneliness she must have endured during all that time, and when she was gone, the empty house standing by itself, no one visiting, no one to rouse, move or displace anything. Was this possibly the same as the unknown sailor found dead, kneeling in prayer, trapped in isolation in the anchor chain locker, in the bow of the ship? The crew on voyages forever after, hearing the sound of the clanking of the chains, when the sea was calm as a millpond, and nobody up in the forward end of the ship disturbing anything.

The hairs on the back of my neck started to dance about, I smoothed them down with the palm of my hand and felt unerring dampness, then inadvertently placed my hand on my forehead, surprisingly feeling sweat on my brow, yet the room was cold. It was a strange, uncomfortable feeling. I remained standing stock still, only my eyes roaming and searching about the room, patiently waiting for the awareness of some other sense to pass away. It left me at the end of my fingertips, and I unconsciously responded to it by rubbing my hands together. The whole episode ended with me being completely relaxed, although feeling very, very strange. I closed my eyes and waited and waited. Eventually, I returned to the moment, and stared about the room taking time out just to do nothing.

I came out of this haze by unintentionally looking down in the darkness and noticing the binoculars in the bag. I took a pair out and made my way into the right-hand bedroom, pausing at the top of the landing, and whisperingly shouted for Auguste to come upstairs.

When he entered the bedroom, I parted the curtain ever so slightly and pointed. "One of the brothers lives there in that end terrace house across the road, we can just see it from up here without the binoculars."

A shiver came over me, on seeing the front door of the spitting brother's house once again, but with difficulty I managed to continue my words.

"It is the last house on the right, across the road."

He trained his eyes where I indicated.

"Yes, I see it," he said and we closed the curtain.

He followed me into the other bedroom, but before parting the curtain I explained.

"This time we will see the back garden of the other house. It is the semi-detached one with the sort of static caravan on the left. This is the one we are going to blow up, only we are going to blow it up from the front."

He was slightly keener to view this one, and parted the curtain deliberately, studying it for a long time. I also took the opportunity to scan the scene below. Nothing was happening, there was a car parked in front of the static caravan, but no movement of people.

Finally, he closed the curtain. "What about the semi-detached house connected to it, won't we blow that up as well and possibly kill other people?"

"No, the house next to it is empty, nobody lives there at all, anyway after the initial explosion, which will produce more flames than anything else, it will be the fire, the heat and the smoke that will cause all the damage; the house will stay intact. The volatile liquid pouring out of the drum will burn very quickly, and with tremendous sustained force, everybody in the room will burn along with it. They will be unable to escape."

When I finished speaking he hesitated, then hesitated again.

For the first time, I think he saw in pictures what was involved. It was a tense moment, it crossed my mind maybe he was thinking, he couldn't do this. For me it was easy, I had seen the dreadful criminal acts inflicted by these two, they deserved all they were going to get. I was more determined than ever.

This time he put the binoculars to his eyes and looked down at the house again. I decided it was best to leave him and let him watch the house for a while. I went back downstairs.

# Chapter Fifty

Daphers had made a cup of tea and was sitting at the table in the kitchen. As I entered she looked up at me and noticed the expression on my face. I sat down beside her.

"Is everything all right?" she asked.

I replied with slight disdain:

"I have explained to him in detail what we intend to do, and since then he hasn't said very much; maybe he's having second thoughts."

She put a hand on my shoulder.

"Ah, the reality of the situation has struck. When you first told me what you intended, I had the same thoughts." She half-smiled. "He has seen the house and the street so it's all real now. Maybe he needs a few moments like I needed a few moments."

We began getting things ready, but mainly we sat and waited for Auguste to come downstairs. I got a bit fidgety.

"We really should put the pick-up in the barn and start to assemble things."

She smiled. "Give him more time, give him a little longer."

We waited and waited. Eventually, after what seemed like an eternity, we heard footsteps on the stairs.

As he entered the kitchen we both looked up, we didn't mean to, we just couldn't help it. From his facial expression, it was difficult to determine what he was about to say. He knew we were waiting, so he spoke.

"That man down there, 'Mon Dieu', he is a nasty man."

He then uttered words in French, of which I failed to catch the meaning. I glanced at Daphers and she shook her head unable to understand either.

He sat down at the table and announced:

"Some wine would be very good."

I uncorked a bottle and filled three glasses, we all lifted them and drank; he drained his glass completely, I filled it up again.

Daphers and I sat in silence deciding not to ask what he had seen, but to wait for him to tell us, totally unsure he ever would. It must have been horrendous for he was not a squeamish man, he had witnessed brutality before many times; this must have been some sort of viciousness he couldn't or didn't want to speak about.

Standing up I asked, "Can we put the truck in the barn?"

"Yes," he said. "Let's get on with it!" And he grinned and shook his head from side to side.

Outside the wind blew the trees about again, which created just enough disturbance of the leaves to hide any noise. No wonder I liked trees.

I used the keys to open the small barn door. Together Auguste and I rolled the large doors as silently as possible to the fully open position. I climbed into the pick-up and using no lights and a wide turning circle drove nose-first into the barn.

On uncovering the back we discovered the timber base previously fitted hadn't moved, and was still as solid, as a model catwalk. We lowered the tailgate and removed the prepared loose timbers hidden inside and all the ancillary equipment.

Although we couldn't be seen from below, we felt it necessary to creep out to the grassed area in front of the house, pick up the long scaffolding planks and creep back into the barn again. It took several journeys. At this point, we thought it best to as quietly as possible shut the big doors – keeping them closed would reduce any noise we made. I switched on one of the lights and it gave us a tiny glow. It was necessary to wait a moment to get used to the darkness. Four of the scaffolding planks were positioned flat in the back of the truck, along the top of the timber frame and screwed down. These stuck out of the back a long way, which was good for ramming through the double-glazed window. After the timber goalpost had been fitted in position close to the back of the cab, scaffolding planks were erected in the diagonal position, sloping down from above the cab to the end of the truck.

By the time this was finished, it was late. We switched off the light, and exited by the small door and found it was dark outside. Retiring to the house, we ate a lovely dinner, drank lots of wine and went upstairs to the bedrooms with our candles to spy. Auguste and I in the right-hand bedroom with a pair of binoculars each, Daphers in the left-hand bedroom with her small ones. After a while she reported the two youths leaving by car; it was about nine o'clock.

I shouted, "Any sign of the brother?"

"No," she shouted back.

Auguste and I with the candle out, keenly watched the end terrace house. Nothing happened for a long time, then suddenly a light shone through the small window in the front door. We both reached for our binoculars and held our breath. Slowly the door opened and the spitting brother came out, closed the door behind him, then stood looking about.

We levelled our binoculars on him. "Watch him spit," I said.

Right on cue he drew his head back and delivered an enormous chunk of mucus into next door's garden.

"What time is it?" I asked.

"Quarter to ten," Auguste said.

"Yes, they are creatures of habit these two, let's hope they keep the same time tomorrow."

The spitter then walked the short distance down the path onto the road and out of sight, hopefully, and presumably, along to the other brother's house. I nipped through into the other bedroom, trained my binoculars on to the back garden of the semi, saw the light in the kitchen go on, then go out again.

"One of them went into the kitchen for something," said Daphers.

I added, "It might be a couple of beers and a bottle of whisky or both. Tomorrow night the football is on the television, I am banking they will do the same."

We continued spying throughout the evening. Nothing happened until the spitter returned to his own house and the youths came back very late. Eventually, we decided nothing more of any significance was going to occur, so we all retired to our beds.

# Chapter Fifty-one

Daphers was first up the following morning. It was rather chilly and required plenty of clothes to keep warm. By the time I arrived in the kitchen, the other two were sitting at the table drinking tea and eating toast. After greetings and general chat, we got down to the day's very serious proceedings, and the reason why we were there.

It was my turn to speak.

"Everything today must go according to plan. It is very important to get everything ready for tonight. We are only going to get one chance to kill these two brothers and this is it, we must take it, we must not fail."

They both sat and listened with faces of serious intent, and I continued.

"Auguste and I will assemble the complete structure onto the back of the pick-up truck as quietly as possible. When this is about finished I am going to walk the route we will take in the truck tonight, just to make sure there is nothing in the way parked in a silly place."

Immediately Daphers cried out.

"That is too dangerous, Matthew. You can't walk along the road again. What if they see you and recognize you?"

"They won't, it will be dark, and I will walk quickly, I'll be well wrapped up, they will hardly be able to see my face. When I get to their road, I'll walk straight up along the pavement towards the wood then along the path and back here." I looked at her. "I'll be fine. It's got to be done, I'm afraid."

She saw the logic in it and relented. "OK, but when you go be very, very, careful."

"I will. But first, we must complete the assembly of the structure in the back of the pick-up."

She nodded her head in approval and a serious smile appeared.

"Off you go, you two, and don't make too much noise."

Auguste and I went out into a slight wind. Thankfully we could hear the rustle of the leaves in the trees. We closed the small door after entry to stifle any noise. I put the small light on and we began assembling the remaining structure, screwing all the timbers together as quietly as we could.

The work we had carried out in preparation in France paid off, and it wasn't long before we took a step back, and surveyed our handiwork. The flat scaffolding planks were now sticking four feet or more out of the back of the truck, making it look extremely long. The other scaffolding planks were sloping down from above the cab to the end of the truck creating the triangular hole aft of the cab. In the darkish light, the whole thing looked strangely eerie, it was quite a frightening sight.

Auguste spoke up. "I've got a question: why don't we just kill them by going down to the house and throwing two petrol bombs through the window and driving away?"

"Ah, unfortunately, I'm afraid it's not as easy as that, Auguste. We would have to get very near to them, which would be very difficult. Other gangs over the years have tried to rid the world of these two and failed every time. If we threw petrol bombs, none of the bottles would penetrate through the double glazing in the front window and we would ultimately achieve only a load of trouble for ourselves. These two crooks have survived for years by using criminal tricks and sly means. This is the only way."

Still looking at the structure he nodded in agreement. "It is certainly going to surprise them, the shock will probably kill them."

He smiled and turned his face to me. "I think we are ready to roll the drum up to the slope."

It was unexpectedly easy lifting the empty forty-five-gallon steel drum onto the long scaffolding planks sticking out at the back of the pick-up. We clambered on after and pushed it up the sloping planks to the top. I held it there while Auguste screwed one end of the straps in place then threw the two straps over the drum. He went down and crawled in through the triangular hole under the sloping scaffolding planks, and after applying the correct measurement, screwed the prepared wooden quick release mechanism in place. He greased the hole in the wood and pushed the quick-release rod through it, so it protruded through the other side. The rod was then threaded through the eyes of the straps. This enabled the rod when pulled out, to release the straps quickly, allowing the forty-five gallon to roll down the sloping planks with a mighty force and off the end of the truck.

From above the cab I ratcheted the straps tight over the drum, to ensure no movement would take place during the journey tonight down to the semi-detached house. Auguste checked everything and shouted, "OK."

After clambering off the back of the pick-up truck I stared back at the whole assembly.

In front of me was a true monster, much longer and higher than it had ever been before, with the forty five-gallon drum poised right at the top.

I put my hand to my head in amazement and mumbled.

"The next task is the most difficult one of all: we need to fill the drum with all this inflammable liquid."

Auguste lifted his finger in the air and raised an eyebrow.

"I've been thinking about that," he said and went over to his tool bag and opened it; inside was a selection of pipes, funnels and other pieces of equipment.

"It is important we don't spill a drop, as any volatile liquid is very dangerous; working in a garage by myself I learned the importance of preventing fire, and the possible damage it can cause. The gear in this bag will hopefully help, and prevent us from setting alight to ourselves."

Auguste placed the ladder in position at the side of the pick-up to enable him to work upon the flat end of the forty-five-gallon drum. He climbed up and made sure the small plug in the bottom of the drum was screwed in tightly. The larger hole in the flat end we had deliberately positioned at the top of the drum and he commenced fastening his pipe and funnel assembly into this larger hole. When he felt all was right, we fastidiously and patiently began to fill the drum with petrol and diesel from the jerry cans. To sustain a prolonged burn, and to create a substantial amount of heat and flames very quickly, we also added an amount of lamp oil.

Space was left inside the drum for the gases to accumulate, so upon escaping the whole liquid assembly would explode immediately. With this concoction inside there would be no escape for these two murderers.

Auguste removed his pipes and funnel and fitted his specially prepared rubber bung in place. He was most meticulous, making sure no inflammable liquid would escape until the right time. He tied one end of the strong rope we had brought, to the bung, and the other end he tied to the back of the truck, ensuring the bung would be pulled out as the drum entered through the lounge window.

"That's just about it," he said and we stood back and admired the sight.

The pick-up truck was now a very dangerous piece of equipment. It looked ugly, monstrous and out of all proportion. It was now a destructive mobile bomb that was going to be driven by me.

I slowly took my eyes away from the grotesque object and asked Auguste:

"Can you fill a bottle with petrol to make a Molotov cocktail? If I do the driving tonight, can you throw it through the window after the drum?"

"That will be no problem, I will do that," he replied with such enthusiasm, it made me wonder again what he had seen, at that time – it must have been horrendous.

I ventured, "Let's go back into the house and have something to eat?"

Afterwards, Auguste worked inside the barn and finished off bits and pieces. I started my reconnaissance walk, along the path, and down the road to the village, maintaining a brisk pace; turning left and left again then walking past both houses with not even a curtain-twitching. I was pleased there was nothing out of the ordinary, nothing in the way on any of the roads. As I entered the wood to return to the house, I was unable to stop a prolonged angry, teeth clenched smile from arriving and staying on my lips. Tonight would definitely and certainly be the end of these two terrible drug-dealing killers.

# Chapter Fifty-two

When I arrived back at the spy house it was late and darkness was falling rapidly. My mind, when walking through the wood, had been hovering on the question, whether it would be an advantage for tonight's vital raid to have light from the moon. No moon meant less chance of being seen on our escape journey back along the road to the safety of the barn. Whereas a full moon meant it would be far easier for me to gauge the run up to the front of the semi-detached house, before reversing the truck and ramming the scaffolding planks sticking out the back through the double glazed window just at the right spot. On reflection I came to the conclusion we would have to settle for whatever the moon fancied doing tonight.

On entering the kitchen I saw Daphers had dinner ready. We all discussed and agreed, it was best not to have any wine before tonight's well-planned but risky raid.

After eating, we made our way carefully upstairs in the dark. Daphers stationed herself in the left-hand bedroom, watching the back of the semi-detached house, while Auguste and I took our binoculars into the right-hand bedroom, and watched the front of the end terrace house.

It was a good opportunity to ask Auguste about the petrol bomb. He enthused about it.

"I've filled a bottle half full of petrol, and squeezed a rag soaked in diesel into the top as a stopper. When I light the rag, it won't explode until the bottle smashes to pieces; by then it will be through the window and into the lounge."

It was pleasing to hear how confident he was with this Molotov cocktail. If the petrol bomb were to explode anywhere before entering the lounge, it would be worse than disaster.

He continued: "I am going to try and hit the side of the drum exactly after it enters through the window."

"Not before," I said.

"No, not before, or all that liquid will set alight outside the house, and that might blow us all up, and we don't want that, do we?"

He had been thinking about it long and hard, which was a real blessing.

"No, we don't want that," I said solemnly, my thoughts straying to the position of Daphers in the back of the truck, sitting under the forty five gallon drum with all that volatile liquid directly over her head.

He must have been able to make out my thoughts in the darkness, by the expression on my face.

"Don't worry, Matthew, I will take great care with my aim, and my timing."

Phew, I hoped so; it was too late to back down now. So, saying nothing, I put my arm round his shoulders, which made things seem alright.

He smiled and added: "Also, I've taken the bulbs out of the reversing and the number plate lights, as a precaution. We don't want anybody writing anything down."

It was my turn to smile.

We continued our spying of the end house. Nothing happened for quite a while, until Daphers called:

"The little fat brother is on the move."

This was unusual, we needed them to stick to their habits. I quickly went through to her bedroom, parted the curtain a little more and watched. The brother walked past the caravan and knelt down at the base of the small bonfire, he carefully and precisely moved pieces of wood out of the way, raised the lid of some kind of box, lifted out a package, shut the box and returned the wood back to their previous position. He then went to the caravan, which was dimly lit, half opened the door, put the package on the floor, shouted, then shut the door and went back into the house. It was dark and difficult to see the whole operation exactly, but it seemed they had found and made a very good hiding place for their valuable merchandise.

Curiously we both looked at each other and agreed it must be another drug dealing run. We waited and silently watched. It wasn't long before the door in the side of the caravan opened again, and the two boys came out, jumped into their car and roared off out of the drive down the street to wherever the package or packages were required. A thought crossed my mind: 'let's hope they don't come back at the same time we are down there tonight.' It was highly unlikely, the chances were slim; anyway, we are unable to do anything about it.

After that incident, things were quiet. I went back and rejoined Auguste in the other bedroom where we watched and waited. At precisely quarter to ten or very close to it, the light went on and the front door opened in the end terrace house. There, in his full glory was the spitting brother, right on cue.

"Watch him spit," I said quietly.

Sure enough, he looked from side to side, momentarily drew his head back, then turned his face towards next door and gobbed a huge gob right into their garden.

I lowered my binoculars. "Every time I have watched him, he has done that, it is as good as a fingerprint."

My French was getting better, for Auguste understood everything. Then without taking his binoculars from his eyes, he remarked:

"If he is as bad as the other brother, he deserves everything and more than he is going to get. What I saw yesterday from the other brother, was evil."

I still wondered what it was he had seen, but it wasn't the time to ask.

The brother walked down the path, turned right, crossed the street, then went out of sight. I knew he was going to the other house to be with his sibling. He had an additional incentive tonight, being Saturday, the incentive was football, 'Match of the Day' on the television.

It was now just after quarter to ten, and this habit of going to his brother's house at this time every night, was going to be responsible for his death and the death of his brother.

"That's it," I mumbled to Auguste, "everything is now in place, let's you and I go into the other bedroom."

We slowly went through and joined Daphers and watched the garden and the back of the semi-detached house for another twenty minutes. Everything remained still.

When I trained my binoculars on the top of the chimney it was plain to see the tell-tale sign of smoke billowing out, informing us they had a fire – let's hope it was a blazing one. By the trail of the smoke, the wind had not dropped and was still blowing the trees and rustling the leaves.

I was unable to stop the encroachment of a determined smile.

"I think it is time we made a move," I whispered.

We shuffled our way about in the dark, quite expertly now, getting more used to it. Auguste returned to his bedroom to change. Daphers and I stayed where we were and put on the clothes we had brought for the job; the ones we thought we would be most comfortable in for the deadly task ahead. When we were dressed we stood for a moment looking at each other, checking our appearance, paying special attention to our shoes; why this was I don't know, for running and walking were not on the agenda. She had brought special gloves and put them on, then put her hands out to show them.

"I can get a better grip of the quick release rod with these," she said authoritatively.

I told her they would be fine, although I couldn't see them properly in the dark because they were black.

Auguste came into the bedroom, he was dressed in black, which didn't surprise me, including a black woolly hat; I could hardly see him. He sat down on the chair, Daphers and I sat on the bed. I'd left the curtain open slightly, so from my position I was able to see if there was any movement below in the garden.

It seemed the right time for me to talk through the whole procedure.

"OK," I said, "I think we are about ready, let's go through a few things."

They both listened intently; this was now very serious indeed. Getting everything correct was so important.

They both gave me their full attention.

"I will drive down to the road slowly and steadily, taking great care. Earlier, when I walked the route the roads were clear, nothing was in the way, let's hope it stays that way. I have taken particular notice of the position of the house – luckily it is the one with no fence, and with that big bay window in the front, it will be a great target. Also, I've marked in my mind the point at the opposite side of the road where I want to place the front of the truck, before I reverse back through the window."

I took a deep breath, then continued.

"Remember, when we get there, we won't have any lights on the truck and everything around it will be in total darkness. We may have light from the moon, or light from the room inside the house, but that's all."

Stopping for a moment and taking one of Daphers' gloved hands in mine, I spoke in English.

"Look, love, when we arrive at the house, I am going to veer left across the road quite violently; this is the time to hang on as best you can, take a good hold of anything."

She gripped my hand and whispered, "I will do my very best."

That was all I wanted to hear and went on in French.

"After going hard left onto the opposite pavement, I will then turn the steering wheel the other way as fast as I can, put the pick-up truck in reverse, floor the accelerator, and reverse backwards with as much speed as possible, and ram the scaffolding planks through the lounge window."

Both were now listening attentively. "As soon as the scaffolding planks smash their way through the window, you must pull on the release handle as hard as you can, Daphers. This will allow the forty-five gallon drum to roll down the diagonal sloping timbers, and bludgeon its way through the window, spilling out its deadly contents into the lounge."

After a deep breath, I persisted.

"On the way down to the road, Auguste will light his petrol bomb from the flame of a candle, and at the absolute right time he will open the passenger door and throw the lighted Molotov cocktail through the hole we have just made. Now that's all we have to do."

Complete silence descended on the room. We all looked at one another. We were a team and we all needed to do the right thing at the right time. It was an unquestionable gamble, but one we all wanted to take.

"I think I am ready," confirmed Daphers.

"Me too," echoed Auguste.

There was nothing more to be said. I inadvertently looked at my wrist, no watch again and said, "I think it's time we went anyway, so let's go."

We descended the stairs and trooped out into the night. The moon was covered by a passing cloud, so memory, feel and careful manoeuvring were needed. Outside was relatively quiet, only the rustling of leaves could be heard, and the air was tinged with a passing wisp of smoke.

# Chapter Fifty-three

We entered the barn through the small door then as quietly as possible we opened the big door completely. The enlarged size of the pick-up truck was unexpectedly, grotesquely awesome, appearing like a great bovine shadow in the dark. The forty-five gallon drum perched right at the top of the sloping timbers containing all the volatile liquid and gases, looked excessively strange and very pronounced. We three stood before it for a second in amazement and in fearsome admiration. Then, without further hesitation on her part, Daphers climbed the little steps by the side of the truck, turned round backwards, slid herself along through the triangular hole, and finally sat on the toolbox with her back to the cab.

Poking my head after her, I gently said to her: "Are you all right?"

She didn't say anything, just gave me the thumbs up. At that moment I really wanted to kiss her, but instead replied with the same thumbs up.

"Keep a tight hold of the wooden beam on the journey down there; you can see the quick release handle, can't you?"

Again the thumbs up, then she took hold of the wooden beam with both hands.

I moved the steps to one side out of the way and opened the cab door. Auguste was already sitting in the passenger seat, with a candle waxed in position on the top of the dashboard.

He gestured to me. "I've got the bottle half filled with petrol between my feet, and I have soaked the rag at the top in diesel and not petrol, so when I light the candle somewhere about the entry to the road, the petrol won't pre-ignite and flare up."

Feeling he had definitely done this before gave me confidence. I couldn't smell petrol in the cab, only a very slight odour of diesel. I thought of opening the window, but it would ultimately blow out the candle, so I didn't. He had his matches at the ready, and we were all strapped in.

I now had one of those moments asking myself, had we forgotten something vitally important? Was there something we had not thought of?

Deciding it was too late now, I started the engine and put the pick-up in reverse. Auguste and I had previously checked to make sure there was plenty of space behind the rear of the barn for me to move the extra-long truck as far back as necessary, which meant there was also enough space when we returned, for me to take an even bigger turning circle to enter the barn nose-first.

Reversing without any lights in this darkness was not easy, but absolutely essential, because even the smallest light in the night might be noticed up here on the hill. I didn't use side lights either; the short drive along the path between the house and the barn was a dangerously tricky manoeuvre but I managed.

On entering the main road, I switched on the side and main lights, then taking my time drove steady and with patience, watching eagerly for the left turning into the first road. As we approached I took the corner slowly and carefully, and did the same with the next left turn.

We were now in the murdering brothers' road. Everything was clear ahead of me, there were no obstacles or traffic in my way.

The area was as silent as the grave.

Desperately ignoring the quick pounding of my heart, I tried like hell to only concentrate on the picture in front of me, focussing all my attention on the semi-detached house on the right without a fence, the one with the distinct helpful glow in the window from the light in the lounge.

Suddenly knowing the two deadly murdering brothers were inside that room gave me a ferocious lift, and enabled my mind to fix solidly on the target.

With savage calm I drove the monster along the road.

After my slow, quiet arrival at the semi-detached house my calmness totally disappeared and I stamped my foot hard down on the accelerator. The engine in the truck roared and driving instinct took over. At speed I whipped the steering wheel hard left and threw the nose of the truck violently across the road up to the gate of the house opposite. Then with all the force I could muster I thrust the steering wheel back the other way, slung the truck in reverse and at the same time rammed the accelerator pedal hard to the floor. The engine screamed and the pick-up truck shuddered savagely and immediately started to reverse. There was a vicious squeal of tyres, and then, unexpectedly, the truck on its passage backwards hit the kerb of the pavement in front of the house; the truck jumped up in the air which made me wince and for a split second made me think of Daphers sitting underneath all that volatile liquid. Fortunately and thankfully, the monstrosity bounded down again, just as the scaffolding boards bludgeoned their way through the front window of the house. As this happened, I instinctively jammed the brakes on as hard as I could, to stop the truck going through the wall underneath the window and embedding us firmly in the lounge of the house, and burning us all to death. Luckily I managed to stop short.

Automatically glancing in the wing mirror I saw momentarily through the hole where the lounge window had been, the impression of two armchairs inside, and straight after that, heard the sound of the forty-five gallon drum rolling down the ramp, then saw it going at a violent speed through the lounge window hole and into the house.

Daphers had done her part of the job by pulling the quick release rod hard with perfect timing.

The rope must have tightened properly for the bung flew out of the hole of the forty five gallon drum, and at exactly the same time I saw the passenger door open, and Auguste lean out and throw the lighted petrol bomb after the drum.

This action violently jolted my mind and forced me into putting the truck into first gear, and stamping my foot hard down on the accelerator. With all the strength I could muster I spun the steering wheel the opposite way in an attempt to escape the carnage that was happening behind me.

The truck bounced back down on the road as the back wheels cleared the kerb. This happened at the same time as the Molotov cocktail thrown by Auguste burst into flames causing an enormous explosion, throwing huge gouges of flame, some of which tried to find its way outwards and upwards in an attempt to set alight to the roof. At this time I couldn't stop myself from staring into the side mirror again, and saw a flash of fire and flame and the heads of two demented, disturbed, brainsick figures above two armchairs – the sight made me wince slightly, also it gave me added incentive to press down harder on the accelerator.

We had only moved a few yards, when out of the hole where the window had once been, erupted a violent burst of rampaging crimson, orange and yellow flame. More of the volatile liquid had given up its gases, arrived at the party, and produced rampaging heated violence.

It was vital we escape this fearsome catastrophe, so I applied further pressure to the accelerator, and fortunately with screaming tyres, we violently propelled ourselves forward.

Looking left I saw Auguste hanging out of the passenger door, trying with all his might to get himself back onto the truck. As the truck screamed forward it helped him, and he sat back down on the seat, then calmly blew out the candle on the dashboard, as if it was all in a day's work.

As we increased speed along the road, I glanced in the mirrors to see fire burning forcefully in what had been their lounge. The temperature of the heat inside must have been deadly, occasional gushes of flame erupted through the hole but it was now a deathly continuous burn. For both the brothers confined inside the room, it must have been excruciating because of the persistent overpowering heat surrounding them, they were imprisoned in a blazing nightmare. The highly inflammable liquids had done their job.

# Chapter Fifty-four

As I slowed to exit the murdering brothers' road, I said under my breath:

"That is for our beautiful twins." There was no satisfaction from saying it, only a release of anger that had been with me for far too many years.

Continuing to think about it, I drove steadily and cautiously with lights dimmed, first turning right then right again, calmly switching the lights off before entering the driveway to our spy house, then parking the truck alongside the barn.

The moment the truck stopped, my head immediately and uncontrollably slumped onto the steering wheel, and suddenly I started to shake; it took all my power and strength to hold onto the steering wheel with both hands. I glued my eyes straight ahead staring at nothing, desperately trying to focus. I stayed like that for some time, taking deep breaths, trying to help myself to calm down. In the faint background, a concerned Auguste spoke words to me. I couldn't hear properly what he said, and anyway was unable to muster any sort of reply; it was as if I was paralysed.

Eventually, with deliberate concentration, I gathered myself together, and managed to turn and give him an indistinct verbal noise and a forced smile. A great deal of effort enabled me to put the pick-up truck into first gear, and then using a large turning circle I negotiated it through the open doors of the barn, fortunately stopping halfway inside.

Auguste opened the passenger door, and I turned and looked at him trying to unscramble all the thoughts in my mind, watching him through my dazed unfamiliar sight, with eyes not totally connected to the brain. He stared at me in a quizzical strange way, then stepped down from the truck and walked to the far end of the barn and stood waving his arms about, trying to guide me forward into position, like an aircraft into its parking space.

I started shaking my head from side to side in an attempt to clear it, but found it was difficult. Slowly my mind began to function into some sort of normality again. Auguste was waiting and waving. Eventually I succeeded in driving the truck forward without bumping into anything. He held his arms in the air indicating for me to stop; somehow the truck stopped.

I remained sitting in the driver's seat not moving, trying to collect myself. Suddenly I remembered the bounce up the kerb and the possible effect it would have had on Daphers. Jumping out of the cab I peered in through the triangular hole under the diagonal timbers and said.

"Are you all right, love?"

She replied, "That big bump nearly knocked me off my seat! Mind you, it helped me pull the release rod. I saw all those flames bursting out onto the back of the truck and thought it was going to set us all alight.

"Yes, but are you all right?"

"Yes, I'm alright, but it's very dark in here, and I will be very pleased to get out, I can't see anything!"

After helping her out of the triangular hole, we stood and hugged each other for a long time. Tears flowed down our cheeks, all the weight of past years shed itself from us both. We had finally done what we wanted to do. Eventually we were united in a group by the arrival of Auguste, and we three embraced each other, saying nothing.

This moment of elation was interrupted by sirens wailing and we all scurried to the open end of the barn and peered through the holes in the hedge.

Police, fire engines and ambulances were down on the road in abundance. Smoke was still billowing from around the house, and there was a flickering of flames in the darkness. I noticed a faint light in the undamaged caravan, which was pleasing. The structure of the semi-detached house had remained intact, although the kitchen window and the back door were in need of repair.

We watched the scene below for some time; it helped us slowly to calm down. The sirens stopped as the number of vehicles arriving diminished, and the firemen got the blaze under control.

I turned. "Come on," I said, "time to pack things up."

We closed the big doors, and Auguste started to dismantle the timber structure on the back of the pick-up. I could just hear the quiet whirl of the screw gun.

Daphers and I stood by the hedge. For me there was sadness in the air, it was not for those dreadful monsters, but for the memory of our twins and the other unknown girl they had killed, and possibly other people these two monsters had murdered. She must have thought something similar, for she gripped my hand even tighter, looked at me and breathed a steady sigh.

"I would like a drink now."

I kissed her cheek. "You go and prepare it. Auguste and I will get everything ready for an early departure in the morning."

She left with a gentle smile.

We returned everything back into place and fastened the cover in position over the back of the pick-up. In defiance, Auguste and I left the barn doors open to the night air, which now had more than a hint of smoke. We went into the kitchen. The faint glimmer of moonlight allowed Daphers to pour each of us a glass of wine without any lights. It was a special occasion, so we stood and lifted our glasses.

My beautiful wife, with tears in her eyes gently whispered:

"To our precious twins who will never be forgotten."

We repeated, "To the twins."

Auguste nodded in agreement.

We emptied our glasses, filled them up again, opened other bottles and when all the bottles were empty, decided to try for sleep.

I gave instructions. "We need to wake in the morning before first light, so we will set the mobile for five o'clock. We want to be away from here before half past five to allow us to sneak out in the dark without anyone noticing. Let's try and prepare everything before we go to bed? It is important we get the ferry in the morning as early as possible."

With the aid of numerous glasses of wine, we all managed some sort of slumber.

In the morning Auguste peered round the corner of our bedroom door, waving frantically and calling out.

"Your mobile has gone off, it's time to get up."

Then he shot off to get dressed. I swung my legs out of the bed, had a stretch, kissed Daphers. We both put on our clothes as quickly as we could.

Walking across the floor to the window, I parted the curtain just enough to see what was happening down below. It was still dark, there was nothing moving in the rear of the garden of the semi-detached house nor any movement around that I could see, it was as quiet as a graveyard down below.

Looking down on the devastation we had caused, set me thinking and wondering was it possible someone last night could have seen us carrying out this ultra-violent act. It was unlikely they would have seen us quietly arriving, but perhaps somebody in the houses on the far side of the road may have been brave enough to twitch a curtain and catch a glimpse of the pick-up-truck in action. They surely wouldn't see the pick-up leaving because they would be distracted by the destructive happenings inside the semi-detached house, which would be a more exhilarating focal point. The explosion and subsequent fire in the house to them have would been far more interesting than a pick-up-truck. Looking down at the caravan and thinking maybe the woman might have seen something, then quickly coming to the conclusion, no she would have stayed in the caravan and kept her head down.

My thoughts strayed to the callow youth and the spotty youth, and the fact they hadn't arrived back from their night out during our dangerous undertaking, so they couldn't have seen anything last night. But was it conceivable they might have noticed something before last night, a movement or a tiny light or a noise, up here in this spy house, and thought nothing of it at the time, then when talking later, maybe recollect small incidents in the past weeks and unimaginably put two and two together. They had been brought up to be sly, maybe they might just think back and come up here and investigate. They would have to continue living in, or around the semi because their source of income is there. Hopefully the shock of what has happened has frightened them and dulled their senses.

I refocused my eyes and could make out a dormant police car, and a fire engine lurking about on the road. It seems the police were just sitting there, waiting for dawn to appear. Nobody seemed to be in the caravan, the back garden was desolate apart from two unlit bonfires, which I suppose was quite ironic.

Lifting my head away from the window and closing the curtain, I momentarily stood and wondered if the police were observant enough to find the packages secreted under the small bonfire. Maybe what was under there was not so small and maybe very, very valuable.

# Chapter Fifty-five

Hearing Auguste go downstairs, I hurried after him and we joined Daphers sitting at the kitchen table. We couldn't help but look at each other and an impish grin appeared on my face. The other two spotted it; Daphers was the first to follow my grin with Auguste not far behind.

I spoke quietly. "Well we did it. We have done what the police should have done all those years ago, we have stopped those murderers from ever killing again."

I stopped speaking; thought about things then added:

"That was one hell of a journey down there with one or two very hairy moments," and I puffed my cheeks out.

"There certainly were some hairy moments," butt in Daphers. "That bump up the kerb nearly threw me off my seat, I didn't expect it, suddenly up in the air I went, came down, bounced back on my seat, felt the planks crash through the window, and pulled on the lever as hard as I could, and after that heard the drum roll down the slope."

"You pulled the lever at exactly the right time. It was just as I put my foot on the brake to stop all of us going through the lounge window after the drum."

"Putting your foot on the brake pushed me forward, I had to brace myself by gripping the wooden frame. It all happened in a split second."

"Yes, I thought about what was happening to you just before I saw Auguste open the passenger door and throw the petrol bomb at the drum as it flew through the lounge window."

Auguste heard his name mentioned and rather quickly glanced from me to Daphers. We realised in our excitement we had been speaking English, so I quickly gave him a verbal briefing of the aforementioned action.

"Ah, oui oui," and he went on to explain how he couldn't get back into the truck after throwing the petrol bomb, and it was only made possible by me accelerating forward forcing him to fall back onto the seat.

"We've done it," I repeated in French and we all smiled.

Auguste and I donned our coats and went outside into the rather strong wind. Luckily for us it was blowing even stronger than yesterday – any noise we made would not travel far.

In the barn the pick-up truck had returned to its normal size, and now looked like any other. We decided to leave the scaffolding planks inside the barn neatly stacked beside the bench, instead of replacing them in the grass in front of the house, so avoiding the possibility of being seen going in and out. My last task was to make sure the back cover on the truck was fastened down properly. It was surprising how swiftly we were ready to depart.

On returning to the kitchen, Daphers asked if we wanted coffee.

"A quick cup might be nice," I replied.

We drank the coffee and ate a biscuit sitting around the kitchen table. When we finished Auguste went up to the bedroom to prepare for leaving.

Daphers took my hand and slowly and quietly spoke:

"I didn't know how I'd feel when it was all over. I thought, maybe I would ultimately feel sorry for those two, but I don't. I think they should have been caught and punished years ago. I cannot think anything good of anybody who would kill for pleasure and no other reason. They just took people's lives and nobody did anything about it."

A tear unleashed itself voluntarily from the corner of her right eye, I squeezed her hand and waited for her to continue.

"They just killed for killing's sake."

She took an intake of breath and looked directly and deliberately at me.

"I have come to the conclusion we have probably saved lives."

The tears formed in her eyes again and fell down her face as she spoke.

"We are absolutely sure they killed three people; hopefully there weren't any more, but we are not sure."

Further tears ran down her cheeks; she didn't wipe them away but allowed them to flow. I took hold of both her hands, and her tears flowed even more freely.

Auguste returned from upstairs, and I explained to him what Daphers had said. Instinctively he responded:

"It seems as though these two men were running a war against ordinary people, someone had to stop them. In the short time I have been here watching from the window upstairs, I have seen some ghastly things committed by the little fat man. If we have saved any suffering to anyone, it was worth it."

We all sat round the table and grasped hands even more firmly in the darkness.

"It's time to go," I said.

Our bags were already packed and on the floor in the kitchen. I turned off the gas, the electricity at the mains and bagged all our rubbish, leaving nothing behind belonging to us. Made sure the back door was locked, went out through the front door, locked it, then pushed the keys back through the letter box.

I couldn't resist walking behind the barn and having another quick glance through the hedge to the house below. There was very little activity round the garden or in the house of the semi, only a police car poking its nose out onto the road across the drive.

Everything now had to be done in silence, and with as little movement as possible, so no eagle-eyed person down below would see any sign of motion. With the bags stored in the back of the pick-up, I edged myself into the driver's seat and started the engine. Then without lights and as silently as possible, and without any fuss, reversed out of the barn into the clear, wide open space behind, put the pick-up in first gear and with few revs on the engine, drove slowly forward onto the path under the cover of the barn, parked momentarily out of sight, and waited.

# Chapter Fifty-six

Auguste closed the barn doors, snapped the padlock shut, jumped in the pick-up, and with Daphers in the passenger seat we steadily and sedately moved down the drive, switching on the lights as we turned right and entered the road for the ferry to France.

All morning I had been fretting about the likelihood of police visiting us, or maybe roadblocks, but they didn't, and there weren't any. Daphers and I were totally unfamiliar with the actions of the police and knew even less about their procedures, all we knew was all those years ago when we needed them, we were left wanting.

Driving calmly and within speed limits, we quickly separated ourselves from the village, and with every mile my nervousness and anxiety became less and less.

Conversation on the journey to the ferry terminal was limited. We arrived two hours before our sailing time, and so booked the earlier boat. Sitting in the truck in the parking area by the jetty brought my nervousness back, which strayed into the other two. This caused a lot of twitching and glancing at each other, and silence.

In the end, I couldn't stand it any longer and went to the ferry terminal building, bought a newspaper, tucked it under my arm and walked back. Sitting in the truck and casting my eye over it revealed nothing, until I noticed a small headline down at the bottom of a page. It was only a short paragraph, so I read it out loud, translating it into French for the benefit of Auguste.

"A fire occurred in a house in a small village in Kent, two men were burned to death. Everything is pointing to a gangland killing or a gas explosion. That's all it says!"

At this juncture cars started to roll onto the ferry, and we followed. As we made our way onto and over the ramp, we all breathed an enormous sigh of relief. The ferry staff indicated where we should park and we did. We all sat in the pick-up truck for a moment, taking time to enjoy the fact we had done what we intended to do, and as far as we knew, did it undetected. Eventually we slid out of the truck and mingled with everybody else, went up top, found a table and sat down.

Straight away I spoke in English. "I'm glad we did what we did. Auguste was right: the two brothers were evil."

Daphers half smiled and nodded.

We breakfasted on the ferry, Auguste the only one eating well. The crossing was good, and we very quickly docked in the port of Calais. As we entered the French roads we were still saying, 'keep on the right'. We stopped overnight at a hotel further south, leaving the following morning and arriving in Eeee in the early afternoon.

We gave generous thanks to Auguste and before he returned to his garage, asked him if he would help in unloading the truck. He said he would be ready at anytime, then smiled, and said:

"Now the garage is again in my hands I have renewed energy to start afresh."

We shook hands vigorously and I watched him walk out of sight.

It was good to be back in the shelter of the Pyrenees and we drove down the drive and parked in front of our rented house, took our bag inside, entered the kitchen, made a cup of tea, went into the lounge and sat down in comfy chairs.

Again we looked at each other; I spoke quietly to Daphers.

"If the twins had not been murdered, I wonder, would we ever have left England, and now, after what we have done, will we ever return?"

Daphers took a sip of tea, shook her head from side to side and calmly said, "At last after all these years I feel elated as if a very large weight has been lifted from my shoulders. I feel more relaxed somehow, as if all the anxiety of the past years has been swept away. I don't and never will regret anything of what we have done."

"Yes, I feel the same. In the eyes of the law we have done wrong, but all those years ago the law let us down badly, and now I am unable to stop the feeling of elation. Our days from now on are going to be good, no matter what happens."

The following day I drove to Auguste's garage with the pick-up. He was delighted to see me and told me about the work he was going to do in the future. I left him dismantling all the timbers out of the back of the pick-up, thinking to myself, it seems he really has a new lease of life.

Later in the day we took the French car into Toulouse for shopping and I bought several English newspapers.

Back in our rented house Daphers prepared a late lunch and I scanned the papers for accounts of the fire in the house in England and what they thought had caused the fire. Most papers agreed it was an attack by another gang, only one newspaper gave a report of a commercial vehicle being seen driving away down the road just after the explosion.

I sat for a long time and pondered this additional piece of information. Someone had seen us leave the scene of the crime and thought the pick-up-truck to be a commercial vehicle. With all the scaffolding planks sloping down and sticking out the back, I suppose it could easily have been mistaken for a small lorry, but the question was who saw it. Maybe it was just a curtain twitcher, but I put this down as highly unlikely as they would be too frightened to peep round the curtain no matter what happened in the road, they would know if they were caught watching they would suffer consequences. There again it was quite a large explosion and at that time of night they possibly would be awake, so maybe one or more brave ones might have seen something. I presume the police would eventually make enquiries door-to-door along the road and ask for information. I was very pleased the words commercial vehicle had been used to describe our pick-up truck.

My next thought was for the old woman in the static caravan, but I immediately dismissed her as everything happened so quickly, and at the front of the house. Driving with such intensity, I wondered if I had missed something on the return journey? No, there were no other vehicles on the road. Was it possible a person walking their dog had glimpsed the truck from afar? I'm sure the other gangs had a commercial vehicle, I suppose if they wanted one they would steal one. Everything in England had been done correctly and with precision, similar to the time when the hurricane struck the ship. The chances of anyone connecting us with the incident were very remote, we had left nothing behind.

I decided to keep the information and my thoughts to myself, hoping any investigation by the police would be as bad as all those years ago, when they were unable to find any relevant information on those two killers who horrendously murdered our precious twins.

Discussing it with Daphers would cause endless amounts of worry and ingested thought, possibly interfering with our future. So, gathering all the newspapers together, I placed them in a wooden box by the wood burner.

Daphers entered the room and asked, "Is there any further news?"

"No, nothing," I said and gave her a huge smile. "What's for lunch today?"

"Your favourite."

"Oh, how marvellous, I shall open a bottle of wine."

THE END, MAYBE.